What people are saying about

# i heart bloomberg

"Melody offers chick lit readers a bouquet of colorful characters. Kendall and her Bloomberg roommates are guaranteed to brighten up your reading hours. Lovely!"

—Robin Jones Gunn, best-selling author of the
Sisterchicks® novels and *Peculiar Treasures*

"I heart *Bloomberg!* The title fits this lovely, warm story of Megan, Lelani, Anna, and Kendall. Melody Carlson is a master storyteller who deftly captures the heart and yearnings of young women. Readers will connect with the ladies of Bloomberg Place as they strive to find their place in this big world."

—Rachel Hauck, author of *Sweet Caroline*

"*I heart bloomberg* is a delightful story about four roommates renovating their home and their hearts. As the Bloomberg Girls weather the challenges of friendship together, they discover the joys of forgiveness and restoration."

—Melanie Dobson, author of *Together for Good* and
*Going for Broke*

"*I heart bloomberg* reminds me of *Friends*, the TV show, minus the coarseness—a YaYa Sisterhood for my younger Christian generation. The wildly disparate characters compliment each other perfectly. I can't wait to see what else happens to them!"

—Camy Tang, author of *Sushi for One?*

i heart bloomberg

# i heart bloomberg

Melody Carlson

86 Bloomberg Place

David C Cook®

*transforming lives together*

I HEART BLOOMBERG
Published by David C. Cook
4050 Lee Vance View
Colorado Springs, CO 80918 U.S.A.

David C. Cook Distribution Canada
55 Woodslee Avenue, Paris, Ontario, Canada N3L 3E5

David C. Cook U.K., Kingsway Communications
Eastbourne, East Sussex BN23 6NT, England

David C. Cook and the graphic circle C logo
are registered trademarks of Cook Communications Ministries.

This story is a work of fiction. All characters and events
are the product of the author's imagination. Any resemblance
to any person, living or dead, is coincidental.

LCCN 2007941677
ISBN 978-1-58919-104-4

© 2008 Melody Carlson
Published in association with the literary agency of Sara A. Fortenberry

The Team: Andrea Christian, Erin Michelle Healy, Jaci Schneider, Susan Vannaman
Cover Design: The DesignWorks Group, Charles Brock
Interior Design: The DesignWorks Group
Cover Illustration: Rob Roth

Printed in the United States of America
First Edition 2008

1 2 3 4 5 6 7 8 9 10

012608

To Myke Wabs,
a woman who knows all about friendship and houses,
love, mc

# One

# Megan Abernathy

"Three female housemates wanted to share luxurious four-bedroom residence in upscale urban neighborhood. Classic historical house within walking distance of downtown, campus, and shopping. No smokers, no drugs, no pets. $550 a month includes all utilities. One-year lease, no exceptions. First and last, plus cleaning deposit required. Send résumé to Ms. Weis, PO Box 4721, Herrington Heights."

Megan Abernathy folded the newspaper in half and circled the ad with her neon green highlighter pen. Then she read the words again, more carefully this time. This place sounded pretty swanky. And it should be, at $550 a month for just a room! She glanced around her crowded and messy bedroom—one of two in a crummy little apartment she shared with three other young women.

To be fair, it was her roommate's half of the bedroom that looked the worst. Megan's side was relatively neat. Well, other than the plastic storage crates stacked against the wall. But that's what came from remaining in a less than satisfactory housing situation for so long. It had seemed like a smart move a couple years back—a real leap from dormitory living, but still on campus. Now it felt like a jail cell.

Megan kicked a stray flip-flop back to Bethany's side of the room. She had meant to find another place to live after graduation, along with a job. But then Dad got sick in early May. And the summer slipped sideways with his nonstop medical treatments, hospitalizations, and finally, after the doctors admitted they'd exhausted all options, his funeral in late August. Consequently she had no time to think about housing or job possibilities or much of anything to do with her future. And maybe it didn't matter anyway. Maybe she just didn't even care anymore.

"Don't become a martyr," her mother had warned when she dropped Megan back at the rundown apartment a couple of weeks ago. "Your portion of Dad's life insurance can easily help you afford a bigger and better place, sweetheart. You did so well in school, and we never really celebrated your graduation. I'm sure that Dad would've wanted you to—"

"I'll be fine," Megan had reassured her. "I just need to find a job." Her plan had been to get her feet under her before moving to a better place. Of course, she couldn't mention her regrets over not putting in applications for teaching positions last spring. That would only make her mom feel worse. Now it was the end of September, way too late to snag a teaching job. Instead, she told her mom not to worry. "I just want to take a year to figure things out," she said.

"A year can be a lifetime." Mom sighed, then gave her a kiss on the cheek.

"How about you, Mom?" Megan suddenly remembered that her mother was going home to an empty house now, a totally different lifestyle. "Will you be okay?"

"With God's help, I will." Then Mom frowned up at the dismal apartment complex behind Megan. "Just promise me that you'll at least *consider* another place to live. I worry about your safety in this neighborhood."

Now, just two weeks later, Megan wondered if her mom was right about this neighborhood after all. The headlines in this morning's paper reported that another college coed seemed to be missing. Since the sophomore had only been gone two days, a missing-person report hadn't been filed, but the girl's roommate felt certain that foul play was involved, and no family members had seen her either. This was the second female student to go missing in six months. And the truth was, it creeped Megan out. Not having classes to distract her only made matters worse and gave her more time to fixate on things.

More than that, she regretted not giving up her space in this apartment last June, back when she'd begun to suspect that her roommate was turning into a wild child.

Bethany had seemed okay when she moved in a year ago. She was a junior and fairly serious about school, but by springtime things started to deteriorate. Last summer, while Megan was gone, Bethany turned their room into a pigsty and, according to the other roommates, became even more indiscriminate about her male friends and partying habits. At this rate, Megan would be surprised if Bethany would even manage to graduate this year. Megan warned Bethany that her late-night partying could get her into serious trouble, not unlike the poor girl who had been missing since Friday.

Megan used her foot to nudge several stray clothes and mismatched shoes onto the skanky-looking pile of dirty laundry that seemed to be smoldering at the foot of Bethany's unmade bed. Then she liberally sprayed this festering mound with Febreze—her new best friend—and hoped that dirty laundry wasn't combustible. Satisfied that she was keeping the stench at bay, she returned to perusing the classifieds.

She had to get out of here. Whether to escape her raunchy roommate or the fear of some campus criminal, today, she decided, was D-day. D for determination. After slogging around in a slightly depressed slump for the past few weeks, she'd forced herself out of bed first thing this morning and went out to pick up the newspaper. Now Megan was determined to 1) get a job, any job, and 2) move out. And not necessarily in that order. After carefully searching the help-wanted section she had wandered on to the housing ads, which, typical of autumn and the beginning of school, were less than promising. But that one with the "luxurious four bedrooms" caught her eye, and it sounded surprisingly tempting just now. But to send a résumé? Just to rent a room? It seemed a little over the top.

Then again, the house did sound nice. Maybe it would be worth sending her résumé. How much trouble would it be? Just turn on her computer and pull up the doc and print it out. She needed to do this anyway if she was going to apply for those two jobs that she'd highlighted this morning. Easy breezy.

Of course, Megan never liked doing things the easy way. So, after she pulled up her résumé, which she'd edited just two weeks ago, she felt compelled to go over it again thoroughly, tweaking here and there to make sure it appeared impressive enough for this "upscale" and "classic" house that she suddenly felt desperate to inhabit. She imagined herself going to work from a beautiful home where she had a large closet with an organized and well-maintained wardrobe, not to mention a bedroom all to herself, perhaps a master suite? Maybe she would splurge on a bedroom set, even if it was simply from Ikea. And she'd get some cool bedding and bath linens and perhaps an area rug too. It was sounding better by the minute.

After about an hour, she was satisfied, or nearly. She printed out her perfected résumé on pale pink stationery, something she would never do for a job interview because it would look too girly; but she hoped this might get the homeowner's attention. Megan wanted to show this woman that she wasn't just the run-of-the-mill, unemployed college grad. She carefully folded the two pages and placed them in a matching pale pink envelope and, using her best penmanship, addressed it.

Then, not wanting to waste time—it was Saturday and noon was the last mail pickup on this part of campus—Megan hurried out to the mailbox in front of the apartments and slipped it in, pausing to silently ask God to give it his blessing.

"Hey, Megan!" The nasal sound of that voice was familiar—and it seemed there would be no escaping it. Megan turned to see Gwen Phillips, a girl she'd known since middle school, quickly approaching.

"Hi, Gwen," said Megan, forcing a smile.

"I haven't seen you around since graduation," said Gwen as she joined her. "I thought maybe you'd gone home to recover." She laughed. "Or have you moved off campus?"

"No," admitted Megan. She nodded to the dull tan building behind her. "I still live here."

Gwen made a face. "How can you stand that place?"

Megan shrugged. "Actually, I'm thinking about moving out."

"I'm thinking about moving too," said Gwen eagerly. "Especially after hearing about Rebecca Grant being missing now. Her roommate is certain that Rebecca was abducted."

"Do you know her?"

"Not really, but my roommate had a class with her, and she talked to Rebecca's roommate, so it feels like I do."

"It's too bad."

"And it's probably going to turn out just like Amanda LeCroix. Can you believe it was last March that she went missing and they still haven't found her body yet?"

"Her body?" Megan frowned.

"Well, she's obviously been murdered. And who knows what else? Anyway, I don't blame you for wanting to move off campus. I've still got two terms left, but I hate living in a dorm, and it feels totally unsafe. There's absolutely no security whatsoever."

Megan just nodded, trying to think of a way to disengage from Gwen.

In fact, all her instincts told her to end this conversation ASAP. But today's morning devotion had included that bothersome little scripture about loving one's enemies. And while Gwen wasn't exactly an enemy per se—she was actually a fellow Christian—Megan did not consider her a friend. In fact, Megan usually went out of her way to avoid this obnoxious girl. She knew it was wrong, maybe even sinful, not to mention totally judgmental on her part, but Megan seriously disliked Gwen Phillips.

It might've started with that time in seventh grade when Gwen publicly disinvited Holly Benson from a sleepover because Gwen declared her "unsaved." Gwen was one of those Christians who thought if the Bible was a "sword," then she should use it to cut other people into little pieces—people who weren't "saved" anyway. Megan didn't have much patience for that sort of thing.

"Anyway, I've been considering moving off campus myself," said Gwen eagerly. "I mean I still want to be close by, but I've been doing some research and I've found that it's kind of slim pickings around here, not to mention spendy. But, hey, Megan, maybe you and I should consider getting something together. Maybe we could find a small house or a condo or—"

"I … uh … I've already got something in mind," said Megan quickly.

"What?" Gwen stepped closer and Megan stepped back.

"Well, it was an ad I saw, and I've already applied for it, actually." Okay, that wasn't completely true. But at least her résumé was officially in the mail now.

"Which ad?" Gwen queried doggedly. "Where was the place?"

"Oh, I don't know … I mean it didn't have an address. Just a house, you know."

"Was it that four-bedroom, the one that sounded pretty shee-shee and uptown and all that?"

Megan shrugged as if she were unsure, although she was in fact not.

"Well, if that's the one, you might as well forget it. It sounds like everyone is trying to get into it. You won't have the slightest chance."

Megan smiled as if it made no difference. "Yeah, you're probably right."

"So you want to look into something with me then?"

Megan glanced at her watch. "Uh, actually, I need to get going. I'm supposed to meet someone right now, Gwen."

"Well, call me," urged Gwen. "You know my cell number, don't you?"

Megan nodded. "Oh, sure. I've got it."

"See ya then."

"Later," said Megan in a forced cheerful voice. "Take care, Gwen!" Then she turned and ran up the steps to the apartment, feeling a mixture of guilt and relief. She hated lying to anyone. But more than that, she couldn't bear to spend another minute with Gwen Phillips!

Still, she felt like she'd wasted her whole morning as she went back into her smelly apartment, kicking a wadded sweatshirt as she walked through the door. Gwen was probably right—Megan probably didn't have the slightest chance of getting into that luxurious house.

She flopped onto her bed and let out a big sigh. She knew that she should get out of this stuffy room, get some fresh air and some fall sunshine—maybe even put on her running shoes and take a jog. But ever since Dad had died … well, she just wasn't functioning quite like she used to. It was hard to believe that friends had once called her a perennial optimist. Some had even made fun of her—calling her Pollyanna because she could find the bright side of anything. Until this past summer anyway. That's when skepticism had crept in … when she'd started to change.

Megan's degree was in art education, but she'd almost majored in psychology and consequently knew enough about depression to know that perhaps she was dealing with it now. But Megan also knew that, unlike many unfortunate depression sufferers, she had God. Couldn't God stave off depression for her? For the past few weeks, she'd been reading her Bible daily, which was much better than ever before. Shouldn't that make a difference? But even as she told herself these things, she felt that familiar lump in her throat as tears of frustration gathered inside of her.

"Christians aren't immune to sadness," her good friend Jarred had told her recently. "Trying to pretend that you're not grieving won't make the sadness stop, Megan."

"But it's been weeks," she said. "And I know that Dad's with God. He was a Christian, you know."

"I know." Jarred had put his hand on her shoulder, probably practicing his counseling skills. "But you gotta admit that you still miss him, right?"

She nodded, knowing full well where this was going. Jarred was leading a grief therapy group as part of his master's thesis. More and more, he seemed determined to include her as one of his practice cases.

"Come to my group," he urged. "You'd be a real asset, Megan. There are only a couple of other Christians. We need you there."

"I'll think about it," she'd told him. But that was about all she'd done. She looked at the blue flyer he'd given her. It was still lying on the coffee table where she'd tossed it a couple weeks ago. Now it was partially buried beneath her other roommates' piles of junk mail and a couple of old pizza boxes. According to the flyer, the group met on Saturdays at five. She knew she should go, but she also knew that she wouldn't. And she knew that she should probably go outside and take a walk or a run or get a cup of coffee. But she also knew that she wouldn't. Instead, she went back to her smelly room and pulled down the shades and crawled into her bed. Maybe she would burrow in and stay there until Christmas.

# Two

# Lelani Porter

"Another girl has gone missing!" exclaimed Lelani's aunt as she pointed to the front page of the newspaper. "That's horrifying! Oh, what is this town coming to anyway?"

"It's too bad," admitted Lelani. "But hopefully she'll turn up."

"That hasn't been the case with the last girl who went missing." Then Aunt Caroline told Lelani about another college girl who everyone suspected had been murdered.

"Oh," Lelani shook her head. "That's so sad." Then she held up the classifieds section, hoping to distract her aunt. "Listen to this," she said quickly. "Three female housemates wanted to share luxurious four-bedroom residence in upscale urban neighborhood. Classic historic house within walking distance of downtown, campus, and shopping. No smokers, no drugs, no pets. $550 a month includes all utilities. One-year lease, no exceptions. First and last, plus cleaning deposit required. Send résumé to Ms. Weis, PO Box 4721, Herrington Heights."

"You're not considering moving out, are you?"

"Well, maybe."

"Does it give the address of the house?" her aunt asked as she filled Lelani's cup with some aromatic Kona coffee, freshly brewed from what Lelani had brought with her from Hawaii almost a month ago. "It's not on campus, is it?"

"There's no address. Just the PO box." Lelani frowned as she reread the ad. "But they want a résumé. Just to rent a room? What's up with that?"

"I don't know, Lelani. And for that price—was it really $550?—it must be quite a place. I'll bet you could get a one-bedroom apartment for that price."

"Maybe in a nasty part of town."

"Well, for less than $550 a month, I'd make Daniel move in with his little sisters and you could stay in his room and pay me rent."

Lelani forced a smile for her aunt's sake, although she was thinking, *Thanks, but no thanks.* "That's sweet of you, Aunt Caroline, but you guys are already pretty crowded as it is in here." She didn't mention the fact that she hadn't come to the mainland to play nanny to her three young cousins, which had been the way things were going. Lelani suspected her relatives figured it was a fair exchange for nearly a month's worth of free, albeit hectic, housing.

"Well, I'm sorry I don't have more than a worn-out old couch to offer you."

"Hey, I really appreciate your hospitality." Lelani took a sip of coffee. "It's not like I gave you much advance notice."

"But would you really want to commit to a one-year lease, Lelani? That's a long time."

"It might be nice to stay put for a year."

"But what if you change your mind? I mean what if you decide to go back to school? I still can't believe you quit with only two years left to complete your degree." She shook her head with a frown of deep disapproval, a perfect imitation of Lelani's dad back in Maui. Despite the fact that he never went to college, he was not the least bit pleased when his only daughter dropped out of med school.

"Join the club." Lelani sighed and took a slow sip of coffee. Would they ever stop pestering her about this? Whose life was it anyway?

"So, you really don't think you'll change your mind? Finish up your education? Or how about nursing? That's kind of like being a doctor."

"I don't think so." Lelani pressed her lips tightly together. Why had she assumed that by simply leaving Hawaii, she could leave these questions behind? All she wanted right now was a fresh start, a clean slate. Maybe it was a mistake to have stayed with her relatives this long. Didn't they say that familiarity bred contempt? She was starting to hate it here.

"But I remember when you were a little girl, Lelani," her aunt persisted. "You used to carry around your little doctor's bag and wanted to help make people well. What happened to that dream?"

"Dreams change." Lelani looked out to her aunt's tiny backyard, littered with plastic toys and other kid paraphernalia. Right now it looked like Daniel and four-year-old Sophie were about to get into a sandbox scuffle over the ownership of a certain pink shovel. Lelani was trying to think of a way to change the subject. "Hey, didn't Dad tell me that you once wanted to be a ballerina?"

Aunt Caroline threw back her head and laughed. "That was a long time and a lot of pounds ago."

"Right. But you're happy now?" asked Lelani, thinking this was as good a way as any to distract her frazzled aunt.

"Oh, well, you know. It's not easy raising three children under the age of six. And Ronnie is so busy with work. And, good grief, you've heard me ranting enough already to know that I have my complaints."

Lelani nodded, then took another sip of coffee.

"So, do you like your new job then?"

Lelani nodded. "I do."

"Selling cosmetics?" The way her aunt phrased question, she might have said "Selling cocaine?" Then she frowned again, almost as if she were about to go into the "Why did you give up med school?" routine again.

"I actually *do* like it," declared Lelani. "And, in a way, it's not unlike medicine. I am helping women … on the outside. I'm even considering cosmetology school."

"Really? How long does that take?"

"I'm not sure, but not long I think. And the woman who trained me at Nordstrom assured me that some of my med courses would come in handy."

"I would hope so." Her aunt rolled her eyes. They heard a pounding on the sliding glass door, and both looked up to see Sophie's red, tear-streaked, and dirty face. She used both hands to push open the door, wailing that Daniel had thrown sand in her eyes.

Aunt Caroline stooped down, using a paper towel to wipe Sophie's face, causing the child to cry even louder.

"Anyway …" Lelani paused, waiting for Sophie to calm down.

Daniel appeared, loudly proclaiming his innocence. "Sophie threw sand at me first!"

"I think I'll go get that résumé ready." Lelani made a quick exit from the kitchen, leaving her aunt to settle this dispute.

It wasn't that Lelani didn't love her little cousins, she just wasn't ready to play nanny or mommy or whatever—not to anyone. All she wanted was a small place of peace. But finding a quiet corner in her aunt's cracker-box house was going to be a challenge on a Saturday. Not only was Daniel home from school, but Uncle Ronnie was currently parked on the couch that doubled as Lelani's bed at night, and he was deeply entrenched in a football game. But at least he was holding baby Gracie, who appeared to be sleeping through all the noise. Her aunt should be thankful for that.

Lelani gathered up her oversized bag, a real Versace from the days when her future had seemed brighter, and she shoved in her laptop and headed out to face the rest of the world. She was fairly sure she could find a relatively quiet, and at least kid-free, space at the downtown Starbucks next to Nordstrom, where she had been working the past two weeks. As usual, this entailed using the transit system. Although Lelani had gotten somewhat used to the cast of characters she saw on the bus during the week, the weekend seemed to bring out the least savory sorts. After being hit on several times by males between the ages of, say, fifteen to eighty, Lelani had soon learned to keep her eyes downcast and avoid inviting any unwanted advances.

Sometimes she paid a price for being beautiful. Not that she thought of herself in those terms, but everyone else seemed to make a big deal of her looks. Being half Hawaiian—with long and thick black hair, naturally tan skin, large brown eyes, and a decent figure—wasn't terribly unique in the islands. But she seemed to stick out like a sore thumb over here in the suburbs of Portland, Oregon.

To be fair, her looks had posed a problem in med school occasionally. Sometimes her professors and peers didn't take her seriously. In her first year at Hawaii State, she'd actually had a well-meaning teacher take her aside and suggest that she should give up medicine for modeling, because the pay was similar but modeling didn't require such an expensive education.

Not that she'd quit med school because of those minor irritations. No, her story was a bit more complicated than that. And it was a story she wanted to leave behind … back in western Maui.

To distract herself, she pulled out a notepad and listed things she would need to purchase once she started living on her own. Her mother had given her some start-up money, but it wouldn't last long if she got a room at that fancy-schmancy house. Even so, if it was close to downtown,

she could walk to work. And there must be other ways she could econo-
mize. Perhaps she could take on another job on the weekends. Because
being busy sounded like a relief just now.

Finally, she was at Starbucks and seated in a semi-quiet corner in the
back with a grande cup of the day's house blend. Nothing added, nothing
subtracted. Just plain old ordinary coffee. Although she preferred Kona
coffee, she still couldn't figure out why everyone on the mainland had this
curious compulsion to make coffee so convoluted. But at least her java
bought her a bit of privacy, as well as a table without peanut butter and
jelly smears.

After a bit of cautious people-watching, she turned on her computer
and pulled up the file labeled *résumés*, then scanned the various versions
she had customized for different job applications. She finally chose the
one that seemed to best suggest "mature, responsible, dependable grown-
up ready to sign a one-year lease in an upscale house."

Okay, it wasn't how she felt just now, but at least she was moving in
the right direction. Anyway, she hoped she was. Sometimes, especially this
past year, she had felt more and more like an unmanned outrigger out on
the sea, ruthlessly propelled by the waves and the wind with no compass,
no oars, no idea which way to go. She just wanted a place to land, just one
year to settle in and figure things out. It didn't seem like too much to ask.

# Three

# Anna Mendez

"What exactly do you think the word *yuppie* means anyway?" Anna calmly folded a dishtowel, determined to keep her temper in check. Her mother had started tossing that word around at the same time that Anna mentioned she wanted to move out. Her mother seemed to think that calling a person a *yuppie* was an insult, although Anna felt relatively sure it was simply slang for a career person. "I mean, if you're going to call me names you should at least know their meanings, don't you think?"

Her mother laughed, but Anna heard the sarcasm in it. "People used the word a lot in the eighties, although you were too little to understand."

Now this seemed ironic, since her mom had barely been speaking English in the eighties herself. Anna folded a washcloth and told herself to be patient. Laundry was not a task she enjoyed, and she'd only volunteered in the hopes of getting on Mom's good side today—a goal sliding further out of reach. It never failed: whenever Anna mentioned getting a place of her own, Mom went ballistic. "Well, I think *yuppie* is a bit archaic," said Anna. "That means old-fashioned and outdated."

"That's only because you were a *bambina* then." Mom smiled and ruffled Anna's short, wavy hair as if she were still five years old.

Anna tried to ignore this aggravation as she folded a fluffy white bath towel into neat thirds, exactly how she'd been taught when she was a preschooler and she "helped" Mom to clean other people's homes, back before the restaurant took off and money started rolling in.

"You still haven't told me what you think a yuppie is, Mom."

"Oh, I'm not sure exactly … but I think it is a person who tries to get ahead in the world … to get more money … to dress better, you know what I mean?"

"So, what's wrong with that? You and Dad do that all the time." Anna shook out a pillowcase with a loud snap. "If I'm a yuppie, then you are too."

"No, no." Her mom's beaded earrings jingled as she shook her head. "We do not go for those designer clothes, *mi hija*, or fancy cars or other luxury things like you do. No, Anna, your father and I are very frugal."

Anna had to bite her tongue now. Hadn't her parents just put in an expensive in-ground swimming pool and spa? Most of the year, thanks to Oregon's rainy weather, the pool was not even usable. But Anna knew their motivation. They wanted to entice their two adult children to continue living at home—one big happy family. Well, not so big, but all under one roof. This seemed especially strange to Anna in an era when other parents complained about their twenty-something kids who refused to leave home. That failure-to-launch thing. You'd think Anna's parents would be pleased at her independence.

"*Yuppie* is slang for *young, upwardly mobile career people*," called her brother from the kitchen. Her guess was he'd been in there simultaneously eavesdropping on their conversation while doing a crossword puzzle.

Anna stuck her head out of the laundry room to discover she was right. Gil, the brainchild of the family, was sitting at the breakfast bar with pencil in hand as he worked on today's crossword challenge.

"Thanks, bro," she called. "It's nice to have an interpreter in this family."

"No problemo, sis." He grinned at her. "Glad to be of help with all of your vocabulary needs."

She laughed. Thanks to Gil, her parents' vocabulary and English skills had greatly improved over the years. But Anna still remembered being embarrassed by them when she started kindergarten shortly after moving to Portland nearly twenty years ago. Although her parents were both legal residents and had been born in this country, some still assumed, based on skin color, that they were illegals or aliens or even "wetbacks," or whatever the current putdown phrase for Spanish-speaking Mexican Americans was at the time. Even after her parents started their first restaurant with her aunt and uncle, and even after it became one of the most popular Mexican restaurants in the area, people made assumptions. It helped enormously when her parents, urged by Anna and Gil, put more energy into learning proper English.

"Thanks for your help, *mi hija*," said Mom after they folded the last of the laundry.

"I don't know why you don't hire someone to do the laundry for you," complained Anna as they went back to the kitchen.

"See?" her mom said victoriously. "That's because you are a yuppie and I am not."

Anna rolled her eyes. "Whatever."

"I think *yuppie* is Mom's new word for the day," whispered Gil after their mother headed up the stairs with her basket of folded linens.

"I guess." Anna poured herself a glass of tea and gazed through the French doors toward the recently installed pool. She had used it maybe a dozen times all summer. And now with autumn here, the pool was covered and the cover was littered with leaves.

"So are you really moving out?" asked Gil as he flipped through the newspaper. He must've finished his crossword already. Anna could never figure out how he did them, or how he did them so quickly. Despite the fact that she had an English degree and worked for a small publishing house, she'd never been able to complete one crossword puzzle in her life. And Gil's forte was numbers. Go figure.

"Not if Mom has her way," said Anna sadly. "She thinks I should live here until my wedding day." She attempted a feeble laugh. "Like that's going to be anytime soon."

"It's just the way she was raised, Anna."

"I know." She groaned. "Believe me, I know."

"And she's worried about your safety if you live alone."

"That's because she watches too much news. She's always reporting on that latest mugging, rape, abduction, murder—it doesn't matter if it occurred in Schenectady, New York; she's certain it's going to happen here and to me. The poor woman is obsessed with crime. Someone should put a block on all the news networks or maybe use a special parental warning. It could say something like, 'Caution: watching this news program could be dangerous to the mental health of obsessive-compulsive Latina mothers of daughters who are about to—'"

"That's why I've been hanging onto today's newspaper," he said as he held up the front page. "Have you heard about this yet?"

Anna stared at the headlines and the photo of the missing girl. "Oh, no." She slowly shook her head as she read the sad news. "Another abduction?"

"Possibly."

"Well, that's the conclusion that our mother will make."

"And it's not exactly in Schenectady either."

Anna sank down onto the barstool across from him. "After that college girl went missing last spring, it took me weeks to convince Mom that I was safe on the streets."

"Believe me, I know." He nodded. "It was the hot topic every single day at the restaurant."

"Now Mom will put up an even bigger fight if I try to move out."

He folded the newspaper over, hiding the horrible headline. "But we can't keep the news from her forever."

Anna sighed. "This is such a setback. I feel like I'll never be able to get out on my own. I mean Mom will barely settle down about one—"

"Hey, how about this?" Gil interrupted her.

"What?" She looked to see what he was talking about.

He still had the newspaper, pointing to what appeared to be an ad in the classifieds. "Mom might go for the idea of you living with other women, Anna. That could be the first step in your flight to freedom."

"Not once she hears the latest missing-girl news."

"But maybe that girl will turn up. Maybe she's perfectly fine. Anyway, listen to this ad." He cleared his throat and read. "Three female housemates wanted to share *luxurious* four-bedroom residence in *upscale* urban neighborhood. Classic historical house *within walking distance of downtown*, campus, and shopping." Then he hurriedly read the last bit, sounding like one of those disclaimers after a pharmaceutical commercial. "No smokers, no drugs, no pets. $550 a month includes all utilities. One-year lease, no exceptions. First and last, plus cleaning deposit required. Send résumé to Ms. Weis, PO Box 4721, Herrington Heights."

"That actually sounds kind of nice."

"It should be really nice for that price. The owner will rake in $1,650 a month by renting the rooms."

"Leave it to you to do the math." But she snatched the paper from him and read it again for herself. "They want a résumé? Isn't that a little weird?"

"You can't blame the owner if it's as plush as it sounds. They just probably want to ensure that no slackers apply."

"I wonder how much I'd need to get in there," she mused aloud.

"Probably around $1,700," estimated Gil. "If the cleaning deposit is about $500, which seems about right for a nice place."

"I can do that." Despite her shopping habits, which had increased with her job location downtown, Anna's savings had been steadily accumulating this year. Thanks to living at home.

"So why don't you?"

She peered at her brother. "You seem awfully eager to get rid of me, bro. What—do you have plans for my room? Maybe an ancillary office or workout room? A place to store your comic-book collection?"

He shook his head. "No. I just want you to break the ice for me. Every time I mention that I'd like to get an apartment downtown, the parents keep telling me to save my money."

Anna read the ad one more time, then firmly nodded. "It sounds absolutely perfect, Gil. I am going to do whatever it takes to get into this house."

"And I'll back you on it," he promised. "Plus, I'll hide this newspaper."

"Like Mom won't hear it on the news anyway."

"We'll try to hold her off for as long as possible. And then we'll play it down."

"Thanks. I know I've already rocked the family boat by refusing to work at the restaurant. But I don't want Mom to disown me if I move out."

"Just make sure you come around for holidays, weddings, and funerals, and it'll probably be okay."

Though he was partially joking, Anna knew he'd hit the nail on the head. Those events, in their family anyway, were not to be missed. Not unless you were hospitalized or doing time. Otherwise, you were expected to show up. And if you didn't show, you could count on the fact that your loving aunts, uncles, and cousins would make inaccurate speculations about your weight or employment status or natural hair color, or else they might start some juicy new rumors about your love life or, in Anna's case, lack of.

As Anna put her résumé into an envelope, she imagined what this lovely home might look like. Being that it was historic, it could be Victorian. There was an old three-story stone Victorian mansion close to town that she would love to get into. It had been completely restored, and the rose garden in the front yard looked like a fairy tale. Not only would it be gorgeous for big parties, it was the perfect spot for an old-fashioned wedding. Not that wedding bells were in her future. No. Anna had managed to bungle that one royally. Yet, here she was more than a year later and still not quite over it, still trying to move on, hoping to forget. Maybe a new residence would help. Now, if only Gil could help to buffer the news of that missing girl.

Four

# Kendall Weis

"Good grief," said Kendall. As she held up two handfuls of résumés, others spilled down onto the coffee table. "It's like half of the women in town want to live in my house."

"Yeah, right." Marcus snickered as he sprawled out on her new ecru chenille sectional and reached for the remote. She wanted to tell him to keep his feet off the furniture, but they'd only been dating for a couple of weeks and, so far, she sort of liked him. Or mostly. On the plus side, he had a decent job and although his parents were divorced and each remarried, they seemed to have plenty of money. On the minus side, he didn't seem to worship her as much as she'd like. But she might be able to get him to change all that ... if she played her cards right. If not, she could toss him back. Because Kendall knew, almost better than anyone, that there were *lots* of fish in the sea.

"How will I ever make up my mind?" she said as she skimmed yet another résumé and sighed.

"Just let them see the place," said Marcus as he flipped through the channels. "It's nothing like that ad you created. Have you ever considered writing fiction for a living?"

"No, but thanks for the vote of confidence." She scowled at him. "What was wrong with my ad? The house is historic, it's in an upscale neighborhood, close to downtown—"

"Luxurious?" He actually laughed now.

"It will be," she protested. "I just need a little money to fix it up some."

"Why don't you forget that whole roommate thing, Kendall?" He sat up and gave her an appealing smile, reminding her of why she'd found herself attracted to him in the first place. Blond, tan, white teeth, well built … what's not to like? "Just let me move in. The house is paid for. If you like I'll pay rent."

"Thanks, but no thanks." She picked up a pale pink résumé and carefully read it, placing it in the to-be-considered pile.

"Why not?" He came over now and started to massage her shoulders. "I'm an easy keeper and I come with some fringe benefits."

She shrugged him off and stood up. "Look, Marcus, we've been through this already. I've only known you a few weeks and I have no intention of living with you. End of conversation."

"I could help you fix things up around here," he suggested. "My old man taught me a thing or two. I can be pretty handy."

She rolled her eyes. "Yeah, right. Your dad is a CEO. What does he know about tools?"

"He has a workshop," argued Marcus. "He used to make birdhouses."

She chuckled. "Fine, then why don't you make me a birdhouse and we'll see how it goes from there." She waved a résumé at him. "Now, if you don't mind, I've got work to do. I want to get my interviews set up for Saturday and—"

"No way," he burst out laughing now. "You're going to make these chicks do interviews? Are you totally nuts?"

"No, I just happen to be particular. I'm not signing one-year leases with girls I don't like. We have to be compatible."

"I think if they're willing to shell out the bucks, you should get along just fine." He nodded to a slick white garment bag still hanging on the hall tree by the front door where she'd left it. "Looks like you've been to Camille's recently."

"They just got in some Dolce & Gabbana and I got a sneak preview yesterday."

"Looks like you got more than that."

She gave him a look that was meant to shut him up and, fortunately, it worked. Or maybe it was ESPN. Still, it was none of his business how she spent her money. And if he wanted to make it an issue, she would quickly show him the door. He wasn't *that* cute!

She finally worked the pile of applicants down to ten and promptly began calling. Her plan was to meet with them at Starbucks on Saturday. Inspired by a "Who's Your Real Friend?" quiz in *Cosmo*, she had her interview questions all worked out.

"An interview?" said the first call recipient, a bank teller named Lucy. "Just to rent a room?"

Kendall put a black checkmark on Lucy's résumé. "Well, if you're not interested, I have plenty of other applicants to—"

"No, no." Lucy sighed loudly and Kendall put a second checkmark on her résumé because she disliked loud sighs. "That's okay. I'll come," the woman said.

"Okay then," said Kendall, knowing full well that Lucy was probably a loser and a total waste of time, "I'll schedule you for nine on Saturday." Maybe Lucy would be like a test run—Kendall could warm up her interviewing skills on her.

"Nine in the morning?"

"Yes. I have a number of interviews," said Kendall with a chilly tone. "I'd like to finish them before noon."

"So where is your house?" asked Lucy eagerly.

"My house?"

"Yeah, for the interview."

"Oh, I'm not conducting interviews at my house."

"Why not?"

"Well, it seems a little risky, don't you think? What if someone is posing as an applicant, but is actually a deranged stalker? I wouldn't want that person to know where I live."

"Oh, yeah, I guess that makes sense. So where is the interview?"

"Starbucks downtown, by Macy's."

"Okay ... but how will I know you?"

Kendall smiled to herself. This was easy. "I'll be the tall blonde wearing Dolce & Gabbana."

"Dolce and what?" asked Lucy. Kendall put a third black checkmark on her résumé and considered canceling the interview right now. Then she reminded herself that it would be good practice.

"Never mind. Just look for an attractive tall blonde in the back."

"Oh. Okay."

Fortunately most of the other phone calls went more smoothly. And for those who weren't answering, she left brief but explicit messages. Before long, she had her list and everything was all settled.

"So, you're really going through with this?" asked Marcus as he turned the sound up on the football game. She'd told him to mute it while she made her calls.

"Of course. Why not?"

"And this is your alternative to getting a real job?"

"No." She frowned at him. Why hadn't she noticed he was so nosy? "I'll get a real job ... eventually ... when I find something I like."

"Well, maybe you could be a professional shopper," he teased, "you're good at that."

She smiled now. "Thank you. But I think I'd rather do something in personnel. I happen to be a highly intuitive person when it comes to reading people."

Marcus looked skeptical. "Like your friend Shara?"

"What's wrong with Shara?"

"Nothing," he said quickly. "That is, if you don't mind hanging with kleptomaniacs. They tend to make me nervous. I guess it's that old guilt-by-association thing."

"She only did that once," protested Kendall.

"That you know of."

She considered this. He was probably right. "Even so, Shara was fun. You have to admit that. And she's the one who introduced us." Kendall leaned down and ran her fingers through his hair. "You can't fault her for that."

"No, I can't." Then Marcus reached up and grabbed her, pulling her down onto the new sectional and into a wrestling match, which Kendall wasn't enjoying too much. Besides, he was messing up her hair. Sometimes she wasn't too sure about this relationship. And yet it was better than being without a guy.

She extracted herself from him and then frowned. "Besides, Marcus," she said as she smoothed down her mussed hair, "I'd think you'd be glad to know I'm getting roommates."

"Why's that?" He picked up the remote again.

"Haven't you heard about that other missing girl?"

He nodded. "Yeah ... so?"

"Don't you worry that something like that could happen to me? I mean, here I am living all by myself in this big old house. What if I became the next victim, Marcus? What if someone kidnapped me?"

"I don't think getting roommates automatically protects you from being abducted, Kendall. You still need to be more careful. And I've warned you about shopping at night by yourself."

She smiled now. "So you do worry about me then!"

## Five

# Megan

Megan frowned at her image in the bathroom mirror. Talk about a bad hair day. Maybe it had been a mistake to try to straighten out her red curls today. Sure, it had worked on Wednesday when she'd interviewed for a job. But today was rainy and already the damp air was wreaking havoc on her hair. In a last-ditch effort she dampened it down and, this time using hair gel, she squeezed and twisted until it finally took on a shape of its own. Not her best look perhaps, but better than that previous limp mess. She retouched her makeup now, cleaning the drip lines her wet hair had made on her blush and adding another layer of ash-brown mascara to her pale lashes.

She had a strong suspicion that this Kendall Weis person was highly into appearances. Hopefully, Megan's new Marc Jacobs jacket and Joie jeans would make the grade. She normally didn't go for expensive designer wear, but when Kendall had mentioned Dolce & Gabbana, Megan knew she had to toe the line. And today she was toeing the line in Stuart Weitzman boots. A splurge, perhaps, but Megan had convinced herself the purchase was more than that. It was an investment in her future. Besides, the boots hadn't seemed to hurt her interviews this week. Already she had an appointment for a second interview with the interior designer. She felt hopeful.

Megan checked her watch. The downtown bus should be here in about ten minutes, but with this rain, she'd better take an umbrella. That's when she noticed Bethany's umbrella still open by the door. It was a handsome Burberry in the traditional Brit plaid and would look great with her brown jacket. Also, considering that Bethany had made such a commotion when she came home totally wasted at three in the morning, Megan decided to borrow it. With Bethany's hangover she probably would never get up in time to notice it anyway. Besides, Bethany had borrowed Megan's things, without asking, numerous times.

As Megan rode the bus downtown, she felt more nervous about this appointment than she had for her job interviews earlier in the week. Why was that? Maybe because she felt so desperate to get out of that apartment. Or maybe she was turning a page, moving on in her life. Whatever it was, she knew she needed to place the outcome in God's hands. Despite her funk or depression or grief or whatever it was, she knew that without God, she would make a mess of things. And so, riding on the muggy bus, she silently asked God to either open or close the door to this new housing opportunity. And she promised to accept whichever way it went. Even though she felt like she really wanted it.

The bus stop was about a block from Starbucks, and the heavy rain had diminished to a steady drizzle by the time she was in front of the coffee shop. According to her watch, she was five minutes early. Perfect. She paused underneath the awning to catch her breath and steady herself. She intended to do this right. That would require confidence and friendliness. She could do that.

"Megan!" exclaimed a voice from behind her.

She turned around to see Gwen Phillips just emerging from Starbucks. "Oh, hi," she said casually.

"What are you doing here?"

Megan shrugged. "Getting coffee?"

Gwen shook a finger at her. "I know exactly what you're doing! You've got an interview with Kendall, don't you?"

Megan didn't know what to say.

Gwen got closer, lowering her voice as if someone was interested in this conversation. "I just had mine."

Megan blinked. "You're interviewing for a room?"

Gwen nodded with a big grin. "And I feel really good about it. I'm pretty sure that I'm in. Now if you get in too, we'll be roommates. Can you believe it? That will be so cool, Megan."

"Yeah." Megan swallowed hard.

Gwen slapped her on the back. "Go in there and get 'em, girl."

Okay, now Megan was tempted to run in the opposite direction, but decided, no, she would not let Gwen get the best of her. "Thanks," she told Gwen. "I think it's time for me to—"

"Kendall is that gorgeous blonde woman in the blue—"

"I know who she is," said Megan, although she'd never seen her before.

"Good luck!"

"Thanks, Gwen." Then Megan pushed open the glass door, took a deep breath, and decided to simply get through this thing as quickly and as painlessly as possible. Kendall was easy to spot. And Gwen was right about one thing. This girl was gorgeous. In fact, she had the kind of looks that Megan usually shied away from. So coifed and groomed and impeccably dressed that she resembled a full-grown Barbie doll. And in Megan's experience, girls like this were usually shallow and mean. At least in high school. To be honest, she hadn't had much experience with them since those days. So maybe she was being judgmental.

"Hello," said Megan as she approached the table. "Are you Kendall?"

"I am." Kendall smiled warmly and extended her hand, giving Megan a firm handshake. "You must be Megan Abernathy. Won't you sit down? Do you want a coffee?"

"I'll get one on my way out," said Megan as she settled herself in a chair.

Kendall's brows arched with interest. "Now, I couldn't help but notice you were talking to another applicant on your way in here. Do you happen to know her?"

"Gwen Phillips?" asked Megan with uncertainty, although she knew full well who Kendall meant.

"Yes. Is she a friend of yours?"

Megan couldn't help but frown. "I do know her, but I wouldn't exactly call her a friend."

"Oh?"

"I know it probably sounds terrible, but I don't really get along with her that well. In fact, if you've decided to rent to her, which is totally your choice, I think I might as well save you the time of interviewing me. I don't have any desire to live in the same house as Gwen." Megan reached for her purse, preparing to leave.

"No, don't go," said Kendall. "I have no intention of renting to that obnoxious girl. I was just checking to see if you were friends."

"Oh." Megan felt a mixture of relief and guilt. "I hope I didn't say anything to make you decide against Gwen. I'm sure some people totally love her. I think it might be kind of a chemistry thing—like oil and water—we just don't mix."

Kendall laughed. "Well, we must have a similar chemistry, because I don't care to mix with Gwen either. She seriously got on my nerves."

Megan considered this. She doubted that she and Kendall had the same chemistry, but knowing that Gwen was out of the picture relieved her.

Kendall glanced down at the pale pink résumé, which Megan was already starting to regret. The pink stationery had been a gift from an aunt and probably not that reflective of Megan's personality. Oh, well. "So you majored in art ed?"

"That's right."

"But you're currently unemployed?"

"My father passed away this summer. That was a distraction to looking for a teaching job."

"I'm sorry."

Megan nodded. "Anyway, I've been interviewing and I feel positive about working for a design firm."

"Really?" Kendall's brows arched again. "May I ask which one?"

"Sawyer & Craig. I have my second interview on Tuesday."

"Sawyer & Craig?" Kendall nodded. "Impressive."

"It's only an assistant position, but I think it would be interesting. And I'd probably learn a lot."

Kendall frowned slightly now. "But what if you don't get the position? How will you pay your rent?"

"My father had a good insurance policy. I have a fair amount in savings."

"Oh, well, that's good."

"But I do plan to work. I *want* to work."

Then Kendall asked some slightly weird questions about friends and relationships and what-ifs. Megan did her best to answer honestly, but she felt that some of them were a bit too personal and even invasive.

"Just so you'll know," said Megan finally, "I'm a Christian. So if that's a problem or anything, I'll—"

"Not at all. I like that you don't party or invite boyfriends for overnighters. As far as your religion, well, you could be Islam, Buddhist,

Hindu, whatever … as long as you mind your manners and don't try to convert me, I don't really care."

Suddenly Megan wondered if this was such a good idea. Perhaps she should've looked into sharing housing with Christian girls. She knew of several, including Gwen, who might be possibilities. But then Megan remembered the scripture about not putting your light under a bushel basket. She also remembered her prayer on the bus. God could open or close this door. She would leave it to him to decide.

"Well, that pretty much takes care of it."

"So," said Megan, slowly standing and wondering how she'd rated on Kendall's scale of interviewees. "Will you let me know?"

"Of course. I plan to make my decisions by the end of the day. I'll call you tomorrow and tell you—one way or another—which way it went." She extended her hand again. "Nice to meet you, Megan."

Megan shook her hand and tried to read what was behind those bright blue eyes, but this girl had such a smooth veneer that Megan couldn't see past it. As Megan was leaving, she realized she had all kinds of questions for Kendall. But she'd never had the opportunity to ask them. Talk about a one-sided interview. Well, maybe it made no difference. Megan suspected she wasn't the sort of roommate someone like Kendall Weis was looking for. Whether it was her looks or prestige or personality, Megan felt pretty sure she would not measure up. And perhaps it was for the best.

# Lelani

"You're Hawaiian?" asked Kendall shortly after Lelani had joined her at the table in the back of Starbucks.

Lelani nodded. "My mother is Hawaiian. My dad is from the mainland. Iowa, in fact."

"What took him from Iowa to Hawaii?"

"He went to Maui for a vacation straight out of high school and never went home again. He loved surfing and the people and he met my mom and they got married, and now west Maui is his home." Lelani cleared her throat and sat up straighter. She knew that wasn't an answer that would impress someone like Kendall. "Actually, he started a small business there when I was a baby," she continued. "A snorkeling shop. Now he has a chain of about thirty shops, located in Maui and Lanai and Molokai." Okay, now she sounded like a commercial.

"So what brings you to Oregon?" asked Kendall.

"I have relatives here. And I wanted a change. I love Maui, but I wanted to experience the mainland for a while. I guess I just needed a break."

"You were a premed student?"

"I was … but I decided to go in a different direction."

"Working at Nordstrom?" Kendall frowned. "Don't get me wrong. I am a faithful Nordie customer. But going from premed to—what?—sales? It seems a little strange."

"I'm considering going to cosmetology school," explained Lelani. She forced what she hoped looked like a sincere smile. "I like helping people, and it's fun making women look more beautiful. I'm even considering becoming an esthetician."

Kendall nodded. "Yes, I hear there's good money in that, and your premed training would probably be helpful."

"My thinking exactly."

"Which line do you sell?"

"Do you know about La Prairie from Switzerland?" A month ago, Lelani didn't know a thing about this incredibly expensive line of beauty products herself.

"Oh, I adore La Prairie!" Kendall's eyes grew wider. "Their moisturizer is to die for."

"Some women swear by the skin caviar product."

"I've heard it's amazing. And perhaps you might share some of the latest beauty secrets with your roommates?" Kendall had an almost childlike hopefulness now.

"Certainly. It would be my pleasure." Lelani felt more optimistic now. It was obvious that someone like Kendall could appreciate a job others might put down. "I could probably even bring home some of the sample products, you know, so you could try them out and see how you like them."

"That would be fantastic."

"Have you smelled their Silver Rain perfume?"

"I'm not sure."

Lelani held her wrist up for Kendall to take a whiff.

"Ooh, that is scrumptious."

"I can get you a sample."

Kendall looked like she was about to jump up and cheer. But her expression turned somber. "But what if you decide it's a mistake coming to the mainland?" she queried. "What if you get homesick? Or you decide you want to return to medical school? Would you try to break your lease?"

"No." Lelani firmly shook her head. "I am committed to spending a full year here. I wouldn't break my lease." But even as she said this a small wave of homesickness washed over her. "Although I might go home for a visit. Just a week or two. Perhaps in the spring. But then I'd come back."

Kendall brightened. "Any chance you'd want a friend to tag along?"

Lelani smiled. "Of course. That would be wonderful. My parents have a large home right on the beach. You would be welcome."

"One more question," said Kendall in a voice that sounded serious enough to make Lelani feel nervous.

"Yes?"

"Do you get an employee discount at Nordstrom?"

"Of course."

"And would you share that benefit with, say, a very good and very discreet friend?"

Lelani smiled with confidence. "I don't see why not."

Kendall reached across the table and shook her hand now. "I think I can say for sure that you are getting a room in my house."

"Speaking of your house, when do I get to see it?"

"Tomorrow. I will invite all the tenants over to fill out the paperwork and sign the lease." Now Kendall frowned and Lelani felt nervous again. "I'll call you about the time," said Kendall quickly, glancing at her watch.

"Time for another interview?" ventured Lelani.

Kendall nodded. "Yes. I need to keep this moving."

So Lelani thanked her and, as she was leaving, she believed she spotted the next interviewee. A petite Hispanic girl with short wavy hair that framed her face like a pixie—a very pretty little pixie. "Are you next?"

asked Lelani as she paused to get in line for a coffee.

"Is that Kendall Weis?" the girl asked, nervously fidgeting with the strap of what looked like a real Prada bag, not one of the knockoffs that so many girls were sporting these days.

Lelani nodded. "Don't worry, she puts on her pants every morning the same way as you do." Okay, it was corny but something she'd heard her dad say hundreds of times.

The girl laughed. "With long legs like that, I seriously doubt it."

For some reason Lelani felt a connection to this girl, maybe because she resembled her old school chum Oliana. "You'll be fine," she assured her. "Just relax. And if it helps, tell her that you're my friend."

"Does that mean you're in?" the girl asked.

"I think so."

"Wow, thanks. My name is Anna. Anna Mendez."

"Good luck, Anna. And in case you need it, my name is Lelani Porter, I moved here from Maui about a month ago, and I work at Nordstrom."

Anna's brow creased as if she was mentally taking this all down. "Hey, I thought you looked familiar. I'll bet I've seen you at Nordstrom."

Lelani grinned. "Of course, we're old friends, remember?"

# Seven

# Anna

"Your parents own the La Casa Del Sol?" asked Kendall with what seemed genuine interest. "I've eaten there a lot."

"Yes. They've owned it for about fifteen years. "Also, they own Casa Del Rey in downtown Portland—they started it up about five years ago."

"So …" Kendall seemed to study her closely. "Are you a good cook?"

Anna laughed. "Well, I suppose so. Not as good as my mom, but I pretty much had to learn how to do everything."

"What's your specialty?"

Anna shrugged. Cooking really wasn't her favorite thing, but if it would help get her foot in the door … "My dad thinks I make the best tamales."

"I love tamales. Do you use cornhusks and everything?"

Anna laughed. "Yes. Cornhusks and everything."

"But you're working at Erlinger Books?"

"As a children's book editor," proclaimed Anna proudly. "My degree is in English."

"Interesting."

Now there was a long pause and Kendall was just looking at Anna's résumé, which Anna feared was fairly mediocre. She was even more afraid that this less-than-impressive interview was about to end.

Inspiration struck Anna. Okay, maybe it was a stupid idea, but Anna decided to go for it. "Excuse me for asking, Kendall, but are you a model or an actress or something?"

Kendall looked up from the résumé with curiosity. "No … why do you ask?"

Now Anna just shook her head as if in amazement. "Well, you're just so beautiful, I thought maybe …"

Kendall smiled now. "Well, thank you." She glanced over Anna's shoulder as if looking for someone. Probably the next interviewee, so she could send Anna packing. "Speaking of beautiful, did I notice you talking with Lelani?"

Anna nodded. "Yes. And you're right; she's beautiful too." She held up her hands as if to make a hopeless gesture. "I suppose it would be crazy for someone like me to want to share a house with two beauties like you and Lelani. I wouldn't dare bring a guy over—"

"So you're friends with Lelani?"

Normally Anna despised lying. But then again, hadn't Lelani just befriended her? "I haven't known her for long," admitted Anna.

"Well, she hasn't been here for long," added Kendall.

"That's true. Can you believe she'd leave Maui to live here?"

"No. In fact, it worried me a little. But she assures me she wants to commit to a one-year lease." Kendall peered at Anna. "How about you?"

"I don't have a problem with that. I've been wanting to move out for a couple of years now, but my mom is kind of overprotective. Especially with this recent thing about another missing girl."

Kendall nodded. "Yes, that's not looking very good for her."

"It's so sad." Anna felt genuinely sorry for the girl, but she also felt sorry for herself and the way her mom had been hanging that whole thing over her head all week, warning Anna again and again to be careful and not to go out alone and just being generally paranoid.

"It's one of the reasons I've decided to take in roommates," said Kendall. "Safety in numbers, you know?"

"Absolutely." Anna nodded eagerly. "In fact, I think it's probably the only way I can move out with her blessing—or at least without some sort of ugly and unresolvable dispute."

"And there's a certain security about sharing housing with respectable women. That's why I'm conducting such thorough interviews."

"Yes." Anna nodded. "I'm sure my mother would be very impressed."

Kendall smiled. "Well, it is partially because of my grandmother. She gave me the house, but with stipulations as to how I could use it."

"Such as?"

"No live-in boyfriends. No crazy parties. And only housemates that my grandmother would approve."

"So is she going to interview us too?"

Kendall laughed. "No way. I think she trusts me on this. Although I wouldn't be surprised if she popped in from time to time just to check in on us."

"I think my mom would like your grandma."

"And probably vice versa."

"So when do you think you'll make up your mind on this?" Anna twisted the strap of her purse more tightly now, controlling the urge to bite her lip—a bad habit that she'd given up years ago. Maybe she should just cut her losses and make a quick getaway.

"Is that Prada?" asked Kendall.

"What?"

"Your bag."

"Oh, yeah."

"Nice."

"Thanks. It was a graduation present from my mom."

"She has good taste."

"I think my aunt helped her pick it out. She's the one with the taste in the family. Although I'd like to think I could learn." She grimaced.

"It's not that hard."

"Maybe for you, but I'm not like you, Kendall. The truth is, I'm kind of fashion challenged." She brightened now. "But maybe if you rent me a room some of your style will rub off on me."

"So, Anna." Kendall peered curiously at her now, making Anna feel like a bug under a microscope, like maybe she should just crawl away. "What would you bring to the table?"

"What?" Anna felt defensive. "Okay, don't take this wrong, Kendall, but as a renter of a room in your house, I would bring my rent money to the table."

Kendall nodded. "I'm sorry, that came out wrong. But there are a lot of applicants. Tell me why I should pick you to rent to."

"Well, I'm tidy. I'm responsible. I'm a pretty good cook, although I don't plan to be in charge of cooking. I'm usually pretty cheerful. And I play guitar."

"You play guitar?"

"Yes, and I sing too." Anna didn't admit that sometimes she sang opera in the shower—a habit that her college roommates hadn't always appreciated.

"Cool." Kendall wrote something on the bottom of Anna's résumé, then smiled and extended her hand. "Thanks for playing along. I know it probably seems silly, but I really want girls who will be compatible."

"No, no, that's okay. I understand," Anna assured her. Maybe this had gone better than she'd assumed.

"So, I'll call you, okay?"

"Cool."

Anna thanked Kendall for considering her, then put her purse strap over her shoulder and, holding her head high, walked away. But as she reached the door she noticed a beautiful blonde who appeared to be waiting for the next appointment. Anna actually blinked to see this girl. She could have been Kendall's sister. Well, that settled it. Anna didn't have a ghost of a chance now. Maybe her mother was right. Maybe she should just keep living at home.

Anna felt like giving up as she slowly walked to her car. The sky was dark and gray, probably about ready to let loose again, but she didn't care. She was only going home. Home to where her mother would probably remind her of what unsafe times they lived in. Really, why had she even wasted her time trying to fit into a world that obviously did not belong to her? Why force her way onto people who obviously didn't want her? Her mother was probably right about her being a yuppie too—in that Anna always did seem to be striving for more, asking for too much, trying too hard to be fulfilled, appreciated, accepted, and liked.

And yet part of her felt indignant too. When had she developed this give-up mentality? This twisted attitude that only the beautiful can land on top? If applying to rent a stupid bedroom in some supposedly glamorous house was nothing more than a beauty pageant, well then, why should she care?

But she knew why she cared so much. And she knew exactly where these warped ideas had been conceived. As usual, she would blame it on Jake. If he hadn't made those promises to her. If he hadn't told her she was his one and only, the love of his life, the most beautiful woman on the planet. If he hadn't sworn his loyalty, his devotion, his never-ending love—well, then her heart never would've been broken.

In his defense, and he certainly needed it, maybe he would've still felt that way if Kayla hadn't come along. Beautiful Kayla, not so unlike

Kendall or Lelani or even that nameless girl who was waiting for her interview, waltzed in and stole Jake's heart. Anna never had a chance. Jake had
made his apologies, taken the blame, but then he'd moved on. And when
he did, he left Anna behind. And that's where she'd been stuck for more
than a year.

She reached the parking lot just as the rain came splattering down.
She ducked inside her compact car and inserted the key into the ignition.
But instead of turning on the engine and simply driving home and acting
like everything was just fine—the way she had done so many times
before—Anna leaned her head against the steering wheel and just cried.
As rain pounded on the roof of the car, careening down the windshield
like it had passed through an open floodgate, Anna cried.

Then finally, when she was finished and had blown her nose and
wiped off her wet face, she took in a long, jagged breath and decided it
was time to quit blaming everything on Jake. Even if she didn't get to
share a house with a bunch of Barbies—and would she even really want
that anyway?—she would find something suitable. Some place where she
fit in and could feel good about herself. Because Anna was ready to set old
things aside today. She was ready to move on to something new.

# Eight

# Kendall

"I need help and I need it now," pleaded Kendall. She'd just called three of the girls she met today, informing them that they'd been chosen for the privilege of living in her "luxurious" home, and then she realized that it really wasn't looking all that great.

"What on earth is wrong?" asked her older sister, Kate.

"I've got renters coming tomorrow."

"You're renting Nana's house?"

"Housemates," she said quickly. "I'm getting housemates to share expenses."

"What expenses?"

"What difference does it make?" Kendall regretting calling her sister, but she didn't know anyone else who knew about things like furniture and decor. Kate, twelve years older, had a gorgeous home—and Kendall needed her expertise now.

"Does Nana know about this?"

"Of course. And in case you've forgotten, Nana gave the house to me." With conditions, but Kendall didn't need to say what her sister already knew.

"And that was probably a mistake."

"Thanks."

"So what kind of people are you renting to anyway?" asked Kate.

"Very nice, professional young women. I had them send me their résumés and do interviews and everything."

There was a brief silence. "Well, that sounds more intelligent than usual."

"And considering the criminal element in this town, and the way young women seem to be going missing every few months, I'd think you'd be happy for me to have housemates, Kate."

"I suppose it could be sensible." But Kate still sounded somewhat skeptical. Sometimes Kendall wondered if and when anyone in her family, besides Nana, would ever take her seriously.

"So will you help me then?"

"What do you want me to do, Kendall?"

"I need you to go shopping with me."

Kate laughed. "The shopping queen is asking *moi* for help?"

"I'm not shopping for clothes or shoes or bags," snapped Kendall. "I need to get things for the house. You know, cool things to make it look really nice. I don't know much about that."

"Oh, well, that sounds like fun. When did you want to do this?"

"Right now!"

"Right now, as in today?" Kate made that sucking noise between her teeth, never a good sign. And Kendall could imagine her sister's brow furrowing—an expression that Kendall had warned her would bring on premature wrinkling.

"I had today in mind," admitted Kendall.

"That's impossible."

"Okay, how about tonight?"

"I can't."

"Tomorrow morning?"

"No. Tom and I are about to head out. He got us reservations at the coast. I'm sure it wouldn't occur to you, but tomorrow's our anniversary."

"Happy anniversary." Kendall's voice fell flat now.

"Thanks a lot."

"So what should I do then?"

"I don't know, Kendall. What exactly is it that you want to accomplish?"

"I just want to make the place look good."

Kate laughed. "In one day? You must be crazy."

"Yeah." Kendall looked around the dingy living room and knew Kate was probably right. "I got a new sectional," she said meekly.

"What color?"

"Kind of white-ish. I think it was called ecru."

"Well, that's a start."

"But it looks pretty boring. And now that beige carpet in here looks shabby."

"That carpet *is* shabby."

"I got a new coffee table too."

"What style?"

"I don't know. It's square and made of wood."

Kate laughed again. "You're hopeless, Kendall."

"Thanks."

"Okay, let me think. For starters, get some colorful pillows and a throw to put on the sectional. And a couple of interesting lamps to warm the place up. And if you buy any furniture, you might want to consider something in mission or craftsman style, and if you need it by tomorrow—which is absolutely nuts—you'll have to go with places like World Market, Pier 1, or the home-improvement stores. And for the kitchen things, I saw that Macy's has a big sale on—"

"Wait, wait," yelled Kendall as she dug through her Michael Kors bag for paper and pen. "I need to write this down."

For the next thirty minutes, Kendall attempted to get her sister's recommendations on paper, but by the time she was finished, she had a mess of almost unreadable notes, plus a throbbing headache. What had made her think she could pull this off?

"And don't forget about curb appeal," said Kate as they were about to hang up.

"Curb appeal?"

"Yes. Clean up the porch. Get a couple of outdoor chairs, if you can find them, and put out a pot of plants."

"A pot of plants?"

"Yes, like ornamental cabbages. That should probably last until Thanksgiving."

Kendall wrote this down and wondered how in the world she could possibly accomplish all this in the next twenty-four hours.

"Good luck," said Kate in a tone that suggested Kendall would need it.

"Have fun at the coast," said Kendall, although she secretly wished that her brother-in-law Eric would suddenly get some big legal case that would force him to cancel this untimely celebration.

As soon as she hung up, Kendall called Marcus.

"What's up?" he asked sleepily.

"Did I wake you?"

"Just having a little afternoon nap."

"I need help."

"With what?"

"Shopping."

He laughed. "Since when do you need help shopping?"

"Since I started buying big things. I need someone with a pickup."

"So, you want me for my truck?"

"Something like that. If you help me, I'll buy you dinner."

"Okay, you talked me into it. What'll I do?"

Kendall suggested they meet at World Market. "I'm heading there now. My sister gave me a list of stuff to buy and I might as well get started."

Kendall knew that this shopping spree was going to involve using plastic, and she only had one card with a significant amount of credit left on it. Still, she told herself, this was an investment. By the time she collected rent and deposits from the three renters, she would have more than enough to cover today's expenses and more.

It was her first time in World Market, but as soon as she started looking around, she knew that Kate was absolutely right. This place had everything—furnishings, dishes, rugs, mirrors, pillows, the works. And the prices weren't bad either. Kate had warned her that these weren't "investment" pieces, but under the circumstances, they would have to suffice. By the time Marcus arrived, she had already made several selections, and a salesgirl had told her about a credit plan that would give her a ten percent discount on everything. Kendall was getting into this!

"Is that all you've got?" asked Marcus when he found her back in the kitchen section putting a set of wine glasses into the cart.

"This is like my fourth cart," she explained. "The others are parked up in front for when I check out."

He rolled his eyes.

"Also, there are some bigger furniture items. In fact, maybe I should pay for those items so you can get them loaded in the pickup and take them to my place."

It was eight o'clock by the time Kendall had completed her shopping, including several trips to deliver the household items to her house, and she was exhausted.

"What about that dinner you promised?" asked Marcus as she piled the last of the Macy's bags in the living room, which already looked like a hurricane had hit.

Kendall was tempted to beg out, but she knew that might put this relationship in peril, and she wasn't sure she wanted to lose this guy yet. Especially after all the help he'd been this afternoon. Plus, she knew that some of the furniture items she'd purchased today had "some assembly required."

"Name the place," she told Marcus. "Then you call ahead while I clean up a bit." Who knew that putting together a house could feel like running a marathon? And, here, Kendall had thought she was a pro at shopping.

Kendall's bedroom was on the second floor. She had used the room since she was a little girl and visited her grandmother here. Unfortunately, not much had changed in this room since then either. But at least it was private and right next to the upstairs bathroom. She noticed her clutter of beauty products lining the shelves and vanity and realized she would soon be sharing that bathroom with someone else. She changed her outfit, going to the other bedroom, which she was currently using as a closet annex, and it hit her that she'd need to find another place for her clothes as well. Maybe she hadn't planned this as carefully as she'd thought.

"I'll think about that tomorrow," she told herself as she freshened her blush and lip gloss, gave herself a generous squirt of Gucci Envy, then hurried down to join Marcus.

After a leisurely dinner, and after Kendall had paid the bill, she gave Marcus an enticing look and invited him to come home with her.

His brows lifted hopefully. "Sure, that sounds great, babe."

"So, are you pretty handy then?" She leaned over the table with a coy smile.

"Oh, yeah," he said with a firm nod.

"Good," she said sitting up straighter. "I need help putting that furniture together."

Marcus groaned and leaned back in his chair. "I don't know, Kendall. It's getting kind of late."

She scowled at him now. "Fine. I'll do it myself."

He glanced at his watch. "Well, I guess I could give you an hour or two." He shook his finger at her. "But then you'll owe me."

She smiled again. "That's okay. I'll think of some way to repay you."

As it turned out, Marcus helped her put things together until well past midnight. Even by then, they were only partially done.

"Unless you're letting me spend the night, I'd better go," he said sleepily.

"No, you're not spending the night." She looked at the clock she'd just hung in the kitchen. It was nearly one. "And I'm so tired that I'll probably start making more dumb mistakes like when I put the table legs on backward."

"That was from not reading the directions," he pointed out as he slipped on his jacket.

"Yes, I did learn something, didn't I?"

He leaned over and kissed her. "That they put those instructions in the box for a reason."

"And in twelve different languages too." She smiled up at him. "Thanks for helping."

"Don't forget, you owe me now."

She nodded seriously. "As soon as you need help putting furniture together, I want to be the first one you call."

He frowned and she knew that was clearly not what he had in mind. Of course, she didn't really care either. She'd learned enough times—the hard way—that guys pursued her more intensely when she wasn't giving it away. And this time she planned to stick to her guns. "Thanks again," she said as she walked him to the front door.

She closed and locked the door, then turned around to see the huge mess of cardboard and plastic and Styrofoam that littered the living room, along with bags of kitchen items that still needed to be stowed away. "Tomorrow," she muttered as she turned off the lights and trudged up the stairs to collapse in her bed.

But tomorrow morning came and, as usual, Kendall had difficulty getting up. It was nearly noon by the time she crawled out of bed, and even then it took her a moment, when she saw the mess downstairs, to remember exactly what was going on here.

"Renters," she said aloud as she shuffled into the kitchen to search for her coffeemaker. The countertops were lined with boxes and dishes and things—the sorts of things she had no idea where to place. Why hadn't she asked Kate about that?

But she cleared a spot by the sink and as her coffee dripped, she attempted to put some of the things away. For the next several hours, Kendall plodded along, but it seemed that every time she solved one problem, she created another. For instance, she got the dishes put away, but then there was no place for the glasses. But perhaps that was because she'd gotten too many dishes. So she put some of them into the pantry, which made less room for food, and so it went. How were people supposed to know how to do such things? Had there been some college course she'd missed before she'd dropped out midway through her third year? Eventually she simply stuffed things wherever they would fit. Out of sight, out of mind.

After all, today was all about first impressions. Functionality was secondary. So, pretending that she was "dressing" the house for a big date, she simply put out the things she thought made it look good and decided not to worry about the cupboards or closets. And she stowed everything else in the garage.

She was in a race against the clock, and Kendall was afraid the clock might win. She'd invited all her renters to see the place and meet each other at five o'clock. By now she was fully aware that her house description in her ad might've been misleading, but her hope was to charm everyone into seeing past the minor flaws of the house and to recognize its potential. She'd even ordered a special dinner from a new French restaurant that was supposed to be delivered at six. Her plan was to significantly wow these women, have the table beautifully set, with candles even, and then serve this fantastic meal. Before they left for the evening, she expected them to have signed the one-year lease and handed over their checks.

Piece of cake. Or so she hoped.

# Nine

# Megan

"So when can I see the house?" Megan had asked after Kendall informed her that she'd been selected as a renter.

"Sunday at five," said Kendall. "The other girls will be here too, I'll show you all around, and then we'll have dinner together."

"That sounds great," said Megan with real excitement.

"And you can start moving in whenever you want," said Kendall. "Even though it's not quite October yet, I've decided to let you all move in next week. You get a few days free."

"That's great. I already have someone interested in taking my spot in this apartment," said Megan. "I can't wait to move in."

"The address of the house is 86 Bloomberg Place."

"I've heard that Bloomberg Place is a nice neighborhood," said Megan.

"Yes, and it's not far from town."

"It'll be great to just walk to work."

"So, I'll see you tomorrow."

"At five," said Megan. After she hung up, Megan actually hopped around her tiny apartment bedroom and did a happy dance. Things were definitely looking up. Megan was tempted to sneak over to get a peek at 86 Bloomberg Place, but it was raining cats and dogs out there, and she had no intention of getting onto that smelly, damp bus again.

Fortunately, Sunday's weather, while gray, seemed less foreboding and, after church, Megan rode the bus downtown, got herself a coffee, and sort of meandered on over to Bloomberg Place. Okay, the truth was, she felt somewhat like a stalker and seriously hoped that Kendall wouldn't be around to spot her. That would be embarrassing.

Still, Kendall had been somewhat mysterious, requiring résumés, interviews, a special meeting and dinner today. Megan felt that it was worth getting a sneak preview. Besides, she told herself as she turned onto Bloomberg Place, what if this Kendall was some kind of scam artist? What if she planned to take their money and run? Megan wanted to have a good heads up before she got herself into something she'd regret.

She walked about a block before she arrived at 86 Bloomberg Place, and when she saw the house, she thought she must have made a mistake. Perhaps the house number wasn't on right. Maybe a numeral was missing or one had flipped upside down. But then she looked at the houses, much nicer houses, on either side and across the street, and realized that, no, the address was probably correct.

Even so, this rundown house didn't seem anything like the ad's description. Megan racked her brain to remember the exact phrasing, but could only come up with words like *historic* or *upscale neighborhood*, and those descriptions were mostly true. The bungalow style home did appear to be fairly old, and the surrounding neighborhood actually was quite nice. And the house, in its own way, was charming with its generous front porch and craftsman-styled columns and lead-glass windows. But Megan also knew that something about that ad had been misleading. She just couldn't put her finger on it. Oh, yes, something about *luxurious*.

Of course, she hadn't been inside the home yet, but she found it hard to believe that this one-and-a-half-story house, while sweet, would be considered luxurious. Perhaps the interior was completely restored. Although if the exterior was any indication, Megan didn't think so. The siding appeared to be in need of paint, and the front yard had been sadly neglected, especially compared to the other well-maintained homes on this street. 86 Bloomberg Place was a bit of an eyesore. But something about the house tugged at her. It obviously needed someone to care for it. Still, that rent. It just didn't seem to match up.

And yet Megan had always been fond of bungalow-style houses. And the idea of sharing one wasn't disappointing, but perhaps the rent was a bit steep. They could sort that out this evening.

Finally, feeling like a real stalker, although she was standing across the street, pretending to be sipping her now empty cup of coffee and waiting for—what?—she decided she better move on before a suspicious neighbor called the police.

Megan walked slowly down the street, admiring the various styles of architecture. How unusual and interesting that one neighborhood could be so diverse. Her dad would've appreciated a neighborhood like this. Being an architect, he often complained about developments where all the houses looked the same. Sure, maybe the paint colors differed or the floor plan was flipped, but those houses seemed to be about conformity and cost-efficiency. Her dad used to jokingly wonder if people ever got confused after a hard day's work and walked into the wrong house, or got lost trying to remember what made their house different. Meanwhile, her dad had tried to design houses and buildings with personality and unique features that made them memorable. And he, like her, had been fond of bungalows.

Remembering these qualities about Dad made Megan miss her mom. So, as she slowly walked back toward town, she decided to call. Megan hadn't intended to inform her mom about this possible move until she was actually in the house. Now she felt like she needed advice and encouragement from someone who loved her.

"Oh, it's so good to hear your voice, sweetie," said Mom. "What's up?"

Megan explained about the housing situation and how she'd sent in her résumé and been interviewed and the works. "It's a bungalow and probably about eighty years old. The paint's a little peely and the yard needs work, but it's actually really cute."

"Oh, it sounds delightful."

"It would be nice not to share a room with anyone," admitted Megan, not mentioning the rent. "And it's in a really great part of town. Bloomberg Place."

"Oh, I love that neighborhood. That's fantastic, honey. I'm so happy you're getting out of that apartment complex. I keep thinking about that missing girl—both of those girls. And I can't help but worry about you. Although I do pray. Still, you getting a room in a nice neighborhood, well, it's an answer to my prayers!"

"So you think I should go for it then?"

"Of course. Absolutely."

"It's not as cheap as the apartment."

"Sometimes you have to choose safety over finances. I know your dad would have agreed with me on this."

"And I do have a job interview—actually it's the second one."

"Where?"

"Sawyer & Craig. I'd only be an assistant, but I already met with Cynthia Sawyer and she seemed to like me. I meet with Vera on Tuesday."

"That is so wonderful to hear. Things are really looking up for you. I actually know Vera Craig from my college days. In fact, you can tell her that if you like."

"Meaning that's a plus?"

Mom laughed. "Of course. I wouldn't tell you to mention me to someone if we'd been enemies. We were only casual friends, but I did like

her and think she liked me. And I'm sure she knows who your dad was—
if you want to drop that little tidbit. It never hurts, you know."

"Thanks, Mom. That's helpful. I actually think it would be kind of
fun to work there. Not as a career, but just until I can get a teaching position. I'm sure I'd learn a lot about interior decorating too."

"And I'll bet you'd be really good at it, Megan. You've always had such
a good eye for color and design."

"Kendall, that's the girl who's renting the rooms, said I can move in
this week, even though it's not October. So maybe I'll try to get settled
tomorrow. Just in case I get hired at Sawyer & Craig."

"Want some help?"

"Sure. You know I don't have that much, but I'd considered renting a
small moving van. It's not like I can haul my stuff over there on the bus."

"Now that would be something to see." She laughed. "How about I
take you to breakfast tomorrow morning, and then we'll attack it
together."

"Thanks. That sounds perfect."

"See you then."

Megan felt much better after she hung up. Oh, she wanted to think
of herself as secure and independent and able to make decisions like this
on her own. But losing Dad last summer had sort of rocked her world.
And things she'd once felt confident doing didn't come so easily now.
Having Mom's support wouldn't be such a bad thing. Like the soloist had
sung at church this morning, "No man is an island." Megan knew that
had been part of her problem this past month. She'd isolated herself. She'd
made an unhealthy choice, but all that was about to change.

Ten

# Lelani

"Lelani?" called Aunt Caroline from the kitchen. "Could you watch Gracie for me while I take Sophie and Daniel to Jennie Lynn's birthday party?"

Lelani popped her head out of the garage/laundry room into the kitchen. "Sure."

"I'd take her along, but she'll be so ready for a nap by then." Her aunt used a dishcloth to swipe something green and slimy from Gracie's pudgy face, then extracted her from the high chair.

"No problem." Actually, Lelani was pleased at the prospect of having the place to herself for a couple of hours. Peace and quiet were hard to come by in this house. "But I do have that appointment at five," she reminded her aunt. "That means I'll need to leave here by four fifteen to get there in time."

"Ronnie should be home by four," said Aunt Caroline. "But we should be back long before that anyway." She glanced at the kitchen clock. "In fact, we should get going. I wonder if Sophie and Daniel are ready yet."

"How about if I take Gracie," suggested Lelani, extending her arms for the baby.

"She needs to be changed and—"

"And she needs to be cleaned up some more too, don't you Baby Gracie?" cooed Lelani as she tickled the baby's still messy face. "How about if I give her a bath?"

"Oh, would you?" Aunt Caroline looked so happy Lelani thought she was about to cry. "That would be fantastic. She didn't get one last night, and by the time we get home, I'll be—"

"Don't worry," said Lelani. "Gracie shall be squeaky clean by the time you get home."

"You are an angel!" Then her aunt got a very sad expression. "I don't know what I'll do if you leave me, Lelani. It's been so wonderful having you here. Are you sure you want to move out? What if we made room for you?"

"Where?" Lelani looked around the already crowded and cluttered spaces.

"Maybe we could put all three kids in Daniel's room. It's actually the biggest."

"Oh, I don't know."

"But you're family, Lelani. Family should stick together."

Lelani didn't know what to say.

"Well, think about it anyway," said her aunt as Daniel and Sophie came tearing down the hallway. "We need to get going."

Soon Lelani had the house and baby Gracie to herself. She partially filled the bathtub off the master bedroom, since that's where all the baby paraphernalia was, and before long Gracie was clean and sweet-smelling. Her eyelids were getting droopy as well. Lelani tucked her into the crib that was wedged into the tiny room she shared with Sophie, and within a minute, the baby was fast asleep. Lelani stood there for a bit just watching the sleeping infant, and a great big lump grew in her throat. She heard her aunt's words replaying through her head. "Family should stick together … Family should stick together …"

Maybe that was true. But maybe it wasn't always possible. Blocking these thoughts from her head, Lelani tiptoed out of the bedroom, quietly shut the door, and returned to do damage control in the bathroom, sopping up the splashes with a used towel as she let the water drain from the tub. Then she put the tub toys back in the basket, and just as she was giving the tub a much-needed wipe down, bending over to scrub off what seemed like months' worth of soap scum, she heard footsteps.

"What have we here?" said her uncle as he stood in the doorway.

"Oh?" She looked up in surprise. "I was just cleaning up after—"

"Is lovely Lelani going to take a bath in my tub?" he asked in a teasing voice.

She stood up quickly now, dropping the sponge and realizing that her T-shirt was fairly soggy from bathing Gracie and cleaning the tub. "Excuse me," she said, crossing her hands over her wet T-shirt as she moved closer to the door, which he was blocking. "Aunt Caroline said you wouldn't be home for—"

"No need to run off, Lelani." He placed a hand on her shoulder now, smiling at her as if they were old friends. "Why don't you sit down? We can have a little chat. I hear that you're thinking about leaving us and I—"

"Excuse me," she said as she shrugged his hand off her shoulder. "But I was just cleaning up after Gracie's bath. I'm done now."

But he still didn't budge from where he stood blocking the door. "No need to be so unfriendly." Now he got what looked like a hurt expression. "Have I done something to offend you? It seems you're always avoiding me." This time he reached up to touch her cheek.

She cringed. "Please, Uncle Ronnie. Let me through."

And then to her horror, he actually grabbed her. Not in a malicious way, but more like he expected her to return his embrace. She stiffened and gave him a firm shove. "Do not touch me," she hissed at him with narrowed eyes.

"Ooh," he said in a taunting tone. "You're even prettier when you get angry. Real fire in those black eyes." And he reached for her again. But this time she doubled up her fist and took a hard swing, landing the hit right smack on her uncle's nose. Stunned by this, his hands flew up to his face, and she blasted past him and straight to the hall closet where she had been keeping her things. She jerked out her duffel bag and began ripping her clothes from hangers and stuffing them inside.

"Hey, you don't have to go nuts on me," said her uncle from behind her. "I was just trying to be friendly."

She turned and glared at him now. "That is not what I consider friendly."

He rolled his eyes and waved his hand at her. "Oh, you Porters and your superiority complexes. You all think you're better than everyone."

There were so many things she could've said just then, but she knew it was pointless. "Baby Gracie is taking a nap. Your *wife* and children will be home in about an hour. I am moving out now and I will pick up the rest of my things later this week." As she pulled on her parka over her still damp T-shirt, Uncle Ronnie protested, saying she didn't have to go and that he was just having fun with her and that she shouldn't take everything so seriously. Finally, when she had her hand on the doorknob, he started to plead with her. "Please, don't tell Caroline about this, Lelani. She won't understand."

She looked him in the eye now, still fuming and suppressing the urge to hit him again. "Fine!" she snapped. "I won't tell her now. But if you *ever* pull something like this on me again, or if I ever hear of you trying something like that on anyone else, you can bet your life I'll tell her." Then she threw the strap of her duffel bag over her shoulder and marched out. Of course, she knew she'd have to make up some explanation for her aunt. But she also knew she was finished there. Maybe some families stuck together, but she didn't have to stick with this one.

Her dad had always said that Ronnie was no good. To be honest, her opinion of her uncle hadn't been much higher. Now it was lower than dirt. She remembered when Ronnie and Caroline came to Maui for their honeymoon but ended up staying with her family the whole time. Some honeymoon. Lelani's dad had said it was because Ronnie was cheap. Not to his face, of course, but it was clear that Dad didn't approve of his baby sister's choice in a husband. Now she had an even better understanding of why.

Still, as she trudged down to the bus stop, she knew she'd miss her aunt and the kids. And yet she knew it would be a relief to get away from them too. Being around them, especially baby Gracie—well, it was just too much too soon.

Lelani had told Kendall that she probably wouldn't move into the house until next weekend since she was working full days all week, but now she would take Kendall up on that offer of a few free days. She just hoped Kendall wouldn't think it strange that all she was bringing with her was a duffel bag.

Lelani looked at the clock at the bus stop. It was only three forty and too early to show up at 86 Bloomberg Place. Besides that, how could she show up looking like she'd just been a contestant in a wet T-shirt contest? Then she remembered the employees' lounge at Nordstrom and the roomy bathroom, well-lit mirror, and the private back entrance. And being that this was Sunday, her regular boss wouldn't be around to ask what she was doing there. Maybe she could sneak in, clean up, change clothes, and be on her way. Why should anyone care?

Even so, she felt nervous as she slipped in through the employees' entrance and up the back stairway. But no one seemed to be around. And, thankfully, no one was in the break room. Before long, she was completely cleaned up and ready to go.

"Lelani?" said Mr. Green as he met her coming back down the stairway. "What are *you* doing here today? I didn't see your name on the roster."

Mr. Green—or Mr. Mean as most of his employees called him—was a lower-level manager, but a person who thought he should be more respected by his subordinates. And he was looking suspiciously at her duffel bag just now. "I wasn't scheduled," she told him. "I just needed to—uh—use the restroom and I thought—"

"What's in the bag?"

Before she could answer, he slipped the strap of the bag from her shoulder and carried it back to the employees' lounge. "It's just personal stuff," she said quickly. "I had some wet—"

"Why don't you let me be the one to determine that," he said as he slapped the bag onto the table and zipped it open. "Employee theft is at an all-time high."

For the second time today, Lelani felt violated by a male. She felt her face burning with embarrassment and rage as he rummaged through her still damp clothes and handled items including bras and underwear until he finally seemed satisfied that she was not a thief. But then he turned and peered at her as if he thought she was mentally ill, and she could just imagine the report he was going to make about this.

"Look," she told him as she crammed her things back into her bag. "I've been living with my aunt and I had just given her baby a bath and I was all wet, and her husband came in and he was making, well, improper advances and—well, I know this doesn't make sense—but I just had to make a getaway. So I grabbed my stuff, but I was still wearing those wet clothes and I have an appointment at five o'clock to rent a room from this very proper woman in a nice neighborhood, and I couldn't walk in there wearing wet clothes and—" She stopped talking now and realized that she was crying.

Then she looked up at Mr. Green and actually saw a trace of compassion on his normally stern face. "Anyway"—she used the damp T-shirt to wipe her wet face—"that's the truth."

He nodded. "I believe you."

"You do?"

He sort of laughed now. "That's not exactly an easy story to conjure on the spot." He pointed to the clock above the couch. It was twenty minutes to five now. "Will you make it to your appointment on time?"

She nodded. "I think so. It's not far from here."

"I was just leaving. I could give you a ride if you want. It looked like it was about to rain again out there."

Okay, part of her was fed up with men and ready to brush him off, and yet a part of her seemed to trust this guy. Besides that, she knew she had a good right punch. "Okay," she said, "that would be nice."

His car was about ten years old, a white Taurus, but it was neat and smelled clean and she didn't see anything dangerous (like chainsaws, axes, guns, knives) when she tossed her duffel bag in the back. She knew she was probably being slightly paranoid, but the two missing college coeds were at the front of her mind. It seemed that every young woman in town was on high alert these days. Still, Lelani trusted her instincts about Mr. Green. He seemed a very conscientious and law-abiding person. And it turned out that his weather forecast was correct too.

"Looks like you were right about the weather," she said as raindrops began to splatter down on the windshield. "The address is 86 Bloomberg Place."

"That's a posh neighborhood," he said as he pulled out of the parking lot and turned on his wipers.

"That's what the ad said."

"You mean you haven't seen the house yet?"

"No, but I met the owner and she seemed nice." Lelani sighed. "And I guess I'm a little desperate for a place to live." Then, as he drove, she told him about the application process and how she'd been worried she wouldn't get in. "I even promised to take the woman home with me when I go back to visit Maui—I wonder if that came off as a bribe."

He chuckled as he turned onto the street. She glanced over and thought it was unfortunate that most of the salespeople at Nordstrom assumed he was so mean. He actually seemed rather nice now that she had the chance to know him.

"Here you go," he said as he pulled up in front of what looked like the least impressive house on the block.

"Are you sure that's right?" She stared hard at the house. It didn't look anything like what she'd expected.

"You said 86 Bloomberg place, didn't you?"

"Yes." She looked at the overgrown yard, the house in need of paint, and frowned.

"Is something wrong?" he asked.

"No. It's just that I thought it would be, well, a little fancier, you know." She shrugged. "Not that I really care about that so much. I mean, as long as it's clean and safe, I'm sure I'll be just fine with it."

He smiled at her. "Well, good luck. And, by the way, I'm sorry if I came across as a bit abrupt in the employees' lounge earlier. But it is true that some employees steal from the company."

She looked him straight in the eyes now. "I wouldn't do that, Mr. Green."

He nodded. "I believe you."

She thanked him and retrieved her bag from the backseat. Then she grinned at him and, crossing her fingers, waved as he drove away.

"Here goes nothing," she said to herself as she marched up the walk. Of course, myriad misgivings set in as she was about to ring the doorbell. What if this was some sort of strange setup or possible scam? What if she had made a mistake in her assessment of Kendall? What if Kendall was somehow related to the missing young women in this town? Okay, that seemed totally ridiculous. Still, Lelani felt uneasy as she rang the bell. But then again, she reminded herself of Uncle Ronnie. How safe was that little setup?

_Eleven_

# Anna

Anna's mother exploded. "I can't believe you want to waste all that money just to rent a room!"

Anna had just broken the news, and her mother's reaction was more extreme than Anna had anticipated. She'd started out ranting about crime and safety issues, reminding Anna that there were now two, not just one, missing girls in their town. When Anna argued that living with three other women would be safe and that she would be closer to her job and not driving across town, where she could possibly get in a wreck, Mom detoured down the financial route. She acted appalled that Anna was willing to pay $550 a month to rent a room. Of course, Anna hadn't even mentioned the cost of the deposits or the one-year lease yet. In fact, she now had no intention of doing so.

"It's my money," said Anna, openly irritated. She had given up on defusing this conversation.

"And you want to throw away your hard-earned money like that?"

"Renting a room in a nice house within walking distance of my job is not throwing my money away, Mom."

"It is when you have free room and board right here."

"I don't want to live right here."

Her mother's black eyes smoldered like two hot coals, and Anna knew she'd stepped too far over the line. She also knew there was no turning back.

"*What?*" demanded her mom. "So, are you too good to live with your family now?"

"You know that I love my family," Anna backtracked. No good would come of hurting Mom over this. Family meant more than anything to her mother, and to dismiss it lightly would only create a mess that would take weeks, maybe months, to clean up. "And I love this house and I'd like to come and visit … but I just need a little more independence. Besides, I'll save money on gas by living closer to—"

"Your car gets excellent gas mileage! You said that's why you needed such a tiny car—a car that I still feel is completely unsafe, not that anyone listens to me."

"Yes, but that's not the only reason I want to—"

"I just do not understand you, *mi hija*. After all your father and I have done for you. And expensive college and the new car for your graduation present and we just put in that swimming pool so you kids could—"

"I never wanted that pool," said Anna. "You put it in because you wanted it, Mom."

"So are you saying that you're willing to throw away good money just because you don't want to live at home with your family? You'd rather live with strangers than us?"

"It's not like that, Mom."

Her mom made a huffing noise, turned her back to Anna, and pretended to busy herself with scrubbing the already spotless sink.

"I just need some space—"

"*Space?*" Her mother reeled around, waving her hands widely. "This house—this house has almost four thousand square feet of space! That's almost a thousand square feet per person living here. When I was growing up in my family's home—a family of nine—our space was not even half as big as this kitchen!"

"Oh, Mom." Anna rolled her eyes. How many versions of this story had she heard over and over again?

"And you want to pay $550 a month just to rent one small bedroom so that you will have *more space?*" Now her mother started speaking in rapid Spanish, using expletives that she would never tolerate in English, and that's when Anna knew this whole conversation was pointless. Why had she even bothered? Last night she had tried to win her father over to her change of address, but as usual he took the coward's way out, which was to agree with her mother before he made his quiet escape to work.

"Mama, Mama, Mama," said Gil as he emerged from the family room. Anna suspected he'd been lurking there this whole time, probably enjoying the fact that she was breaking the ice for him. So much for moral support!

"Do you know about this?" she demanded. "Have you heard of your sister's half-baked plan to throw away good money to rent a room?"

"Calm yourself down, old girl ... before you have a stroke." He went over to where their mother still hovered near the sink, wringing a dish towel in her hands and acting as if her whole world was crumbling. Sometimes Anna wondered why her mother hadn't pursued a career in acting instead of cooking. Mom began to mutter in Spanish again, but she quieted down as Gil slipped a comforting arm around her shoulders.

"It's not the end of the world, Mama," he calmly assured her.

"Yes," added Anna. "You're acting as if I'd signed up with some sci-fi cult where we all plan to meet the mother ship and fly off into space to mate with aliens. Good grief, Mom, I'm simply moving downtown with three other mature and responsible career women."

"You do not even *know* these women," protested Mom. "You said so yourself."

"I met two of them," said Anna meekly. "They seemed nice."

"Seemed?"

"Mom," said Gil soothingly. "Anna is an intelligent person. You've raised her to use good judgment. And she just needs a chance to spread her wings a little. I'd think you'd be glad she's living with other women her age. What if she were getting an apartment by herself? Or even worse, what if she wanted to move in with a boyfriend?"

Their mom looked truly aghast now. "Anna would not do that."

"Yes, I would," said Anna stubbornly. "Okay, maybe not the moving in with a boyfriend part. But I was thinking about an apartment of my own."

"A young woman is not safe on her own," insisted Mom. "We already have two missing college girls … and they are about your age, Anna. A lone girl isn't safe in this town and you—"

"Then just be happy that I won't be living alone. I'll have three responsible and mature housemates. The woman I'm renting from did extensive interviews. Her grandmother owns the house and has very high standards, Mom."

"And the house is in a respectable neighborhood," Gil pointed out.

"A *safe* neighborhood," added Anna, although she wasn't entirely sure of this. "And it's not on campus."

"And I'll help her move her stuff over there," offered Gil. "If it makes you feel better I can check the place out and report back to you."

Now the irony of having Gil, almost three years her junior, offering to look out for Anna like this was slightly insulting. And yet she knew it was simply a cultural thing. Males just got more respect. But if it helped her case, she wouldn't complain.

"That would be good," admitted her mom.

"Anna lived away from home during college," he pointed out. "You managed to survive that."

"But I was so happy when she came home." Now Mom had tears coming down her cheeks as she reached for Anna. "*Mi hija*, I just do not want to lose you."

Anna hugged her mom. "The only way you'll lose me is if you hang on too tightly, Mom. You should know that makes me want to run in the opposite direction."

"I know, I know." Mom used the rumpled dish towel to wipe her cheeks, slowly nodding. Then she peered at Gil. "And you'll take Anna's things, like you said, and you'll make sure the place is a good place?"

He smiled. "Yes, Mama, count on it."

"Well." She sighed. "All right. I guess it's okay for Anna to move out."

Anna knew it would seem strange to someone who didn't understand their culture that she, although twenty-five and college-educated and gainfully employed, still needed her mother's blessing to make a decision like this, but she knew that she did. Yet even as she thanked her mom, Anna felt that some of these family ties were more like shackles and bonds and, more than ever, she felt the need for distance.

"I'm going over to see the house and meet the other women," said Anna, noticing that it was already four. "The owner, Kendall, is fixing us dinner."

"You haven't seen the house yet?" Mom looked perplexed and ready to go for round two.

"It's okay," said Anna quickly. "It's in a great neighborhood and I already know it's really nice."

"And we need to get to the restaurant," Gil said to Mom. "I heard the place is going to be hopping tonight."

Mom nodded. "Yes, there is an engagement dinner at seven and …" She looked sadly and then longingly at Anna. "Oh, *mi hija*, if only it was for—"

"I have to run," called Anna as she made a dash toward the stairs now.

No way did she want to hear her mother's lamentations over the fact that Anna wasn't the one in need of an engagement celebration tonight. Anna seriously needed some space—and she needed it pronto!

She scurried up the stairs, going straight to her bedroom, which really was quite spacious with its walk-in closet and private bath and jetted tub. Okay, her room really wasn't the problem, and she might miss parts of it, including the view of a wooded hillside out her window. Her parents had purchased this house when she was in high school, and it really had been a great place to live, but as much as she liked this room, it was too close for comfort—to her family anyway. And sometimes, like just moments earlier, she felt as if she could barely breathe. So what if her new room wasn't as nice as this—although she expected it would be—it would be preferable to being under Mom's thumb. And it would be one giant step toward freedom and independence.

She dressed carefully, choosing what she hoped was one of her more stylish outfits, a simple pair of black wool pants topped with a blue sweater set. The sweaters were cashmere, which she hoped that would suitably impress the fashionable Kendall Weis, who was way out of Anna's league. Both Kendall and Lelani were the kind of girls that Anna would normally observe from a distance, wondering what it would feel like to live in such beautiful skin. Especially back in her adolescent days when Anna was prone to acne. Fortunately those days had finally passed. Still, she didn't like anyone to look at her complexion too closely.

Anna was surprised that she'd been selected as a roommate, and she had no intentions of jeopardizing Kendall's decision by showing up tonight looking like the true fashion klutz that she was. She'd even bought a new pair of black suede boots after her interview yesterday—the sales-girl had assured her that they were all the rage, plus their nearly three-inch heels made her look taller and, she hoped, slimmer. And they were Prada.

The name alone seemed to suggest status. And Kendall had commented on her Prada bag, so Anna knew that Kendall knew the difference. Of course, the boots had cost about a month's rent, but Anna's savings account was still nicely padded from living at home the past couple of years. And it would be worth it. She knew it would be worth it.

She'd even washed her car, which now seemed silly since it was raining again, but she wanted to make a good impression when she pulled into what she imagined would be nice long driveway.

As she made her way down Bloomberg Place, however, she realized that, while the houses on this street were nice in an old-fashioned sort of way, they were not as big or fancy as her parents' home. Still, she didn't care. This was her first step to freedom.

Then when she actually found 86 Bloomberg Place, she thought there must be some mistake. With its unkempt yard and shabby exterior, this was by far the worst looking house in the neighborhood. Perhaps, in her excitement, she'd written down the address incorrectly. Yes, that had to be it. So, she decided to drive up the street again, going slowly so that she could check her notes more carefully. But she couldn't find another house with a similar address. She returned to the rundown house and noticed a tall, slim woman who looked a lot like Lelani walking toward the porch with a flowered duffel bag slung over one shoulder and determination in her steps. This had to be the right place. She didn't want to think about what her mother's reaction might be when she saw it. She'd probably laugh and say, "I told you so."

# Twelve

# Megan

Megan arrived at 86 Bloomberg Place soaked, thanks to the rain, and a few minutes late. She felt a little nervous as she rang the doorbell, but standing up straight, she told herself this was no big deal.

"Oh, Megan, you're here," said Kendall as she swung open the heavy wooden door. "Come on in and meet your new housemates."

Megan stepped into the house and felt dismayed to see that the interior, like the exterior, was in need of a little work and updating. The walls were a depressing shade of pinkish beige and the carpet, which was well worn, was a few shades darker. But at least the furnishings were somewhat bright and cheery, although the arrangement was all wrong. The sectional was wedged into the darkest corner, and the living room was dominated by a bulky TV on an old dresser.

Kendall introduced Megan to the other two girls—an exotic beauty from Hawaii, Lelani Porter, and a pretty Hispanic girl named Anna Mendez. They both seemed nice and, unless Megan was mistaken, as nervous as she felt.

"I was about to give them the tour," said Kendall. "But now we can all have it together."

The house was actually a bit bigger than it appeared from the outside, but still it wasn't anything like the impression Kendall's ad had presented. She led them from the living room to an unfurnished sunroom with dirty windows that looked out over a dismally overgrown backyard, then on to the kitchen with nice leaded windows, also in need of a good scrub. The floor was covered with old linoleum that was curling in places, and the countertops were a plastic laminate that dated back several decades. Megan's best guess was the seventies. The appliances were the same era too, and brownish in color. Some might call it retro, but in Megan's opinion it was totally wrong for this craftsman-style bungalow.

The dining room wasn't too bad. So far it was the only room with what had to be the original wood floors showing. And the mission-style table and chairs were attractive as well as complimentary to the house.

"Nice place settings," said Anna as they all stood before the table, which was set for dinner, complete with flowers and candles.

"Anna's parents own the Casa Del Sol restaurant," said Kendall.

"And Casa Del Rey," added Anna.

"So, are you a good cook?" asked Lelani.

"I'm okay." Anna nodded in a way that suggested she was probably a great cook but didn't want to brag.

"I'm not much of a cook," admitted Kendall. Then she laughed. "But don't worry, I ordered out for our dinner tonight."

"Well, you do set a pretty table," said Megan. "That dinnerware is perfect for a craftsman-style house."

"That's what the saleslady told me," said Kendall. "She helped me pick everything out, including the placemats and napkins."

"Very nice." Megan just wished the rest of the house were this nice.

"Ready to see the bedrooms?"

The girls nodded eagerly, then Kendall took them down a hallway where two decent-size bedrooms flanked a somewhat small bathroom.

"I'm guessing there are hardwood floors underneath that carpeting," said Megan as they looked at one of the rooms. "Would you mind if I removed the carpet from the room I rent?"

"I guess not," said Kendall. "Is that hard to do?"

"It involves some work," said Megan. "After you get the carpet and pad out, you have to pull up staples. Hopefully the wood is in good shape, but it might need some refinishing. But the payoff, I think, is worth it."

"Wow, it sounds like you know a lot about this stuff," said Anna.

"She's working with Sawyer & Craig," said Kendall, "just the best interior-design studio in town."

"Well, I don't actually have the job yet," admitted Megan. "But I have my second interview this week."

"So how do you know about hardwood floors?" asked Lelani.

"My dad was an architect who occasionally did some building and remodeling, and I learned some things through him."

"I like the color of the tile in this bathroom," said Lelani.

"Really?" Kendall frowned at the green tiles. "I thought it was kind of dark myself."

"I think it's kind of soothing," said Lelani as she ran her hand over the top of the vanity.

"Actually, it goes perfectly with the house," said Megan. "I'm sure it must be original." She bent down to look more closely at the grout lines. "And it's actually in pretty good shape. Whoever put this down the first time must've done it right."

"Well, the upstairs bathroom is a little more cheerful," said Kendall. "Ready for the rest of the tour?"

They all agreed and, like a mini parade, followed Kendall up the stairs, which were unfortunately covered in the same ugly beige carpeting. Megan felt sure that even if the hardwood beneath the carpeting was worn, it would be greatly preferable to this horrible rug.

"That's my room," said Kendall as the girls peeked into the cluttered space that was obviously in use. "I had to toss some things in there that I'd been storing in the other bedrooms." She quickly closed the door and moved on to the bathroom, which like the one downstairs, was tucked between the two bedrooms. But this one was tiled in a coral pink shade and cluttered with a variety of beauty products.

"Ooh," said Anna, "that's a pretty color."

"I like it," said Kendall as she kicked a used towel aside. "Sorry, I didn't have time to clean up in here."

The fourth bedroom was pretty much the same as the others. "Well, that's it," said Kendall. She smiled at them. "Anyone want to put dibs on a bedroom yet?"

"I like this bedroom," said Anna. "It sort of reminds me of my room at home … I mean because it's upstairs. But if someone else wants—"

"No," said Lelani quickly. "I'd like to be downstairs. And I like that bathroom too. That green tile feels sort of like Maui to me."

"Downstairs works for me too," said Megan. Actually, she was relieved not to share the second floor with Kendall. She suspected that Kendall might be the type to spend a lot of time in the bathroom.

"Well, that was easy," said Kendall. "Anna and me up here, and Megan and Lelani downstairs. Do you guys want to flip for the room?"

"I don't really care which one I get," said Lelani as they trekked back down the stairs.

"Neither do I," said Megan. She thought she might prefer the one in the back of the house, since it seemed the most private, but she didn't want to be selfish.

Just as they reached the first floor, the phone rang, and Kendall dashed across the living room to answer an old-fashioned dark green phone with a curly cord.

"You can't?" she said in a disappointed tone. "But you said you—" She paused to listen, and a deep frown creased her forehead. "Yes, well, I guess I can do that. But you know, if you expect your business to succeed, you should deliver what you promise." Then she hung up. "I'm going to have to run out and pick up our dinner myself," she said in an aggravated voice.

"Do you need help?" offered Anna.

"No," said Kendall. "Why don't you all just make yourself at home while I'm gone. There's some wine chilling and some sodas and things in the fridge. You guys help yourselves. I should be back in about twenty minutes."

The house got quiet after Kendall left, and Megan wasn't sure what to do, but Anna went straight to the kitchen. Megan and Lelani followed, watching as Anna opened the fridge and removed a bottle of wine. "This is a good pinot gris," she said. "Any takers?"

"Sure," said Lelani, pulling up a stool at the tiny breakfast bar.

Megan normally didn't drink alcohol but didn't want to seem unfriendly. "Just a little for me," she said.

Anna was opening cabinets now, obviously searching for wine glasses. "Look at this," she said, laughing. She pointed to an overly full cabinet, packed with various dishes and food items and an assortment of other odd things. "I think Kendall needs some organizational help in the kitchen." Anna finally located the wine glasses, then opened the bottle.

"Uh, what do you guys think of the house?" asked Megan quietly. "I mean in general. Is it what you expected?"

"Not exactly," said Lelani. "I mean Kendall's ad made this place sound, well, you know. A lot nicer."

"My thoughts exactly," agreed Megan.

"Not that I'm complaining," said Lelani quickly.

"No, of course, not," said Megan. "I actually like the style of the house a lot."

"The rent is too high," said Anna as she handed them their wine glasses.

Lelani nodded. "I sort of wondered about that too. I mean, Kendall has obviously tried to fix this place up with some new furniture and things."

"It doesn't matter how much you gussie up a pig," said Anna in a matter-of-fact tone, "it's still just a pig."

Lelani laughed at this, but Megan felt slightly defensive for the sake of the house. "Obviously this house needs some work," she said, "but it does have some potential. The original woodwork is really beautiful."

"Even so, Kendall misrepresented the house in her ad," said Anna. "She set us up to expect something far nicer than this."

"But I really need a place to live," said Lelani.

"So do I," admitted Anna. "Although I still say the rent is too high."

"Even so," said Lelani. "I'm not going to rock the boat."

"I'm with you on that," Anna agreed, then she held up her wine glass. "To new housemates?"

"Yes, to new housemates," echoed Lelani with a faint smile.

Megan lifted her glass with a bit of uncertainty, but as they clinked them together she got an idea. First she took a cautious sip of the wine. Then she decided to go for it. "You know what I think we should do?" she said.

"What?" asked Anna.

"And if we all agreed and stuck together on it, well, it might work."

"What might work?" asked Lelani.

"Let's ask Kendall to reduce the rent in exchange for some home improvements," said Megan eagerly. "We can all work together to remove that horrid carpeting, and we can refinish the floors, if they need it, and paint the walls and just basically fix the place up so that it'll be more like the house she described in that ad."

"How much work do you think that will really entail?" asked Anna.

"Not that much," replied Megan quickly. "I know you guys have jobs, and I hope to have one soon, so I realize we'd have to do the renovations on our off time. But I'm willing to roll up my sleeves."

"So am I," agreed Lelani. "And I have weekends off."

"What do you do?" asked Megan.

Lelani explained about her job at Nordstrom and how the college girls liked getting the weekend hours. "Which totally works for me," said Lelani, pausing to take a sip of wine.

"I have weekends off too," said Anna. "I work for Erlinger Books."

"Doing what?" asked Lelani.

"I'm a children's book editor," said Anna proudly.

"That sounds like fun," said Megan.

"It's also work," Anna replied. "And I'm not sure I want to spend all my spare time remodeling someone else's house."

"Not remodeling," said Megan. "Just a little sprucing up. And the payoff will be having a much nicer place to live. Can you imagine that living room with gleaming hardwood floors and a nice coat of, say, Tuscan Gold on the walls?"

"Are you an interior decorator?" asked Lelani.

Megan laughed. "No. But I did take some design classes and my major is art ed. Some people think I have a good eye for these things." She glanced around the kitchen. "Really, this house has a lot going for it, but it needs some help."

"It might be fun," said Lelani, glancing hopefully at Anna.

"Would you teach us a little about interior design?" asked Anna with interest. "I mean, you should see the things my mom picks out." She laughed. "Not exactly Elvis paintings on velvet, but not too far evolved from there either."

They all laughed. And once again, they clinked their glasses together, this time in a pact to get Kendall to lower the rent and agree to some renovations.

"You'll have to be the one to present our case," Anna told Megan.

"And she's just pulling in," said Lelani from where she was standing near the kitchen window.

"Let's just hope this works," said Megan. She glanced at her two new friends. "We need to present a united front, girls."

"All for one and one for all," said Anna.

"Dinner is about to be served," announced Kendall as she emerged through the side door, balancing a small stack of white boxes.

"Need any help?" offered Lelani.

"Sure," said Kendall. "There are a couple of bags still in the car—in the backseat."

"How about in here?" asked Anna. "Do you need help?"

"Yeah," said Kendall as she set her boxes on the counter. "How about if you arrange this food in an attractive way, Anna?" She smiled at her. "I'm sure you know all about *presentation*." She turned to Megan now. "How about if you fill the water glasses? There's an ice tray in the freezer." Kendall hung her damp trench coat on a hook by the door, then pulled out a kitchen stool. "And I will pour myself a nice glass of wine."

Before long, they were all seated in the dining room, and Kendall looked supremely pleased with herself—almost as if she believed she had actually cooked this dinner—and they began to eat.

"This is delicious, Kendall," said Lelani. "What's it called?"

"I can't say it in French," said Kendall, "But in English it's roasted duck with apples and porto sauce."

"It's really good," said Megan. "Where's it from anyway?"

"Have you seen that new French restaurant with the blue awnings?

Chez Simone?" asked Kendall as she buttered her bread. "Their ad said they delivered, but apparently their delivery guy was sick, and I'd already placed the order. Naturally, I was pretty irked at them, but when I got there Simone came out and apologized personally. And he even reduced the bill and threw in dessert, so I suppose I'll keep ordering takeout from them after all."

"What kind of dessert?" asked Anna.

"Crème caramel custards with raspberries."

"Yummy," said Megan. She decided it would be best to wait until after they finished dinner to present their proposal to Kendall. For one thing, she didn't want to spoil Kendall's meal, but besides that, she hoped that Kendall, feeling happy and full, would appreciate the sensibility of this recommendation. So, as her potential housemates made small talk about jobs and background and whatnot, Megan pretended to listen, nodding occasionally. For the most part, though, she used this time to formulate what she hoped would be a good offensive, putting together the various points that she thought might convince Kendall that this really was a good idea. Because, despite the shabby condition of this neglected old house, Megan actually wanted to live here. And she knew it would feel good to see this house restored to something reflective of its original grace and beauty. Somehow, she had to inspire that same vision and desire in Kendall.

Thirteen

# Kendall

"You want me to lower the rent?" demanded Kendall. "And you haven't even moved in yet?" They'd just finished dessert and were having a great little visit with coffee in the living room when Megan decided to spoil everything.

"I just want you to listen to me," said Megan.

Kendall sat back down, crossed one leg over the other, and pressing her lips tightly together simply glared at Megan. Who did she think she was anyway?

"We discussed this while you were getting—"

"You were talking behind my back?" Kendall stood up again, pacing and staring at the three young women she had so carefully selected. "I cannot believe this."

"Please, just hear us out," said Anna in a quiet voice. "We weren't talking about you behind your back. We were simply questioning the condition of the house in regard to the ad you placed in the paper."

Megan nodded. "Yes. We don't want to accuse you of false advertising, Kendall, but your description of the house was somewhat misleading."

"I have to agree," said Lelani. "I had expected something ... well, a little more luxurious."

"That's right," said Anna. "You actually used the word *luxurious* in your ad."

"I did?" Kendall tried to remember exactly what the ad had said, besides the money part. She had that down. "Well, I suppose *luxurious* was a bit of an overstatement."

"For instance, this carpeting." Megan was standing now too, pointing to a darkened spot in the beige carpeting. Kendall had thought the coffee table disguised it, but in this light, it wasn't hard to see.

"I meant to get everything steam-cleaned," she explained. "This used to be my grandmother's house, and she had a beagle named Lulu with an incontinence problem." Anna made a slightly disgusted face and Kendall realized that was too much information. "Anyway, I can still get it cleaned."

"Why not get it removed?" Megan suggested. "And in return for a rent reduction, we can do it ourselves."

"It's one thing for you to take out the rug in your bedroom," said Kendall, "but I can't allow you to do the entire house."

"Why not?" asked Megan.

Kendall shrugged. "What if there's something wrong with the floors beneath the carpet? I can't afford to have it all replaced." Kendall was thinking she couldn't afford to take less rent money either. The whole point of renting rooms was to supplement her income, an income that was currently nonexistent. Why was everything suddenly going sideways?

"I can start with my bedroom," said Megan. "It should be a good indicator as to the condition of the wood floors."

Kendall frowned. She was having serious second thoughts about renting to Megan now. She didn't need this kind of inconvenience. The whole point in doing this was simply to raise money, and now Megan was suggesting she forget all about that.

"It would be an investment in your house," persisted Megan. "Your property value will go up with these improvements."

"And we're all willing to help out," said Lelani. "I actually like to paint."

"It sounds like a great big headache to me," said Kendall.

"But just imagine how great this house could look," said Megan, waving her arms as if she thought she was Vanna White showing the contestant the next prize on whatever that stupid game show was called. "With gleaming wood floors and fresh paint in a good color, your new furnishings would look totally awesome in here."

Kendall just shook her head. She'd already spent way too much on furnishings—furnishings she'd hoped would impress these girls. Now all they could do was complain. What was the matter with them anyway?

"This just doesn't add up, Kendall," Anna piped in. "I've done the math. With four women paying the amount of rent you're expecting to get here, we could rent a fantastic house with all the amenities—we might possibly come up with a down-payment and even buy one."

Kendall sat back down and sighed. Her ship was sinking fast.

"I actually like this house," said Megan. "I mean it's not like what you described in the ad, and even if it was in great shape, I seriously doubt you could get more than $400 a month from anyone. But I do think it has charm and personality. It just needs a lot of TLC. And you've got three new friends here who are willing to roll up their sleeves and help you with it."

"That's right," said Lelani. "Can you imagine what you'd have to pay to hire someone to do what we're willing to do in exchange for rent?"

"No." Kendall didn't want to imagine that. She didn't really care about that. She simply wanted some congenial roommates who had no problem paying the rent—period. Instead she got Miss Fix-It and friends.

"Seriously, Kendall," Megan continued. "Who do you think you could get to come in here and pay $550 a month for a room and shared bath in a house that's as rundown as this one?"

"I had dozens of responses to my ad."

"Yes," said Anna quickly. "But that ad was misleading."

"Perhaps that's why you didn't let us see the house before we sent in our résumés and did our interviews," suggested Lelani.

"And now that we've seen the house …" Megan frowned. "And well, we think there is room for some negotiation."

Kendall felt trapped. As much as she hated to admit it, she knew they were probably right. Marcus had said the same thing.

"Remember what you told us about Chez Simone tonight?" said Megan.

"What?" Kendall looked up at Megan with narrowed eyes. Why hadn't she seen that this girl was going to be such a troublemaker?

"Well, you were ticked at him for advertising something he couldn't deliver."

"So?" Kendall fluffed one of the new pillows, then set it next to her.

"So he apologized and renegotiated the cost of your dinner."

"And threw in dessert for free," added Anna.

Kendall was mentally tallying up how much she'd already invested in her little business venture. The furnishings and kitchen things, tonight's dinner—which wasn't cheap—the ad in the paper, getting the lease agreements all ready to sign, not to mention her own precious time. She'd even paid to have keys made, putting them on special little rhinestone key rings of different colors. And now they not only wanted her to invest more, they wanted to pay her less.

"I suppose you could always start over," said Megan. "Call up the other applicants and go through your interview process again, then wait and see if they're more impressed with the condition of your house than we are."

"What I said about the neighborhood was true," insisted Kendall. "And the location was true."

"Yes," agreed Megan. "And those are good things."

"But saying this house was luxurious." Anna scowled. "Well, I don't want to hurt your feelings, but compared to this house, my home— including my bedroom suite—is about ten times nicer than this."

"So why are you moving out of your house?" demanded Kendall.

Anna sort of shrugged and looked uneasy. "I just need some freedom from my family." Then she got a stronger look in her eyes. "Good grief, I am twenty-five years old and a college grad and I have a great job. I think I deserve to live away from home."

Kendall held up both hands. "Sorry. I was just curious."

"So, what's it going to be?" asked Megan. "I can't speak for Anna and Lelani, but I'm willing to shop around for something else if you can't at least—"

"Fine, fine." Kendall felt cornered and outnumbered. Most of all, she didn't want to go through that whole interviewing process again—and what if it ended up like this or worse? "We can renegotiate."

"Do you have some paper?" asked Megan as she fished out a pen from her bag. "We should play with the numbers a little to see what works."

Soon they were all sitting at the dining room table again, watching as Megan made estimates on the cost of things like paint and materials she thought would be necessary to improve Kendall's house. Despite reservations, Kendall was starting to get into the spirit of things. She actually liked the idea of having her house fixed up and looking pretty. And she couldn't argue the point that improvements would increase its real estate value, although she knew that her grandmother had set stipulations on when Kendall would be allowed to sell it.

Finally, the girls agreed on the details. To start with, the rent would be reduced to $400 a month. In exchange for labor, they would receive their first month's rent for half price. And they reduced the deposit amounts to a flat $1,000 per renter with the agreement that this money would be used to purchase the paint and materials needed to complete the renovation in a timely fashion.

"What exactly *is* a timely fashion?" asked Kendall, as Anna, acting as secretary, added this new information onto the lease agreements.

"Well, for starters, I think we should give ourselves a full month to finish the interior renovations. By then it will be November, so we'll probably need to put off the exterior painting until spring."

"Oh." Kendall considered this.

"But you should keep the leftover deposit money in an account so that you can buy the exterior paint and stuff later on down the line."

"Of course." Kendall nodded, but she was thinking that it wouldn't be anyone's business where she kept the deposit money or how she used it. She'd probably have a job by spring anyway, and she could easily buy paint and whatever with her income at the time it was needed—if it was needed.

Finally, the contracts were signed, and the girls all handed her their checks for a total of $3,600—just a little more than half of what Kendall had expected to be receiving at this time. Not only that, but according to the agreement, most of this money had to go back into the house.

"I'm going to take you up on the offer to move in early," announced Anna. "My brother offered to help me tomorrow."

"And my mom's going to help me move my stuff tomorrow too," said Megan.

"And, if you don't mind, I'll camp here tonight," said Lelani. "I brought some things."

Kendall opened a drawer in the kitchen, extracted the keys and fancy key rings and handed them over, one by one, to her new renters. "Here you go," she said in a flat voice. *"Mi casa es su casa."*

"Ooh," gushed Anna as she hugged Kendall. "Pretty key ring. Thanks!"

Kendall brightened a little at Anna's enthusiasm. Okay, maybe this wasn't such a big mistake. After all, these girls—well, except for Megan the tyrant—seemed really sweet. And it would be nice having room-mates. Besides, starting with November, their rent—only $1,200 now—would help supplement Kendall's income. Plus, she wouldn't be expected to do all the housekeeping now. That in itself had to be worth a lot. And maybe some of them would want to cook. Kendall despised cooking and usually ate out, which really tended to add up. She'd gotten all those dishes and things for the kitchen as an incentive for someone, not her, to take a culinary interest.

Fourteen

# Megan

"Where's your car?" asked Anna as she and Megan went out the front door.

"Oh, I don't have one."

"How will you get home?"

"The bus."

"At night?" Anna looked shocked by this confession.

"I do it all the time," admitted Megan.

"Isn't it dangerous? Don't you worry about ... well, surely you've heard about the abductions of the college girls?"

Megan shrugged as she buttoned up the top of her coat. "You can't live in fear, Anna." Okay, the truth was that Megan wasn't that comfortable riding the bus at night. Plus, she'd promised her mom that she wouldn't.

"Well, tonight, I'm giving you a ride," announced Anna.

"Thanks." Megan wasn't about to argue with her. The truth was she couldn't wait until she no longer had to ride the bus to town. That alone was a huge motivation for moving into Kendall's house. Megan pointed to the little red car parked on the street. "Is that yours?"

"It is."

"It's so cute."

"It's an Austin Mini."

"It's so tiny," said Megan as Anna unlocked the door. "It's good that you're small."

"It's roomier than you'd think."

Actually, it was roomier. But still, small like Anna. "I'll bet it gets good gas mileage."

"Up to forty on the highway."

"Cool." Megan leaned back and sighed. She was relieved to get the evening over with. "How did you think it went tonight? I mean with Kendall and the whole renegotiation? Do you think she hates me now?"

"She seemed pretty ticked. But it's not like she could deny that you made sense. $550 a month for that place was totally nuts."

"I actually think $400 is generous."

"Especially in its current condition." Anna glanced at Megan as she stopped for the traffic light. "Do you really think we can fix it ourselves?"

"Of course."

"I don't want to sound like I think I'm a spoiled princess or anything, but I'm really not used to doing things like that."

Megan had already noticed Anna's long and perfectly manicured nails—a strong hint that this girl was not into manual labor. "I'm sure you can learn," said Megan. "And you might be surprised to find that it's fun."

Anna nodded, but her expression didn't look convinced. Megan directed her across town to the apartment complex. "You live here?" asked Anna.

"Pretty bad, huh?"

"Oh, I don't know. My mother would have a fit if I moved into a place like this."

"My mom's not too crazy about it either."

"It's probably good that you're moving then."

"That's for sure," said Megan. "Thanks for the ride."

"See you tomorrow," said Anna. "I have to work, so I won't be actually moving in until after five."

"See you then." Megan waved and hurried up the stairs to her apartment. She never liked coming in after dark and always made sure she had her key ready to put in the doorknob.

"Speak of the devil," Bethany announced as Megan entered the apartment and saw that all three roommates were home tonight.

"Thanks," said Megan as she unbuttoned her coat.

"So, are you really moving out?"

"I am."

"Good," said Bethany.

"Thanks again." Megan wondered how she'd put up with Bethany for a whole year. The sooner she was out of here the happier they'd all be.

"Because I found a new roommate who can't wait to take your place."

"Lucky girl."

"Who says it's a girl?" smirked Bethany.

"That's what we were just discussing," said Claire with a disgusted expression. Claire was a senior but had been in the apartment the longest. She considered herself to be the one in charge, although the residents disputed that fairly regularly.

"Who cares about gender," said Bethany, "as long as he pays the rent?"

"I care," said Erin. "I happen to like walking around in my underwear sometimes."

"I'm sure Todd will like it too," Bethany shot back.

"Good luck," said Megan, directing a sympathetic glance to Claire and Erin.

"Thanks a lot," said Claire. "This is your fault, you know."

"It's not my fault. I already lined up Stacy. It's up to you guys whether you take her or not."

"Well, Bethany doesn't like her," said Erin in a snippy tone.

"Since when does that matter?" asked Megan. Hadn't they forced Bethany on her when Allison moved out?

Soon they were all arguing, and Megan made a quick getaway to her bedroom, where she continued to pack her belongings. Her plan was to be ready for a fast exodus first thing in the morning. At this rate, and if her roommates continued to squabble, she'd be in bed and hopefully asleep before Bethany decided to call it a night. The sooner she got out of this place, the happier she'd be.

Of course, once in bed, she started to worry about Kendall. She could not ignore the several tense moments this evening. Megan felt fairly certain that Kendall did not like her and probably regretted choosing Megan to be a housemate. Hopefully, Megan could win her over tomorrow. As badly as she wanted out of this apartment, she didn't really like the idea of jumping into another situation that could turn into something as contemptuous or worse. Oh, she hoped she hadn't made a mistake. And then, she prayed she hadn't.

The next morning, Megan got up early. She wanted to do one last check throughout the apartment to make sure she hadn't forgotten anything important. She'd already promised to leave a few things behind, including her old twin bed and matching dresser, as well as a toaster and a set of baking dishes. Maybe this would suffice as a peace offering for Claire and Erin. She did feel sorry for them getting stuck with Bethany and her boyfriend. That would change the dynamics in the apartment considerably. But that was their problem now.

Before long, her mom arrived, and after they ducked out for a quick breakfast, they came back and hauled all the boxes and plastic crates downstairs, packing them into the full-sized van that Mom had borrowed from a neighbor.

"Miracle of miracles," said Mom as they stuffed in the last load. "If we can get this door shut, I think it's all going to fit."

"Good thing I left the bed and dresser behind," said Megan.

"But now you'll need to look for some bedroom furniture," Mom pointed out. "Where will you sleep tonight?"

Megan hadn't really considered this. Mostly she'd been wondering how long it would take to remove that nasty carpet and what sort of condition the floor might be in underneath it. "I'll figure it out," she told Mom as they got into the van. Then she gave her directions. As her mom drove, Megan told her a bit about last night's confrontation and getting the lease renegotiated.

"Good for you," said Mom.

"I guess, but now I'm worried that Kendall will have an ax to grind."

"It sounds like you were simply being fair and honest. Why should she fault you for that?"

"Because she wants money?"

Mom laughed. "Tell her to get a job."

"She said she's going to, when she finds the right thing. The problem is that she's sort of, well, you know, the Paris Hilton type."

Mom frowned. "You mean the type who parties a lot, spends too much money, and drives under the influence?"

"No, not exactly like that. More like the attractive, stylish, entitled, blonde, princess type."

"Oh." Mom nodded like she got this.

"But she's nice too. In a slightly self-centered way."

"You're sure you want to move into this house, Megan?" Mom's voice sounded concerned now. "I think they have that three-day rule for renters. Like when you buy a house. You can change your mind and stop payment on your check and—"

"No," said Megan firmly. "I want to do this. And I actually think it's going to be fun to fix up the house."

"Well, if it doesn't work out, you can always move back home. You know that, Megan." Mom sighed. "I hate to admit it, but I've been frantic about you since the latest abduction. Oh, I try to pray and I try to keep my worries in check, but every time I hear the latest news, about how they're searching for those two girls…. They suspect there's a connection, you know, that there could be more missing girls. I just wish you were safe at home with—"

"I know this is hard on you, Mom. But really, I'm just fine. And I'm perfectly safe. And, if it makes you feel better, I'm trying to be extra careful too." For some unexplainable reason, the idea of moving back home sounded to Megan like failing. Also, it would limit her job choices, or force her to get a car—and Megan hated to drive. "I think it's going to be fun living with these girls. And if I get that job I'll be able to walk to work."

"Yes." Mom nodded. "That all makes sense."

"I feel like something really good is going to come out of this too," Megan assured her. "Like maybe it was God who directed me to the house, to these girls. Who knows what might happen within the course of a year?"

"Yes. I've had that thought too, Megan."

"So you see? I really do think it's the right thing for me."

"But I may sell the house," said Mom sadly.

"Seriously?" Suddenly Megan didn't feel so sure of herself. Was Mom selling the house simply because Megan didn't want to live at home?

"It's too big for me … by myself." Mom sighed. "But Martha told me I should give myself a year before making any major decisions."

Martha was Mom's counselor friend. "I think that sounds wise," said Megan. "And who knows, maybe after a year, after my lease with Kendall ends, I'll want to move back home."

"Really?" Mom sounded hopeful, and this made Megan feel like a fraud. She had no genuine intentions of moving back home. Not really. Still, a lot could happen in a year.

"That's it," said Megan. "That tan bungalow with the overgrown yard."

"Oh?" Mom frowned slightly as she pulled in front. "Goodness, it does need some work, doesn't it?"

"But it's actually quite charming," said Megan.

"I suppose it has potential."

"I'll admit it's been neglected," said Megan. "And the carpeting is horrid and the walls are this grungy beige." But even as she said this, she felt as if she were being disloyal to the house. Mostly she felt it just needed a little TLC. "Come and see it for yourself."

Unsure as to whether she should simply walk in or not, Megan first rang the doorbell and then knocked loudly, but when no one came, she slipped in her key and entered.

"Hello?" she called out, but no one answered. Lelani might've already gone to work. And perhaps Kendall, after discovering that her get-rich-quick scheme wasn't panning out, had gone out job-hunting herself. One could hope.

Mom was a good sport about the house. And as Megan talked positively about some of her plans, giving her mother a quick tour of the first floor, Mom began to see the potential too. And at some points she seemed almost enthusiastic. Although she did mention more than once that Megan could always move back home if things didn't work out right.

"Thanks," said Megan. "It's nice to know I have a safety net."

"So, do you really want to move all your things into your room if you're just going to rip that carpeting out?" asked Mom. "That's like moving twice."

"I know." Megan considered this as she surveyed her bedroom, the one in the back of the house—the one she wanted but hadn't claimed.

She'd been surprised to see Lelani's duffel bag in the other bedroom, with some pieces of clothing already hanging in the closet.

"And that carpeting …" Mom's nose actually seemed to be twitching at the smell. "You don't really want to put your things in there with it still down, do you?"

"Not really."

"Odors are hard to get rid of, you know."

"Well, maybe we could just put my clothing and personal things in the hallway or the sunroom for now," suggested Megan. "And I'll stick some of my other crates out in the garage. Kendall showed us where we could store some things. Just until I know what to do with them anyway. Then, after everything is unloaded, I think I'll go ahead and attack that carpeting."

"Why don't we attack it together?" suggested Mom.

"Really?" Megan peered curiously at her mom. "You actually want to help?"

Her mom smiled. "Why not?"

"Well, I was going to run over to the hardware store to get some gloves and maybe a tool or two," said Megan, peering down at the gross rug with some uncertainty. "To be honest, I'm not totally sure how it's done, although I know that it has to be doable."

Mom chuckled. "How about we both go to the hardware store and ask for some advice?"

So a little before noon, Megan and her mom arrived back at the house, equipped with gloves, particle masks, pliers, a cutting tool, and a special kind of crowbar that the salesman promised would "pop off the baseboards like magic." Of course, it wasn't long before Megan was wishing for some real magic. Ripping out carpeting involved hard, dirty work.

"I'm afraid I'm going to be sore tomorrow," said Mom as they heaved the last of the nasty carpet pad out into the backyard.

"Don't overdo it," warned Megan. "I mean, I really appreciate your help, but you don't have to stay if you—"

"I'm not quitting," declared Mom. "But I do think we could use some lunch. I'm starting to fade a bit. Can I interest you in taking a break?"

"How about if I start pulling up staples while you go pick something up for us?" suggested Megan. Seeing the golden brown grain of the wooden floors was somewhat invigorating to her, and the idea of getting this task completely done was highly motivating at the moment.

"It's a deal."

Megan worked fast and hard while Mom was gone, but she was only half done when her mom returned with deli sandwiches, which they ate in the dining room. They had just finished up and returned to the bedroom to remove the last of the staples, when they both heard a noise upstairs.

"Is someone here?" asked Mom with alarm.

"I don't know." Megan paused to listen to what definitely sounded like footsteps overhead. "I thought everyone was gone," she whispered.

"Do you think it could be a burglar?" Mom's eyes were wide as she picked up a tool like a weapon.

Megan wouldn't admit it, but she was thinking about the two missing college girls—what if their abductor was in the house? Should they try to make a quick break? As the sound of quiet footsteps came closer, Megan picked up the crowbar that she'd used to remove the baseboard and, like her mom, wielded it like a weapon as they tiptoed out into the hallway. Megan was about to tell her mom to run for it when she saw Kendall, coming around the corner wearing pink fluffy slippers and a white terry bathrobe, with a big white towel turbaned around her head. Not a very threatening sight.

"Good morning," said Kendall cheerfully.

"Don't you mean *good afternoon?*" asked Megan in a perturbed tone. Why hadn't Kendall answered the door earlier? Or made herself known? What kind of games did this girl like to play anyway?

"Morning … afternoon … whatever." Kendall just shrugged. Then she looked at the tools that were still being held up—threateningly wielded like weapons of house destruction. "What's going on here?"

"I didn't know you were home," said Megan as she sheepishly lowered the crowbar. "We heard footsteps and thought maybe someone had broken in."

"Who did you think it was?" Kendall chuckled now. "The campus killer?"

"Well, you young girls can't be too careful," said Mom in a no-nonsense voice.

Then Megan introduced Kendall to her mom.

"So what's up with the tools?" asked Kendall. "I mean other than beating off intruders."

"We've been taking up the rug in my bedroom," explained Megan.

Kendall rolled her eyes and nodded. "So that's what all the noise was about."

"You heard that noise but didn't come down to investigate?" asked Mom with a curious frown.

Kendall shrugged again. "I figured it was just one of my new tenants moving in. Nothing to get worked up about. Although it did interrupt my beauty sleep." She smiled and patted a pretty pink cheek.

"Sorry," said Megan quickly. "I really did think you were gone, but I guess I should've checked first." She suddenly remembered her resolve to patch things up with her landlord before their relationship got any worse. She hadn't made a very good start at it.

Kendall blinked her big blue eyes. "Gone? Where would I be gone to at this time of day?"

Megan wanted to point out the possibilities but didn't. "Anyway, we're almost done with the noise down here."

"Good. I don't suppose anyone made coffee?"

"Sorry," said Megan.

"I figured."

"Nice to meet you," called Mom as Kendall shuffled toward the kitchen.

"Princess type," said Megan quietly.

Mom nodded and giggled. "I see what you mean."

Then they went back to the bedroom, where Megan smiled down at the fruit of their labor. "Wow, that floor looks pretty good, doesn't it?" she said. "I mean, I don't think it'll even need to be refinished."

"It actually seems to be in great shape," admitted Mom as she bent down to pull out a staple that Megan must've missed. "I think all you'll need to do is use some of that wood cleaner that the salesman recommended."

So, for the next hour, Megan replaced the baseboards and Mom pulled out the remaining staples and by four o'clock, the floor really did look almost as good as new. Megan hugged her mom. "I really, really appreciate your help," she told her. "I had no idea you were such a hard worker."

"That's because your dad usually took over projects like this."

Megan nodded. "Yes. And sometimes I would help him."

"Those times are gone now, honey."

"I know. But I couldn't have done this without you today." Megan felt closer than ever to her mom right now. She also felt close to tears. "Thanks so much, Mom."

"I'm glad I could help." Mom patted her on the back. "And I'm proud of you, Megan. Just look at what you've accomplished."

Megan looked at the dingy beige walls now. "But I just thought of something."

"What?"

"I should've painted the walls while the carpet was still down. Then I wouldn't need to use a drop cloth."

Mom laughed. "There's that good old twenty-twenty hindsight again."

"Hey, how much longer do you have that van for?" asked Megan suddenly.

"As long as we need it," said Mom.

"Are you too tired to go to Ikea?"

"I don't think so," said Mom. "What's Ikea?"

Megan chuckled. "You're going to love it."

As Mom drove the van to the city, Megan explained that the store carried Scandinavian and contemporary furnishings and all kinds of cool stuff at some fairly economical prices. "I thought I might get myself some bedroom furniture and bedding and maybe even an area rug."

"Ooh, this does sound like fun," said Mom. "I love shopping for household things."

Now Megan's only challenge would be not allowing her mother's taste to override her own. Fortunately, her mom was so enthralled with the giant Ikea store that they quickly went their own separate ways—her mom to the dining room section, where she hoped to find a new kitchen table set, while Megan made a beeline to the bedroom area.

Megan's plan was to paint her bedroom a comforting sage green and to purchase some bedroom furnishings with straight simple lines, in a light natural wood tone. And it didn't take long to discover she'd come to the right place. In just a little more than an hour, she had made all her furniture selections and picked out bedding, lamps, a mirror, candles, an area rug, and even some artwork for the walls. She couldn't wait to get back to the house to put it all together.

"The table I wanted was out of stock, but I ordered it," Mom told her as she drove the loaded van back to the house. "You were lucky they had what you wanted right there at the store."

Megan nodded. "It feels like God is smiling on me right now."

Mom chuckled. "Well, I hope you'll feel that way when you've put it all together. I never saw anyone pick out a room's worth of things that quickly. Which reminds me, don't you have that interview tomorrow?"

"Oh, yeah!" Megan slapped her forehead. "I had totally forgotten the interview."

"Well, make sure you don't overdo yourself tonight," said Mom. "You want to put your best foot forward for that interview. I don't want to scare you, but Vera is very concerned about appearances."

"Appearances, you say?" Megan looked down at her grimy sweatshirt and jeans then let out a groan as she noticed her dirt-encrusted and broken fingernails.

"Just put your best foot forward," Mom reassured her as she pulled up in front of the house. "Then pray about it. If it's meant to be, it'll be. Right?"

Megan nodded, although she wasn't so sure now. Still, for Mom's sake, she put on an air of confidence. "You're right," she said. "If it's meant to be, it'll be."

# Fifteen

# Lelani

"Do you need some help?" offered Lelani when she saw Megan and a woman—she figured it must be Megan's mother—lugging a long, bulky box up the steps to the house.

"That'd be great." Megan paused at the top of the stairs, pushing a strand of hair from her eyes as Lelani picked up the other end of the box and helped to maneuver it through the front door. She was just getting home from work and, although her feet were killing her, it was obvious they needed a hand.

"You were just in time," said the woman breathlessly as she and Lelani continued to carry the back end of the heavy box down the hallway. "I was about to expire."

"Wow," said Lelani when they finally set the long box in Megan's bedroom. "Look at what you've done already, Megan. That floor looks fantastic."

With a big smile, Megan put her hands on her hips and nodded. "It turned out pretty nice, huh?"

"I'll say. Now I really want to do the same thing to my room."

"I can help you," said Megan.

"Cool," said Lelani. "It feels so much cleaner without the carpet."

"Yeah, the floor is cleaner, but I'm a mess." Then Megan introduced Lelani to her mother, explaining how helpful she'd been today.

"Nice to meet you, Mrs. Abernathy." Lelani shook her hand. "Megan's lucky to have your help."

"Lelani is such a pretty name. Please, call me Linda," said Megan's mom. "That way I can pretend I'm just one of the girls, too." Then she rubbed her back and grimaced. "Although I feel more like I'm ready for the geriatrics ward at the moment. I hope I didn't strain anything vital."

"I recommend a nice hot bath and some ibuprofen," suggested Lelani.

"And you should listen to her, Mom," said Megan. "She was in med school."

"Was?" Linda peered curiously at Lelani.

"Yes. I sort of took a detour," explained Lelani. "I just needed a little break."

"Her home is Hawaii," said Megan. "And so she decides to take a break here."

Linda laughed. "Well, at least it's a change, eh, Lelani?"

Lelani smiled. "Absolutely." She looked around Megan's room, which had various boxes piled on the shining hardwood floor. "Do you need any more help?"

"Sure, if you don't mind," said Megan. "There are a couple more bulky boxes in the van."

"Just let me change my shoes," said Lelani, "then I'll be a new woman."

The three of them quickly emptied the van, then just as Linda was driving away, a big diesel pickup pulled up, followed by a tiny red car.

"That must be Anna's brother," said Megan. "Have you seen Anna's car yet?"

"It's so cute," said Lelani. "Like a toy car."

Anna hopped out and quickly introduced them to her brother, a good-looking guy named Gil. Within minutes, the four of them were unloading Anna's things from the back of the pickup and carrying them upstairs. And if Lelani thought Megan's things were heavy, Anna's were a lot worse. Plus they had the stairs to contend with. But finally they dumped the last of it in Anna's room, leaving a number of the larger pieces lined up along the hallway. Lelani was curious how all that furniture would possibly fit in the bedroom with any space left to walk, but she figured that was Anna's problem now.

"Before you get everything into place, you might want to check out Megan's room," suggested Lelani.

"Why?" Anna shook out a pale pink pillow and set it on her dresser. "She's already removed her carpet."

"Yes." Megan held up her grimy hands as if to prove it. "It was hard work, but totally worth it."

Anna frowned. "Well, I'm not sure I'm ready for that just yet."

"That's okay," said Megan. "We can focus on Lelani's room next."

"Great," said Lelani. "A friend at work offered to loan me some bedroom furniture. He plans to drop it here on his day off on Thursday. Is that too soon to get that rug ripped up?"

"No problem," Megan assured her. "And it'll be easier to do without having the furniture to contend with."

"I think you're going to be sorry, Anna," her brother warned. "And don't call me if you need to move all this stuff again." He winked at Lelani now. "I should warn you guys, Anna doesn't care much for hard labor."

Anna punched him. "Thanks for the help, Gil. Don't let us keep you."

"That's okay," he said, still grinning at Lelani. "I'm not in any big hurry. By the way, Lelani, if you need a hand taking out that carpet or moving anything, feel free to call. Anna can give you my number."

Now Anna actually took her brother by the arm and led him out of the room. "Listen, Gil, I know you want to stick around and admire the house and all, but I'm sure that you have other things to do. Thanks so much for your help though."

Megan laughed, then lowered her voice. "I think Anna's brother wants to get better acquainted with you, Lelani."

"No," Anna told Megan as she rejoined them. "I think my brother has fallen hopelessly in love with Lelani."

"Kind of looked like it to me too," agreed Megan.

"You guys!" scolded Lelani.

"Seriously," said Anna. "I thought his eyes were going to pop out and roll across the floor."

"Well, that offer of help was tempting," said Lelani. "But I wouldn't want to give him the wrong idea."

"Don't worry," said Anna. "I'm sure he already has the wrong idea. And I won't be surprised if he pops in with some pretense to visit me from time to time now."

"He seems nice," admitted Lelani, although she had no interest in getting involved with a guy right now, no matter how nice.

"He actually *is* fairly nice, for a little brother anyway." Anna laughed. "In fact, he's the one who is usually pursued by the girls."

"How old is he?" asked Megan.

"He's only twenty-three, but he's always been on an academic fast track. He got his MBA when he was twenty-two."

"He must be super smart," said Megan.

"He's definitely smart. Although I'm not too crazy about his career choice."

"What's that?" asked Lelani.

"He manages both of our family's restaurants."

"I think that's pretty impressive," said Megan, "especially considering his age."

"And it's good experience," pointed out Lelani.

"I guess," said Anna. "But not for me."

"But I'll bet your parents appreciate having their son involved," said Lelani.

"For sure." Anna glanced down the hallway now. "Hey, has anyone seen Kendall today?" she asked.

"I saw her this afternoon," said Megan, "after we woke her up."

"She slept in until afternoon?" Anna looked shocked.

"Apparently," said Megan. "I knocked on the front door, but she didn't answer and I just assumed she was out. So my mom and I were crashing around downstairs taking out that carpeting and making all kinds of noise. I'm surprised she didn't wake up a lot sooner."

"Did she get mad at you?" asked Anna with concern.

"She didn't seem terribly mad," said Megan. "Although she did mention that we disturbed her beauty sleep."

"How much beauty sleep does she need?" asked Anna.

Megan laughed. "Who knows?"

"Maybe I kept her up too late last night," said Lelani. "We talked until pretty late." She didn't admit that it was Kendall who did most of the talking, keeping Lelani up much later than she had wanted. But Lelani had felt slightly indebted to Kendall for allowing her to crash on her couch like that. And she couldn't exactly send the owner of the home off to her bedroom.

Still, Lelani would be so glad when Mr. Green dropped off the bedroom set. He had noticed the dark shadows under her eyes this morning and inquired about her new housing situation. When she'd told him about couch crashing last night, he had immediately offered her the use of what had once been his daughter's bedroom set.

"It's slightly juvenile," he'd admitted, "but I think it's a good mattress."

She was surprised to learn that he had a grown and married daughter. He didn't really seem that old. But it was sweet of him to loan her the set. Especially after witnessing the scene that her aunt had caused earlier.

Lelani didn't even want to think about how Aunt Caroline had stormed the cosmetic counter this morning. Mr. Green must've known straight off that her frumpy looking aunt couldn't possibly have been a legitimate La Prairie customer. And so he had approached, discreetly inquiring if there was a problem.

"You got that right," Aunt Caroline had snapped back at him. "The problem is Lelani. She's my niece and had been living with me and then she just up and disappears. For all I knew, she might've been kidnapped and murdered."

Mr. Green had nodded knowingly. And Lelani was relieved that she'd already told him a bit about her previous living arrangements.

"Perhaps you would like to take your break now, Miss Porter," he had politely suggested. Naturally she took him up on the offer, asking her aunt to meet her at Starbucks to talk about this in private. But as she hurried to punch out for her break, she was tempted to hide out in the employee lounge. The prospects of being subjected to her aunt's foul mood over coffee was not terribly appealing.

"What on earth were you thinking of to run off like that without telling anyone?" her aunt demanded as soon as Lelani sat down to join her.

"Didn't Ronnie tell you anything?"

"Of course. He said he came home and you were gone. I cannot believe you'd run off and leave poor baby Gracie like that, what kind of person—"

"Leave baby Gracie *like what?*" Lelani felt alarmed now. Had someone harmed the baby?

"I mean all alone like that." Her aunt scowled darkly. "I thought you were more responsible than that, Lelani."

"Gracie wasn't alone," insisted Lelani. "Ronnie was there."

"Not when you left the house."

"But I—"

"And you can't imagine how worried and shocked I was. For all I knew someone might've broken in and kidnapped you. You could've been the next missing girl. I tried your cell phone and it was turned off and—"

"My battery was dead and I couldn't find the charger."

"Because you left it at my house!" She shook her head with disapproval. "I was so concerned about your whereabouts that I called your mother, Lelani. I told her about the recent kidnappings and how I didn't think you'd just abandon poor little baby Gracie like that without good—"

"You called my mom?" Lelani felt shocked that Aunt Caroline would go to such an extreme. Especially considering how the two women weren't exactly on speaking terms.

"That's right. I did call your mom. And come to find out, my little Gracie wasn't the only baby you abandoned."

Lelani could feel her heart pounding in her temples as she bit into her lower lip, waiting for her aunt to continue.

"Yes, I know your dirty little secret now, Lelani. I know why you quit med school, why you left Hawaii and came here."

"It's not a dirty little secret." Lelani kept her voice even, but she really wanted to scream that this wasn't any of her aunt's business.

"Having a baby with a married man? Abandoning that baby with your parents? Dropping out of school? Running away? I'd call that a dirty little secret, Lelani. Certainly, it's not something you're proud of. And you obviously didn't come forward with that information, did you? No, I had to find it out for myself. And then I had to come over here looking for you. Just to be sure that you hadn't been kidnapped. Do you know how I felt when I saw you standing behind the cosmetics counter, acting like nothing whatsoever was wrong?" Her aunt's face was red with anger now.

Lelani looked down at the table. What was there to say? What difference would it make?

"If I had known you were that kind of a girl ..." Her aunt exhaled loudly. "Well, I wouldn't have taken you into my home or allowed you to spend time with my children. And the thanks I get from you, after I trust you and help you, is that you run off and leave my baby unattended. You don't call, you don't come home. What was I supposed to think?"

"Is that what Uncle Ronnie told you? That I left the house before he got home?"

"Oh, Ronnie assured me that you'd make up some phony baloney story." Her aunt narrowed her eyes at Lelani. "And he even told me why you'd do it."

"Why I'd do what?"

"Why you'd try to blame him. Ronnie didn't want to, but eventually he told me how you'd been coming onto him ever since you moved in with us. He told me how sometimes, like if I was gone or busy with the kids or doing laundry, he told me how you'd start rubbing his shoulders and flirting and how you'd push yourself up—"

"That is a big fat lie."

Her aunt laughed now. "Yes. That's exactly what he said you'd say."

Lelani considered telling her aunt the ugly truth now. Telling her how it was Uncle Ronnie who had come on to her, how he'd found her cleaning the bathtub in their bedroom, how Gracie had been down for her nap, how Lelani's T-shirt was wet from giving the baby a bath, and how he'd been the one to proposition her. But then she thought, why bother? Her aunt wouldn't believe her anyway. Besides, her aunt had enough problems—she was the one married to a loser.

"And, just so you know, Lelani, I told your mother everything. I told her about how you'd run out on my child and how you acted around my husband too. I told her what a little tramp you are."

Lelani stood now. Her fists clenched into balls as she pressed her lips together, trying desperately to hold her tongue. She did not have to stoop to her aunt's level.

"I'm sorry I ever invited you to stay with us," said her aunt, also standing. "I thought I was a good judge of character. I guess I was wrong."

"I guess so," said Lelani in a tight voice. "If you will excuse me, I have to get back to work now."

"Oh, yes, you go off and sell your hoity-toity over-priced beauty products." She shook her finger at her. "Just don't forget that beauty is only skin deep, little girl. And what lies underneath your skin is dirty and nasty and ugly." Then her aunt had turned on the rundown heels of her dowdy shoes and marched out of the coffee shop.

Lelani just stood there for a while, silently fuming, until the girl at the counter finally asked her if she needed something. "No, thank you," she had muttered. Then attempting to compose herself, she slowly walked back to Nordstrom, punched back in and returned to the La Prairie counter.

Later, Mr. Green inquired as to how things had gone with her aunt. She told him the truth, or most of it, managing to keep her answer brief and professional. And he had simply nodded in a compassionate and caring way that made her appreciate him even more. Of course, Mr. Green knew what it felt like to be mistreated and misunderstood by others. That was some comfort. But even so, the memory of her aunt's harsh words still stung.

"What do you think, Lelani?" Megan was asking her.

Lelani was jerked back into the present. "Think about what?"

"Anna's going to put her furniture into place now," explained Megan.

"And that's a problem?" asked Lelani, still trying to remember what they'd been discussing.

"I just thought Anna might want to rip out her carpeting first, you know, before she moves everything in here." Megan pointed to a heavy dresser that was still in the hallway.

Anna seemed to consider this. "I know that probably makes more sense, but mostly I just want to get settled in tonight. I want to sleep in my bed. And if the color of the carpet gets to me I might just get an area rug to cover it with."

"If there's anything left to cover," said Megan doubtfully. "By the time you get your things in place there might not be much rug showing anyway."

Lelani wanted to point out that the room might smell better without the old carpet, but then this room actually seemed to have been the least affected by the pet odors and stains. Perhaps the grandmother's dog hadn't been allowed in here.

"Well, let us know if you need any help with those heavier pieces," said Megan as she and Lelani left.

Back downstairs, Lelani paused in the doorway of Megan's bedroom to admire the pretty wood floor again. "That really looks great, Megan."

"And it'll be even better when I paint in here."

"I'm starved," admitted Lelani. "I think Anna's going to be busy for a while, but do you want to run out and get a bite to eat with me? Maybe we could bring her back something."

"How about getting something delivered?" suggested Megan. "I'm so grungy right now that I'd hate to go out without cleaning up first. But, before I shower, I really need to get some things put away."

"Sure, we could get something delivered," said Lelani. "Kendall has a whole stack of take-out menus in the kitchen."

"Great."

"Do you like pizza?" asked Lelani tentatively.

"Are you kidding?" Megan grinned. "It's a relief to know you're not some health freak or doing the latest no-carb diet. After sneaking a peek in Kendall's fridge, I'm a little worried that she might be one of those naked-green-salad-and-water-only kinds of girls."

"Or maybe she just doesn't like to cook," suggested Lelani. "What kind of pizza do you like?"

"Just about anything that doesn't involve anchovies."

"I'll check with Anna too."

"What about Kendall?" asked Megan as she reached for her bag and opened her wallet.

"Maybe we can order enough for four and if she's not into pizza, we can either pig out or have leftovers."

Megan handed her a twenty. "Sounds good to me. Here, put this toward it."

"This is too much," said Lelani.

"I'll cover for Kendall tonight. I sort of feel the need to mend my bridges with her anyway. You know, after hammering on her last night."

"Do you think she's still mad at you?"

Megan shrugged. "I don't know. At least she didn't mention it again today. But I can't totally read her yet. And she seemed pretty furious with me last night. What did you think? You mentioned you guys stayed up late and talked. Did she say anything negative about me?"

"No, not really. I think she's mostly disappointed that she's not making more money."

"She needs to get real and find a job."

Lelani nodded. "She seems to have some slightly unrealistic expecta-tions." Okay, that was an understatement. But she didn't know Megan well enough to lay all her thoughts out. In Lelani's opinion, Kendall wasn't simply spoiled and immature, she was slightly delusional. And she had some serious entitlement issues.

"Well, I'm really just trying to help her," said Megan. "Although I doubt she would believe me. And in the long run, her house will be worth more if she lets us help her fix it up. That is, if she ever sells it. It's a cool house and loaded with potential, but it needs some help."

"And I think you did a great job of trying to get her to understand that," said Lelani. "I appreciated you pleading our case with her. In fact, I think you'd probably make a pretty good attorney."

Now Megan's brow creased as if she'd just remembered something. "Thanks, Lelani. I just hope I can pull off my interview tomorrow. I really want this job, and my mom told me that the designer I'm interviewing with is totally into appearances." Megan helplessly held out her hands and frowned. "And look at me. I'm a mess."

"Yes, but you've been doing a pretty messy job." Even so, Lelani did a quick inventory of Megan. Her clothes, of course, were pretty filthy, but that was easily resolved. And her curly auburn hair was pretty enough, but at the moment it was sticking out in numerous directions, giving her a somewhat clownish appearance—add a red rubber nose and a funny hat and she could join the circus. And Megan's complexion, though clear, was slightly washed out and dull looking. Plus, she was totally void of any makeup, which wouldn't hurt. And her hands, well, they were a total disaster.

"I can tell you think I'm hopeless," said Megan.

"No, not hopeless."

"Just pathetic?"

"Okay, I don't want to offend you, Megan, but how about if I give you a free beauty consultation tonight?" she offered.

"Seriously?" Megan's eyes lit up. "You would do that for me?"

"Of course."

"And I'll repay you by helping to tear out that carpet, and with painting too, if you decide to paint your room that is."

"You don't need to repay me. I just want to do this for you, okay?"

"That would be awesome, Lelani. I so could use some professional help."

Lelani smiled. "Well, I'm not sure that I'm the best professional around, but I have learned a thing or two these past few weeks. And I've got samples of some pretty nice products. Anyway, let me go order that pizza while you do what you need to in here, and we'll start your makeover after dinner."

Lelani ordered a giant pizza, choosing what she hoped was a congenial selection of toppings, no anchovies. Then she changed into sweats and started emptying the dishwasher and setting the table, more casually tonight, with four places just in case Kendall came home. Lelani still wasn't completely sure what she thought about Kendall.

She'd heard a lot of Kendall's history last night and was still trying to make sense of it. Obviously the girl was pretty shallow as well as somewhat immature and inexperienced, not to mention her entitlement issues. But Lelani was trying to understand why she was like that. As the youngest child of five kids, and by a long shot too, Kendall had been fairly sheltered and, in Lelani's opinion, more than a little spoiled. She'd managed to finish a couple of years of college, but unable to decide on a major, she'd dropped out and allowed her parents to support her.

Lelani had been surprised to hear that Kendall's parents even covered what sounded like some staggering credit card bills for a while. Apparently Kendall liked to shop, another understatement. Lelani suspected she was a shopaholic, and her parents had attempted to protect her credit rating from going completely down the drain. But it sounded like their patience and benevolence eventually wore thin, which Lelani thought was totally understandable. Even though Lelani's parents were fairly well off, they would never do something like that for her—she wouldn't even expect it. Not that they weren't generous in other ways. They definitely were.

Her parents. She'd already called them and left a message, just to let them know that she hadn't been kidnapped and that she had moved into a house with three very nice roommates. But she wasn't looking forward to actually speaking to them anytime soon. Perhaps she could put that off for a while. She doubted they would be eager to speak to her either. She didn't even want to think about it right now. Instead, she focused her energy on cleaning the kitchen and trying to figure out what it was that made Kendall tick.

It had been getting pretty late last night when Kendall, probably affected by the second bottle wine, which she had opened during dinner and finished off herself while visiting with Lelani, started to tearfully describe how her parents had "thoughtlessly" sold the family home last spring while Kendall was still living there. They then purchased what sounded like quite a luxurious motor home (Kendall said it cost more than half a million dollars) and "abandoned" her so that they could live on the road. Weary of Kendall's drama by then, Lelani had wondered if Kendall's parents had simply wished to escape their youngest child.

"Dinner?" asked Kendall as she waltzed in the back door. She was wearing pale blue velour sweats and toting what appeared to be a gym bag.

"Just pizza," said Lelani as she filled a water glass.

Kendall frowned. "Pizza?"

"We ordered out," explained Lelani. "Megan and Anna are moving stuff in and they're pretty worn out. Pizza seemed an easy choice."

"Easy if you don't mind lots of carbs and fats."

"Have you been working out?" asked Lelani, hoping to change the subject.

"Yoga." Kendall stood straighter. "Monday, Wednesday, and Friday."

"Good for you."

"You could come too," said Kendall. "The class is from four to five."

Lelani glanced at the clock. "But it's after six."

"Several of us do coffee or green tea or whatever afterward. It's kind of a social thing too."

"Well, I don't get off work that early."

"Ask them to change your schedule," suggested Kendall lightly, as if this were a small thing.

Lelani smiled. "Oh, I sort of like my schedule as it is. It's nice not working weekends or evenings."

"So has everyone moved in now?" asked Kendall.

"Pretty much so. I have a bed and some things coming in a couple of days. But that will give me time to remove the carpeting and maybe even paint. You should check out Megan's room."

"Why?"

"She already took out her carpet, and it looks fantastic."

"Oh." Kendall got a bored expression now, like she really didn't care what they did to the house. Or maybe she was still just miffed at Megan. Whatever it was, Lelani was pretty sure she didn't want to go there.

Just then the doorbell rang. "I'll bet that's pizza," said Lelani as she went to answer it. "You sure you don't want to join us?"

"Well, maybe I'll have one small piece, just to be friendly."

As it turned out, Lelani noticed that Kendall ate more than one small piece. In fact, she ate more than her fair share—not that Lelani was counting, but she couldn't help but notice. She also noticed that Kendall excused herself quickly afterward—going directly to the upstairs bath-room, where Lelani felt certain she heard strange sounds, possibly gagging noises. It didn't take a genius to figure out that Kendall had a little prob-lem with bulimia. Hopefully it wasn't anything too serious. Really, Lelani wasn't that surprised. Just disappointed.

In fact, Lelani felt certain that all of the girls would have their flaws ... and their secrets. Who didn't?

# Sixteen

# Anna

"I'll take you guys up on that offer now, if you don't mind," said Anna. The three of them were cleaning up in the kitchen and loading the dishwasher. "I think I'm ready to move some of the furniture from the hallway into my room. Kendall didn't seem too happy to see it out there. She mentioned that she hoped I didn't plan to leave it there permanently." Anna laughed nervously. "Not that I would. But I didn't think one night of having it out there would be such a big deal."

"I'm ready," said Megan as she hung up a dish towel. "Let's go move some furniture."

"I know I brought too much stuff," Anna apologized as they went upstairs. "But I guess I thought the bedroom here was larger."

"Maybe you should store some of your things down in the garage," suggested Megan. "I put a few crates out there, stacked them up against the side wall so they're not in the way. I don't think Kendall will mind."

"I guess I could do that," said Anna. "Although I don't want my things to get ruined."

"I don't think they'll get ruined," said Megan in a slightly defensive tone.

"What about mice and things?"

Megan shrugged.

"Okay, I'll put some things down there until Gil can stop by and pick them up." Still, Anna wasn't sure what to keep and what to send back. Mostly, she wished she had a bigger room. And she wondered if this idea to move out of her family home was such a smart one after all. Still, she couldn't bear hearing her mother saying, "I told you so."

Anna stood and studied the furniture still in the hallway. "I guess I only really need one of these bedside tables," she admitted. "And that bench is probably not going to fit anywhere."

"Mind if I take a look?" offered Megan. "It might be that you could rearrange things a little."

"How?" Anna peered skeptically into the room. She'd placed her bed in the only spot that it seemed to go, in the center of the room. Her dresser was under the window and the TV cabinet was set up directly across from her bed.

"Want to experiment a little?" asked Megan. "Rearrange things to fit better?"

"I guess." Anna nodded but wasn't too sure.

Then Megan began telling them what to do. She didn't even ask Anna if she agreed, she simply took over. And Anna wasn't sure how she felt about this. Who did Megan think she was anyway? But Anna didn't argue with her as the three of them began to move things around. After about twenty minutes of shuffling and shoving furniture about in a way that made no sense to Anna, she was about to tell Megan to take a hike. But finally it seemed that Megan was satisfied. Or maybe she was just worn out. But the room had been completely rearranged. And to Anna's surprise it actually looked pretty good—and it seemed larger too.

"Wow," said Anna as appreciation set in. She was pretty sure that she was going to sleep well tonight. "How did you do that?"

Megan just shrugged. "I guess I just have an eye for this stuff."

"I never would've considered putting my bed up against the wall like that, but the way you've arranged those pillows actually makes it feel kind of like a couch."

"And now we can put that bench beneath the window," said Megan, "like a window seat."

"Cool." Anna stood back and watched as Megan and Lelani carried in the bench and put it in place.

"And, see, by using your dresser as a bedside table, you get rid of two pieces of furniture that were mostly just taking up space," Megan pointed out.

"Thanks," said Anna. "I never could've made it look like this without your help."

"It was fun," said Megan.

"And now it's time for Megan's makeover," announced Lelani.

"A makeover?" Anna looked at her two new friends with interest. "Why?"

"Megan has a job interview tomorrow," explained Lelani. "I offered to give her a free beauty consultation."

"Not that I need it," joked Megan, holding up hands that looked like she'd been doing yard work or changing motor oil.

Anna nodded. "Yes, those nails are pretty bad. But, seriously, Lelani, you're going to give her a real makeover?"

"More like a mini-makeover," said Lelani. "But I think it'll be an improvement."

"How could it not be?" asked Megan.

"And it's good for me to practice on someone who's not a customer," Lelani told them. "Plus I have some nice samples I can try out on her."

"You mean I'm your science experiment?" asked Megan. "A guinea pig?"

"No, nothing like that," said Lelani. "The products we're going to try are some of the best in the world."

"Ooh," said Megan. "I can't wait."

Anna did not want to be left out of this. And yet she didn't want to be too intrusive either. "I just love watching those makeover shows like *What Not to Wear* or reruns of *The Swan*," she told them. "I think it's so amazing how people can be transformed, and I think it'd be fun to learn some of those tricks." She peered hopefully at Megan. "Would you mind if I watched?"

Megan laughed. "I don't mind if you don't mind. But I'm not sure how much you'll actually learn. I might turn out to be one of those hopeless cases that never make it on the air."

"Of course, you're not hopeless," said Lelani. "But it's getting late and we need to get started. I suggest you hit the shower, Megan. And I'll get things set up."

"Where are you doing it?" asked Anna.

Lelani seemed to consider this. "Well, since our bedrooms aren't really set up ... maybe just the bathroom."

"Give me half an hour to clean up," said Megan.

So Megan and Lelani went back downstairs, and Anna went back to putting things away—or rather trying to put them away. Despite the rearranging, it was still a major challenge to find a place to put everything. Even so, she told herself that she didn't care. It was worth the sacrifice to have this freedom. Besides, she was making new friends. And she couldn't wait to see how Lelani's makeover on Megan would turn out. Who knew, maybe Anna could be next.

"How's it going in here?" asked Kendall as she pushed open the door to Anna's room. Now Anna had neglected to fully close the door, but she still thought it would've been more polite for Kendall to knock before entering. She considered mentioning it to her but decided to overlook Kendall's lapse in manners this time.

"I brought too much stuff," admitted Anna as she set one of her still packed suitcases on the bench. "I think I'll have to send some of this back home."

"I suppose this house is a little short on storage," said Kendall. "I've had a hard time trying to find extra space for my clothes now too. I had been using this bedroom as an overflow closet." She looked longingly around the crowded room as if perhaps she regretted having given up this particular storage space. And, once again, Anna considered the amount of rent she would be shelling out each month for such a small space. Was it crazy? Even so, she wasn't going to dwell on it.

"So, how long have you lived in this house?" asked Anna as she tucked a folded sweater into a drawer.

"I moved here last spring when my parents abandoned me."

Anna peered curiously at Kendall now. "Your parents abandoned you?"

Kendall nodded sadly. "Yes. They sold their house right out from under me, and then they took off to see the world. I didn't have any place to live. And I wasn't even working at the time."

"So that's when your grandmother gave you this house?"

"Yes, I suppose she felt sorry for me." Kendall sat down on Anna's bed now. Anna tried not to flinch as Kendall picked up a big brown teddy bear. Anna wasn't even sure how the bear had found its way to her new digs. Maybe Gil had tossed it in when she wasn't paying attention. Jake had sent the soft, cuddly bear to Anna along with a big box of chocolates when she was homesick during her freshman year at college. She knew she should've gotten rid of it back when Jake broke her heart, but somehow the soft stuffed toy tagged along. And now she told herself it was simply a sweet teddy bear with absolutely no connection to Jake. Still, it seriously bugged her to see Kendall tossing it around now, and it took all her self-control not to snatch him from her thoughtless landlady.

For a distraction, Anna turned her attention back to sorting out what she would keep here and what she would send back home. "So where is your grandmother now?" she asked Kendall.

"She's in an assisted-living place—kind of like a nursing home, only nicer."

"Oh, is she ill?" Anna closed the drawer and turned to see that Kendall was still holding the bear, swinging him by the legs now.

"No, but she's almost a hundred."

Anna blinked. "Almost a hundred years old?"

"Well, she's in her late nineties at least."

"Wow. My grandmother is only"—Anna thought for a moment— "like in her sixties I think."

"Yeah, well, that's about how old my parents are."

Anna tried to absorb this new fact. "Really?"

"Yeah, I was their late-in-life baby—their little surprise package. My mom actually thought she was going through an early menopause, but it turned out she was pregnant with me. I guess we're kind of a weird family. Like I have a niece who's just a couple of years younger than me. And my oldest sister Kim just turned forty-two, which sounds sort of over the hill to me."

"You have a sister who's forty-two? My mom is only forty-four."

"Yeah." Kendall sighed as she swung the bear back and forth by one arm now. "It hasn't been easy."

"Is your family very close?" asked Anna, again suppressing the urge to rescue her bear.

"Not really. I mean everyone likes everyone okay. But I only have one sister who lives in Oregon. The others live all over the country. And my parents, well, who knows where they are right now. Last I heard they were heading for the east coast to see the autumn foliage. Like what's up with driving that far just to see some stupid leaves? We have perfectly good leaves right here in Oregon." Kendall frowned as she finally set the bear aside. "Sometimes I just don't get parents."

"I know what you mean. My parents can be quite a challenge too." Still, Anna wasn't so sure she could relate to Kendall. On one hand, Kendall seemed sort of lucky to have all this independence: her own house and no parents looking over her shoulder. On the other hand, it seemed a little lonely. And strange.

# Seventeen

# Megan

"You have gorgeous skin," said Lelani as she smeared another product onto Megan's face, "your pores are tiny." Megan was seated on the dining room chair that Lelani had managed to wedge up against the bathroom vanity. At the moment, Megan's hands were soaking in something sort of slimy in the sink. She had never been pampered like this but thought it was actually sort of fun.

"I have large pores," said Anna from where she was perched on the edge of the bathtub. "Are there products for that?"

"Of course," said Lelani. "There are products for everything."

"Is this line very expensive?" asked Anna.

Lelani held up the small tube of whatever it was that she was applying to Megan's face and nodded. "This facial masque, in a regular eight-ounce size, is close to two hundred dollars."

"No way!" said Anna.

"I know it seems outrageous," said Lelani. "I was pretty shocked at first too."

"Do you think the products are that good?" asked Anna.

"They're definitely good," said Lelani. "But I'm not sure why they cost so much."

"What do you think, Megan?" asked Anna. "Do they seem worth it?"

Megan sighed. "I don't know much about beauty products, but I have to admit these seem pretty nice. Of course, that might be simply because Lelani knows what she's doing."

"So do you sell very much of these products?" asked Anna.

"You'd be surprised," said Lelani as she checked on Megan's hands. "There are a lot of older women who think nothing of shelling out thousands of dollars just to look younger."

"Sure," said Anna, "like for plastic surgery. My aunt just had her eyes done, and it cost about six thousand."

"No, I mean for products like these," said Lelani. "I had a client just last week who bought a couple thousand dollars worth of La Prairie."

"That's crazy," said Anna. "Does it really work that well? Do they look younger?"

Lelani shrugged as she tore open another sample. "Some of them swear by it."

"So, will I look younger?" asked Megan. "Like sixteen? Because that's not going to help me to—"

"Sh," said Lelani. "You're disturbing the masque."

Megan nodded, determined to keep her mouth closed, as Anna continued to pelt Lelani with a variety of beauty questions. Megan thought that Anna would probably make a good talk-show host. She was chatty and inquisitive. But Lelani was patient in her answers, and Megan could tell that Lelani, even though she admitted she was new at doing this, had done thorough research and seemed to know what she was talking about. Still, Megan wondered why someone as intelligent and capable as Lelani had given up on med school to work in cosmetic sales. It just didn't make sense. And yet, Lelani did not seem to want to discuss it. Maybe in time.

"What's going on in here?" asked Kendall, pushing her head into the bathroom to peer curiously at the three of them. "Some sort of secret society?"

Lelani laughed. "No. I'm just giving Megan a makeover."

"And I wasn't invited?" Kendall made a pouting face.

"Well, it's a little crowded," said Lelani, "but feel free to take the seat on the john if you like."

Megan didn't expect Kendall to accept this weird offer to sit on the toilet seat, but to her surprise, Kendall did. And suddenly Megan was feeling like a sideshow freak. Like maybe she should've sold tickets and invited the neighbors.

"So why is Megan so special?" asked Kendall. "Why does she get a makeover?"

"Because she has a job interview tomorrow," Lelani explained as she soaked a washcloth, then pressed it onto Megan's forehead. "And she promised to help me with my room."

"Why do you need help with your room?" asked Kendall.

"To take out the carpet," said Lelani as she gently began to remove the facial masque.

"Oh, that," said Kendall, as though she had forgotten all about their agreement.

"You should see Megan's room," said Lelani. "It looks—"

"I don't really see why you guys are all wigged out over some carpeting," said Kendall. "It's not really that bad."

Megan wanted to point out how nasty the carpet heaped out in the backyard had actually been, but Lelani had the washcloth over her mouth now—sort of like a gag order, which was probably just as well. Sometimes, like now, Megan felt like gagging Kendall.

"I think a simple steam cleaning should make everyone happy," continued Kendall. "In fact, I'll call them tomorrow and see about setting it up."

Megan wanted to say that was a waste of money, but more than that, she wished Kendall would just leave. She was spoiling everything.

"Megan's face is all red," said Kendall when Lelani finally removed the washcloth. "Is it supposed to look like that?"

Megan stretched her neck to see into the mirror and, in fact, her face was red. "Is it supposed to be red?" she asked Lelani with concern.

"There's always a little redness at first," explained Lelani. "Let's put this soothing moisturizer on now. That should settle it down a little."

But Megan worried. What if she had some kind of allergic reaction to Lelani's expensive products? What if she went in for tomorrow's interview looking like a pomegranate? That should make quite an impression. But the lotion Lelani smoothed over her face did feel soothing. And then she put something cool around Megan's eyes and, despite some questioning comments from both Kendall and Anna, Megan tried to believe that this was going to work out.

Lelani was working on Megan's hands now, first using a stick to push back the skin around the nails and then rubbing something into the nails. Meanwhile Anna and Kendall were discussing the pros and cons of getting a Brazilian bikini wax.

"It really isn't that bad," Kendall was saying. "I mean, what's a little pain for looking good in a bikini?"

"Ooh!" said Anna, like someone had pinched her. "You could not pay me to have my hair ripped out by the root down there. That is totally nuts."

"Beauty shouldn't be painful," said Lelani as she continued to work on Megan's nails.

"Why not?" asked Kendall.

"Because it should start inside of a person," said Lelani.

"I agree," said Megan.

"But how?" asked Anna. "Do you mean by eating the right foods, taking vitamins?"

"No," said Lelani. "It should be a result of how you feel about yourself."

"Then I'm probably a lost cause," said Anna. She stood up and looked over Megan's shoulder into the mirror. "I will never feel beautiful."

"Why not?" asked Megan as she looked up at Anna's softly rounded face and expressive dark eyes. "You're really pretty, Anna."

Anna shook her head. "No, I'm not."

"Yes, you are," argued Lelani. "You have gorgeous coloring and striking eyes, and look at those nice full lips."

"Have you had collagen injections?" asked Kendall, now standing behind Anna and peering into the mirror too.

"Of course not," said Anna.

"But Anna really needs to do something with those bushy eyebrows," Kendall said.

Anna's hands flew up to her brow line. "What?"

"Have you ever heard of tweezers?" asked Kendall.

"For my eyebrows?" asked Anna.

"Unless you've got some hairs growing out of your chin." Kendall peered more curiously at her.

Anna clapped her hand over her chin now. "No!" she snapped. "I don't have hair growing out of my chin."

Megan knew it was wrong, but she wished she could think of something derogatory to say about Kendall's appearance. Unfortunately, it was flawless—at least on the exterior. "Don't listen to Kendall, Anna," Megan told her.

"Fine," said Kendall. "Go around with a uni-brow if you like, Anna. I don't care."

"A uni-brow?" Anna shrieked, leaning over Megan's shoulder to peer more closely at her reflection. "Is that a uni-brow?"

"Maybe you can dress up like Ugly Betty for Halloween," teased Kendall.

"Is it that bad?" cried Anna, still staring at her reflection with a look of horror.

"No," said Megan. "Kendall is just being mean."

"I'm being mean?" Kendall sounded offended now. "You guys are in here having a little makeover party, to which I wasn't invited. You have insulted my house, talked me down on rent, and you accuse *me* of being mean?"

"If the shoe fits ..." Megan tossed Kendall a warning glance.

"Ask Lelani," insisted Kendall. "Does Anna need to pluck her eyebrows or not?"

Lelani looked trapped. "I suppose she could probably do a little thinning."

"Are you just agreeing with Kendall to be nice?" asked Megan, unsure of why she wanted to pursue this. Or maybe Kendall just made her mad. And maybe Megan just wanted to knock Miss Snooty Pants down a notch or two.

"Simply because *some* people have absolutely no fashion sense does not make the rest of us liars," said Kendall in a haughty tone. "Anna has bushy eyebrows. And you, Megan, need to lose weight."

Megan took in a sharp breath. She would definitely need to exercise some self-control now. She mentally counted to ten, reminding herself that 1) she was a Christian and 2) she had just told her mom that it seemed like God wanted her here—to make a difference.

"That wasn't nice," said Lelani.

"But it's true."

"It is true, isn't it?" said Anna, still staring in the mirror, nervously running her fingers over her eyebrows. "I *do* have bushy eyebrows. I guess I just never noticed."

"That's right," said Kendall. "And if Megan took a good long look in the mirror, she'd notice that it wouldn't hurt her to take off a few pounds."

Megan was still trying to control her temper. And she was actually praying for strength now.

"If you want to pluck your brows, Anna," said Lelani carefully, "just make sure you do it the right way. The worst eyebrow mistake that women make is to over pluck. How about if I give you some help another time?"

Anna was still frowning at her reflection. "In the meantime, I have to walk around with a uni-brow?"

"You do not have a uni-brow," insisted Megan. "Kendall was just being mean."

"You mean honest," said Kendall smugly.

"It *was* mean," said Anna. "And it was especially mean for you to say that about Megan. She is not fat."

"By *your* standards," said Kendall.

"Kendall," said Megan sharply. "Anna does not have a uni-brow."

"And Megan is not fat," added Anna. Of course, just hearing the f-word made Megan feel even worse. Maybe she was fat. After all, she had put on that freshman fifteen. Well, maybe not until her senior year. But she hadn't taken it off either.

"Well, Anna needs to clean up that brow line before she does have a uni-brow," declared Kendall. "And Megan needs to cut back on carbs."

"Anna is pretty just as she is," said Megan, pretending to ignore the carb-cutting advice.

"That's right," said Lelani.

"You guys are just being nice," said Anna.

"And Megan is not overweight," continued Lelani.

"And I am just being honest," said Kendall. "Sometimes the truth hurts, girls. Take it or leave it."

Seriously, Megan wanted to slap Kendall now. But she just sat there, pressing her lips tightly together as Lelani finished up her nails. No way was she going to let Kendall get the best of her. She refused to lose her temper on her first night in this house. In fact, maybe that's what Kendall was hoping for. Maybe it was Kendall's way of getting rid of her and finding someone more acceptable—someone who wouldn't rock the boat the way Megan had already done.

"Okay, now I'm going to do your makeup," announced Lelani.

"Makeup?" asked Megan. "Before I go to bed?" Right now, all Megan wanted was to call it a night—and get away from Kendall.

"I just want to show you a couple of tricks."

"Yes," said Anna eagerly. "This is the good part, Megan. This is what I want to learn to do."

Seeing how Anna was distracted from Kendall's attack on her eyebrows by this, Megan decided to be a good sport. Never mind that she was sitting there trying to hold her stomach in to prove Kendall wrong. "Okay," said Megan, feeling helpless. "Show me what you've got."

So Lelani began applying makeup, explaining as she went along. And for the first time ever, Megan thought maybe she was getting it. Lelani was either a real pro or a good teacher, but as she worked on Megan, it all seemed fairly simple and straightforward.

"Because you have fair coloring," said Lelani as she put a soft fawn-like color on Megan's eyelids, "you want to keep your makeup light and natural." Then she continued, explaining each step and using a very light touch.

Finally, she was done. Megan was stunned by the general improvement of her appearance, and the others seemed impressed as well.

"You do look better," admitted Kendall. "Now if you just lost some weight."

"You look fantastic," said Anna. "Really, really pretty."

"And you saw how easy it was," said Lelani.

"But what about tomorrow?" asked Megan. "I mean when I go for the interview—what if I can't make it look like this?"

"I'll help you again in the morning," Lelani offered. "You saw that it was really pretty simple, it won't take long for you to be able to do this on your own."

"I'll have to buy some of these things," said Megan. Then she frowned. "But they're so expensive."

"You don't have to get La Prairie products," said Lelani. "There are lots of less expensive lines. Is there another product that you like?"

"I've always sort of liked Clinique."

"Great. Come by Nordstrom after your interview and I can introduce you to Abby; she sells Clinique."

"It figures you'd like Clinique," Kendall said in that superior tone.

"Why?" demanded Megan hotly.

"Because it's so ordinary."

"What do you like?" asked Anna.

"Lancôme is okay. But I'd like to try La Prairie."

"Well, maybe you should get a job then," said Megan sharply. "So you can afford it."

Anna giggled and Kendall, looking offended, stuck her nose in the air and walked out of the bathroom. Megan let out a sigh of relief.

"Is it just me, or is she a witch?" asked Anna.

"It's not just you," said Megan.

"What are you going to wear for your interview, Megan?" asked Lelani.

Megan shrugged. She hadn't really had time to think about it. "Probably something like what I wore when I interviewed for this house."

She made a face. "Back when I thought I needed to make an impression on Kendall, just so that I could get into what I thought was a fancy, luxurious, upscale—"

"Yeah, yeah," said Kendall, poking her nose back into the bathroom. "And just for the record, that outfit was not impressive. If you really want to get a job as an interior designer, I think you should show a little more style."

"I'm not applying for a designer position," said Megan. "Just an assistant position."

"Fine," snapped Kendall. "Go in there looking like a college student if you want, but I'll bet they want someone who's a little more uptown and a little more sophisticated."

Okay, as much as Megan hated to acknowledge this, she knew that Kendall might be onto something. But Megan also knew that *uptown* and *sophisticated* were not looks she could easily pull off. Plus, she was fully aware that she did look like a college student. After all, that's what she had been these past five years.

"You're probably right, Kendall," admitted Megan, deciding that maybe it was time to start acting more like a Christian. "So, what would you suggest?"

Now Kendall brightened a little. "Well, that jacket you wore to meet me was actually not bad. And those boots you had on weren't bad either. But you need to wear some nice pants or a skirt—not jeans. And then you need to accessorize. Either a scarf or some jewelry or something to suggest that you're at least attempting to grow up."

"Thanks," said Megan, reverting back to her grumpy tone.

Fortunately, Kendall didn't seem to catch it. She was on a roll now. "Come to think of it, I have a scarf that might work for you." She pointed to Megan. "Go get that jacket and something professional looking to go with it. I'll get the scarf and a couple of other things and we'll do a dress rehearsal on you."

Megan was sure that was the last thing she wanted to do tonight, but she also felt pretty sure that she hadn't handled things too well so far. Maybe this was her punishment. As it turned out, it was nearly eleven by the time all three girls had helped to put Megan's interview look together. And, as tired as she was, Megan had to admit, standing in front of Kendall's full-length mirror, that the results were pretty good.

Megan wore her tan tweed Marc Jacobs jacket with a dark brown skirt that Lelani loaned her, combined with a wide leather belt from Anna and a long silk scarf from Kendall. This outfit, combined with her Stuart Weitzman boots and a Prada bag, also borrowed from Kendall, made Megan actually look quite stylish—and grown-up too.

"Thanks, you guys," she told them all. "It looks like it takes a village to dress an idiot."

They laughed, and Megan hoped that this would smooth over the exchange made in the bathroom. Although Kendall's assessment of her weight still stung.

"Anyway," she said, "if I get this job, I'll owe it all to you guys."

"Hey, if you get the job, it's because you deserve it," said Lelani.

"Yes," agreed Anna. "You already aced your first interview."

"Well, if I get the job," said Megan, "how about I treat you all to dinner as a thank-you?" Then she took one last look in the mirror and sighed. She just hoped she could put herself together half so well tomorrow morning.

As Megan got ready for bed, she thought about her new roommates and how the four of them were a fairly diverse mix of personalities. Naturally, she liked Lelani a lot, but she got the feeling that Lelani was holding something back ... like she had this wall up, or perhaps a secret.

Anna was nice, although it seemed she was even more insecure than Megan herself, and yet she could also come across as slightly cocky and bossy. Then there was Kendall. Not only was she unkind, but she was unpredictable too. One minute she was tearing people down, and the next she was acting all helpful. Very confusing. And frustrating.

For the most part, Megan didn't trust her. If Kendall weren't the owner of this house, Megan felt certain that she wouldn't make the slightest effort to befriend Kendall, and she certainly wouldn't placate her like she'd done tonight. And, yet, what could Megan do? It was hard to believe she'd be stuck with Kendall for a full year. That is, unless Kendall got so fed up that she kicked Megan out. And perhaps that would be a good thing. Although she wasn't really ready to give up.

Before Megan went to sleep, she prayed for Lelani and Anna. Eventually, although it wasn't easy or natural, she prayed for Kendall, too. Megan did it only because she knew that she was not only supposed to love her enemies, but to pray for them as well. And, okay, it was a very short prayer, and rather vague, but it was better than nothing. Then Megan asked God to help her through tomorrow's interview.

# Lelani

Lelani awoke suddenly. Still trembling from a nightmare, she told herself that it was just a bad dream and tried to figure out where she was at the moment. Her college dorm? Ben's apartment? Her parents' home on the beach? Aunt Caroline's little cracker box? Oliana's house? Where? Where?

In her dream, which had started out so pleasantly, she'd been enjoying a perfect wave off of Big Beach in Maui. It had been sunny and warm and a magnificent surfing day, but then she'd gotten distracted and lost her balance. Pulled under by a wave, she had thrashed about in the darkness of the sea, as if she'd been caught in a fishing net or seaweed or something that refused to let her go.

She sat up now and looked around the shadows of the room, trying to get her bearings and finally remembering that she had rented a room at Kendall's house and was temporarily sleeping on the couch. Lelani slowly untangled herself from the knitted throw she'd been using as a blanket and took a deep and calming breath. *Just relax. Everything is going to be okay. No big deal.*

Sometimes Lelani could become terrified. It was the worst in the darkness of night and when she was all alone. At times like this she would seriously question everything about herself and about her life. Even though she was trying to block out her aunt's cruel words and accusations, Lelani knew they contained a grain of truth. And so tonight her usual questions seemed even more persistent—more than ever they seemed to demand answers.

What *was* she doing here? Why had she given up on med school and her dreams? Or were those her dreams? Perhaps they were her parents' dreams. And why had she allowed her parents to pressure her into keeping a child she hadn't wanted, and later insisting that she leave the baby with them? Why had she left her home and all that she knew just to come to the mainland? And to do what? What was here for her? What was she running from? Hiding from? At times like this, she would ponder the whole point to life in general. What was the point in even trying?

In the middle of the night when nothing seemed to make sense, sometimes Lelani wondered why she didn't simply give up, give in, surrender.

She hadn't talked to her parents since the time she'd called to let them know that she made it to Aunt Caroline's okay. Not that they would be particularly concerned about her now. Well, aside from Aunt Caroline's crazy phone call. But Lelani's message should have straightened that out. Lelani knew that her parents were glad to be rid of her. It had been their idea for her to leave. They'd paid for the ticket and given her a bit of travel money and more than that, didn't seem to care.

Maybe she'd replaced herself with Emma—a child they could raise as their own. Perhaps Emma would turn out better. Lelani didn't want to think about that. To be fair, her parents had insisted that she take a full year to live away from home, to think about things, to reevaluate and, according to her dad, "to grow up."

Many bitter words had been exchanged during the past six months. Perhaps even more toxic were the unspoken words. She knew her parents held her mistakes against her. She knew she had disappointed them, dashed their expectations. If her punishment was to be banished like this, well, maybe she deserved it. Maybe she would never go back home.

Lelani got up and went into the kitchen. Turning on the light above the sink, she located a glass in Kendall's crazy cupboards and filled it with water from the tap, taking a long, slow drink and telling herself to just relax, calm down. These panic attacks had been an infrequent interruption to life before. Now they were becoming a regular thing. But she knew that deep breathing and refocusing could calm her. The worst thing she could do was give in to it, allow it to grab her and hold her and, like the fishnet or whatever it was in her dream, to pull her down, down, down.

Lelani finished the glass of water. As she sat it in the sink, she noticed an empty wine bottle on the counter. Kendall had started that after Anna and Megan went to bed. Lelani had been trying to go to sleep herself, out on her makeshift bed on the couch, but Kendall had come in with her bottle of wine and two glasses, hoping to entice Lelani into another long-winded conversation where Kendall did all the talking.

But Lelani had begged out, saying she had a headache and needed to get some sleep. Not that it had done much good. Even as Lelani had attempted to doze off, Kendall continued to talk and drink, and drink and talk, telling Lelani far more than she wanted to know. What was wrong with that girl anyway? Well, besides almost everything.

By now Lelani had decided that Kendall was not only unemployed, selfish, lazy, and shallow, but she was probably up to her eyeballs in debt due to her addictive shopping compulsion, plus she had a drinking problem and on top of everything else appeared to be bulimic. It seemed that Lelani had signed a one-year lease with a certifiable nutcase.

But right now she just needed sleep. She fluffed the pillow and tried to focus on something calming and pleasant and carefree. Sunshine, surfing, home. Even so, it took Lelani a long time to return to sleep, and it seemed she had barely dozed off when a gruff voice woke her again, insisting to be let in.

"She's still asleep," said a quiet female voice.

Lelani opened one eye to see what was going on. She spied Megan in her pajamas and apparently speaking to someone at the barely opened front door.

"Who is it?" asked Lelani as she groggily wrapped the chenille throw around her shoulders and shuffled toward the door.

"I'm not sure," called Megan. "Someone who wants to see Kendall. I think it's a neighbor." Then Megan circled her finger around her ear as if to suggest that the person at the door might not be playing with a full deck. Then she turned back to whoever it was and said, "Do you know that it's not even seven in the morning?"

"I need to see Kendall," growled a deep voice.

Now Lelani peered around the front door to see a very old woman in a pink raincoat standing on the porch. "Are you Kendall's grandmother?" asked Lelani.

"Of course I'm Kendall's grandmother," fumed the old woman. "Now let me in right this minute before I call the police. Who are you, and what have you done to my granddaughter?"

Lelani nudged Megan. "We better let her in," she said quietly. "I'll go get Kendall."

The woman was still fuming and growling as Megan let her in. Megan attempted to explain that Kendall had leased rooms to them, but the old lady was not buying it. She seemed to think that they had forced their way in and that they were possibly facilitating her granddaughter's abduction and subsequent disappearance. Lelani excused herself and sprinted up the stairs to get Kendall.

She knocked on the door and when Kendall didn't answer, she went right in. "Kendall!" she said, giving her a firm shake. "Wake up!"

Kendall looked up with blurry eyes. "What?"

"Your grandmother is here."

"Huh?"

"Downstairs. Your grandmother would like to see you."

Kendall groaned and rolled over. "Leave me alone."

For a moment, Lelani considered backing off. Then she remembered how

Kendall had kept her up last night, gabbing on and on despite Lelani saying she needed some sleep.

"No," said Lelani firmly. "Your grandmother is downstairs and you need to go see what she wants *right now!*" Then she jerked the covers off of Kendall and grabbed her by the arm and pulled her out of bed.

Kendall was swearing at Lelani now, but at least she was on her feet and reaching for her robe.

"Sorry to disturb your rest," said Lelani with forced politeness. "But please go speak to your grandmother now." Then she followed Kendall down the stairs. The old woman was sitting in the middle of what had been Lelani's bed. Not that she planned to get in any more sleep this morning.

"Kendall," said the old woman pleasantly, as if it were the middle of the afternoon and she had popped in for tea. "How are you doing?"

Kendall blinked and stared. "What time is it?"

"Six forty-seven," snapped Megan.

"In the morning?" asked Kendall.

"What do you think?" said Megan.

"Why are you visiting me so early, Grandmother?" asked Kendall in a cranky tone.

"I couldn't sleep," said her grandmother. "And I have been worrying about you. So I called a taxi and came to check on you." She pointed a finger at Lelani and Megan. "And complete strangers answered your door, Kendall. Who are these people you've allowed into my house?"

So Kendall introduced Lelani and Megan. "And this is my grandmother, Mrs. Weis," she said politely. "And there's another stranger sleeping upstairs, Grandmother," she added. "Her name is Anna."

"Goodness." Mrs. Weis shook her head as if attempting to take this in.

"I thought you said it was okay for me to have roommates as long as they weren't guys," said Kendall with a yawn.

"Yes, I suppose I said that," said Mrs. Weis. "But you might've told me, Kendall. And you have not been to see me in ages. I was worried about you."

"Why didn't you just call me?"

"I have called you," said Mrs. Weis. "But you never answer your phone."

"Oh."

"And I tried to call your parents, and I get a tinny recording saying that the phone is no longer in service. Why is it no longer in service?"

As Kendall reminded her grandmother of her parents' cross-country motor-home trip, and that they could only be reached on their cell phone, Megan excused herself, making a quick exit.

"Please excuse me as well," said Lelani. "It was nice to meet you, Mrs. Weis."

"Likewise," said the old woman, looking a little forlorn and disoriented.

Lelani felt sorry for her. "Kendall, why don't you offer your grandmother some coffee or something?" she suggested.

"Yes," said Mrs. Weis. "I would like some coffee, Kendall."

Then Lelani slipped out of the living room and went to her barren bedroom, thinking she would simply sleep on the floor. But she just stood there looking at the nasty beige carpeting and reconsidered.

"Why don't you grab some more sleep in my room?" suggested Megan from behind her. "I'm not going back to bed."

"Are you serious?" Lelani turned and looked hopefully at Megan.

"Sure. My bed is probably still warm."

"Thank you!" said Lelani. And to actually be in a real bed with real linens ... it felt like heaven. Her head barely touched the pillow before she was out.

# Nineteen

# Megan

Megan grabbed some things from her room, then took a nice long shower. After that, she slipped into her sweats and, hearing Kendall and her grandmother still talking in the living room, Megan decided to try out the sunroom. She'd found a neglected wicker rocker in the backyard yesterday, cleaned it up a little, and placed it in the otherwise empty sunroom. Now she sat down in it to read.

Shortly after Dad's death, Megan's mom had presented her with his old leather-bound devotional book; she'd found it in Dad's desk and decided that Megan should become the new owner. Megan had recognized the worn brown book instantly, and it felt comforting and familiar in her hands now. Her dad had read through the book so many times that the pages were thin and soft from use. But it felt good to read the same words that had once encouraged her dad. Today they encouraged her.

She had resented being awakened by the loud doorbell earlier, but now she was glad for that early-morning wake-up call. It had been a while since she'd been up this early and, although her interview wasn't until ten, she felt like she would be alert and at her best for it now. She tiptoed past her bedroom, peeking in to see poor Lelani sleeping soundly. Megan had heard Kendall in the living room again last night, trying to get Lelani to chat with her and then going on and on even though Lelani had wanted to sleep. Hopefully an hour or two this morning would help.

Next Megan tiptoed toward the living room. It sounded pretty quiet in there, and when she peeked out of the hallway, it seemed to be vacant. So she made her way to the kitchen, where a partial pot of coffee was still on. Maybe the grandmother had enjoyed a cup of coffee and gone back home. Megan poured a cup for herself and wondered if this early morning-visit was going to be a regular thing. Perhaps she should get a set of earplugs and let someone else answer the doorbell next time.

"Good morning," said Anna as she entered the kitchen and poured a cup of coffee. "Was someone visiting this morning?"

Megan explained about Kendall's grandmother.

"That's pretty weird," said Anna. "Kendall told me her grandmother was nearly a hundred years old."

"She looked like it," said Megan.

"And yet she's out running around this early in the morning?"

"I don't think she was doing much running. But it was early and she took a cab over here. She said she couldn't sleep and she was worried about Kendall."

Anna laughed. "Sounds like she knows her granddaughter." Then she downed her coffee, wished Megan good luck on the interview, and headed out to her job.

When nine o'clock neared, and Megan figured that it was past the time when Lelani liked to get up, she went to check on her. Fortunately Lelani was already moving, and it sounded like she was in the bathroom. Megan decided it wasn't too early to dress for her interview, and she carefully put on the same outfit she'd worn last night. She was just finishing when Lelani knocked on her door.

"Do you want help with your makeup?" she called through the partially open door.

"If you have time," said Megan.

"I do if you're ready right now."

Within minutes, Lelani performed the same miracle she had last night, and this time Megan thought she actually sort of got it.

"Thanks," she told her. "It's starting to sink in."

"Well, I have to run now," said Lelani as she slipped on her watch. "But good luck with your interview this morning. My lunch break is at noon if you want to stop by the store. I can introduce you to Abby the Clinique girl."

"I'll do that," Megan promised.

Megan had already timed how long it would take to walk to Sawyer & Craig, which was about fifteen minutes at a leisurely pace and only ten if she hurried. And, although it was only nine thirty, she decided to head out anyway. It was a nice crisp fall morning, and a few extra minutes in the fresh air couldn't hurt anything. She would have time to pray, too.

As she walked, she asked God to either open or close this door. She really wanted the job, but more than that she wanted what God knew was best for her. Especially after reading today's devotion in Dad's old book, she really wanted to trust God with all the details of her life—both big and small.

She waited to go inside Sawyer & Craig until just two minutes before ten.

"Hi, Ellen," said Megan, smiling at the receptionist she'd met last week. "I have a ten o'clock interview with Vera Craig."

Ellen nodded. "Yes. But Vera's not here yet."

"Oh." Megan wasn't sure what to do now.

"Why don't you wait for her in the consultation room," suggested Ellen. "It's the door over there on the left. And I'll see if I can get Vera on her cell phone."

So Megan went through the door to the left, entering into a room about the size of a large dining room. Centered in the room was a massive conference-style table surrounded by several comfortable-looking chairs. On the table was an interesting selection of fabric, wood, and tile samples spread out as if either Vera or Cynthia had been giving a client a presentation for a room design. Megan toyed with the samples, rearranging them in various ways and imagining that she was the designer showing a potential client how she could transform their house from blah to beautiful.

A tall brunette woman sort of exploded into the room. "Sorry I'm late," she said. She removed a plaid cape, which she tossed dramatically over a chair, along with a leather briefcase and a large expensive-looking purse. "You must be Mary."

"Megan," she corrected, smiling warmly as she stood and extended her hand. "Megan Abernathy."

"Sorry." Vera shook her hand, then took the seat across from her. "As you have probably surmised, I am Vera Craig. And if you don't mind, we'll simply conduct the interview in here."

"That's fine," said Megan, sitting back down and suddenly feeling extremely nervous.

Vera retrieved a file folder from her briefcase, then opened it and seemed to be skimming Megan's résumé. "So you were an art ed major?"

"That's right."

"But you're not teaching art?"

"No. I had a busy summer." Megan stammered for the right words. She didn't want to go into her dad's death. "I wasn't able to apply for a teaching job."

"Oh," Vera's brows arched with interest. "Were you traveling? Did you go abroad? Europe perhaps?"

"Not exactly."

"Yes, well, I always encourage anyone who's interested in design to tour Europe." She waved her hand. "And the rest of the world for that matter. It's all a part of a good education. Have you traveled much?"

"Not really," said Megan uneasily. Had she led Vera to think she'd been abroad last summer? "But I do hope to travel."

"So, tell me about yourself, Megan. What qualifies you to work for Sawyer & Craig Design?"

"Well," she began slowly, "I took a lot of art in college." Okay, that was brilliant. Vera already knew what her major had been. Megan felt seriously tongue-tied. Conversation had come so much easier with Cynthia. She really wasn't sure what Vera wanted to hear. The truth was that Megan hadn't given this interview a whole lot of thought. Mostly she just wanted the job. "And I really do love design and color and style and I—"

"You do realize you're interviewing for an assistant position, don't you? We're not hiring a designer. Surely, you don't think you're qualified to be a designer, do you?"

"Of course not. I, uh, I just think it would be fun to work around such creativity. I think I could learn a lot and—"

"You do realize that this is a job," said Vera sharply. "Not an internship. We would expect you to work at whatever task we assigned to you—no matter how mundane."

"Yes, of course." Megan nodded, feeling even more stupid. "And I would be happy to do whatever you wanted. And I think I could do it cheerfully because I would enjoy working in a creative environment like this. Even if I was just getting your coffee or running an—"

"Well, we aren't hiring an assistant to run and get our coffee." Vera frowned as if she was trying to see what Megan might possibly be good for. "And I don't see that you've done any office work on your résumé. In fact, you don't have much work experience at all, Megan. And waiting tables doesn't really prepare one to work in a design firm."

"But I'm a hard worker, and I'm willing to do whatever needs doing. I mean I don't complain or anything." Okay, Megan knew that had to sound dumb.

"So do you know how to use office equipment?"

Megan considered this. "Well, I know computers and printers, if that's what you mean. And what I don't know, I'm sure I can learn."

"Well, do you know anything about measuring for drapes or carpets or furnishings?"

"I, uh, I think so," said Megan uncertainly.

"How about drafting? Are you able to draw out the dimensions of a room?"

"Yes," said Megan, hoping to appear more confident. "Actually, my dad was an architect and—"

"Well, Megan, just because your father's an architect doesn't convince me that you can draw or read blueprints."

"But I do know the basics. I even considered becoming an architect myself."

"But you didn't?"

"Well, no."

"Is your dad anyone I would know? Does he have a firm here in town?"

"He did. Donald Abernathy Design."

"He's retired now?"

"Actually, he passed away this summer. That was the main reason I didn't apply for any teaching jobs."

"I see." Vera slipped the résumé back into the folder and back into her briefcase as if to hint that the interview was over.

Megan didn't know what more to say. It seemed this interview had gone in a steady downward spiral. Then she remembered how Mom said she'd been friends with Vera in college. Well, it was a desperate measure, but perhaps worth a shot.

"Speaking of my dad," said Megan quickly, "my mother mentioned that she knew you in college."

"Really?" Vera seemed slightly interested.

"Do you recall Linda Abernathy?" Megan tried. "Although she wasn't married then. Do you remember Linda Muhr?"

"Not really."

"Oh." Megan felt like she should simply excuse herself. This interview was definitely not promising. It was like everything was sliding off center. Or maybe it was just a general lack of chemistry—a bad match. Whatever the problem was, it was clear that Vera did not like Megan. And Megan couldn't imagine working for someone so demanding and unfriendly. The woman wouldn't give her a chance.

"Well, is there anything else you'd like to tell me about yourself?" Vera was checking her watch now, reaching for her cape.

"No." Megan forced a smile. "That should cover it pretty well."

"Okay, then." Vera stood and gathered her things. "It was nice to meet you, Megan. If you'll excuse me, I need to meet with a client on the other side of town now." And then just as quickly as she blew in, Vera blew out. And Megan just sighed.

"How'd it go?" asked Ellen as Megan went back through the reception area.

Megan considered saying something like, "Fine," but then decided to be honest. "I don't think Vera liked me very much."

Ellen sort of nodded. "Well, don't be too discouraged."

Megan looked longingly around the handsomely decorated office. It would've been so great to have worked in a place like this. But maybe she would be better off doing restaurant work again. At least she had experience there.

"Will you tell Cynthia hello for me?" asked Megan as she lingered by Ellen's desk. "And please thank her for taking time with me last week." Now she wondered if she would be more polite to simply write a thank-you card. Or would that come across as an act of desperation?

"Why don't you tell her yourself?" said Ellen. "She suggested you pop in after your interview with Vera."

"Really?"

"She's in her office now, and as far as I know, she's not on the phone. Just go tap on her door and say hi."

Megan wasn't too sure about this but decided it couldn't hurt her chances any more than the interview with Vera had.

"Come in," called Cynthia after Megan knocked lightly.

"I don't want to disturb you," said Megan. "But Ellen said you wanted me to pop in and say hi."

"That's right. Tell me, Megan, how did it go with Vera?"

Megan couldn't help but grimace. "Not too well, I'm afraid. I think I showed about as much personality as a fence post."

Cynthia laughed. "Oh, don't worry about that. Vera can have that effect on some people."

"Really?" Megan felt a tinge of hope. "So it's not just me?"

"No, it's not just you. Vera is a brilliant designer, and she's very good with those highbrow sorts who have a need to be impressed. But when it comes to the rest of us, well, Vera can sometimes seem like she's from another planet—or Manhattan, which is actually where she worked for a few years before moving back here."

Megan smiled with relief. "Then maybe I wasn't as hopeless as I thought. You know, I really would love to work here. And, like I told Vera, I'm willing to do whatever is needed. I just think it would be fun to be around creativity. And I do need a job."

Cynthia waved her hand. "You've got one. Just so you know, I'm the senior partner in this firm, and I've already decided to hire you, Megan. I just wanted Vera to feel that she was involved too, like she has a say. I don't like to ruffle her feathers unnecessarily."

"You're really going to hire me?" Megan was incredulous. Had she just imagined it, or had Cynthia offered her the job?

"Of course. With your art background, I felt you were the most qualified applicant. And besides, I like you. But a word of warning, Megan. Tread lightly with Vera. Just so you know, she was in a good mood this morning, but that's not always the case."

"Yes." Megan nodded eagerly. "I'll keep that in mind." She didn't want to think what Vera might be like in a bad mood. And right now, she was so happy that she actually felt tears in her eyes.

"Now tell me, when can you start?"

"Whenever you like."

"Great. Ellen will give you the paperwork to fill out. How about if you come tomorrow at nine. Will that work?"

"Perfectly." Megan had to contain herself from jumping up and down. She could hardly believe this. "Thank you so much, Cynthia."

"Welcome to Sawyer & Craig."

Twenty

# Lelani

"Perfect timing," said Lelani as Megan came to the La Prairie section and pretended to be interested in looking at the expensive product line.

"I got the job," announced Megan.

"Congratulations," said Lelani. "It's time for me to punch out for lunch, but how about if I take you over to meet Abby at the Clinique counter first."

"Cool." Megan was beaming.

So Lelani informed Karen, at Bobbi Brown, that she was taking her lunch break, since they took turns covering for each other. Then she introduced Megan to Abby. Wanting to deliver good customer service, she even suggested some cosmetics and colors that were similar to those she had used on Megan last night. "I gave her a little makeover," she confessed quietly.

"Yes," said Megan, patting her cheek. "Lelani is the only reason I look this good today, but I can't have her doing my makeup every morning."

"And Megan just got a new job," explained Lelani. "She's working for a design firm and she needs to keep up a professional look. I told her you'd get her set up with a system that's a little more affordable than La Prairie."

"That's for sure," said Abby. "Most of us working girls can't afford La Prairie."

"So you'll be in good hands," Lelani told Megan. "And I'll be back in a few minutes." Then she went to punch out and get her purse.

"How's the housing situation going?" asked Mr. Green as she was passing by the office.

Lelani made a slight face, then told him about their early-morning visitor. "It's a real challenge getting much sleep in that place."

"Well, I arranged with my brother-in-law to help me deliver the bedroom set Thursday morning," he told her. "But I know you have to work then. Will someone be at the house?"

She considered this. "Well, the owner will probably be there, although she doesn't usually get up too early. I'll ask her to let you in, or maybe I'll just suggest we leave the door unlocked."

He frowned. "She's okay with strangers coming into her house?"

"She's sort of a strange one herself," admitted Lelani. "But I'll check with her and let you know what works best, okay?"

He nodded. "And by the way, I decided I'm just going to give you that set if you don't mind. My daughter said she doesn't want it and I sure don't want it. Besides, I've decided to turn the spare bedroom into a home office."

"That's awfully generous of you. Don't you want me to pay you for it?"

"No, I'm actually glad to get rid of it and have the space to use. And I don't have time to run an ad. Besides, I doubt that it's really worth much. As I mentioned, it's a slightly juvenile-looking set, but maybe you can paint it or something."

Lelani thanked him and thought, once again, how it was too bad the other employees didn't really know about the other side to this guy. But for the most part he kept his business face on, and when he did converse with employees, he was always rather stiff and formal. Plus, when reprimands were needed, Mr. Green was the one to disperse them. But as

Lelani punched out on the time-clock, she decided she would have to think of something special to thank him with. Maybe something Hawaiian, since he'd expressed interest in that.

By the time Lelani rejoined Megan, Abby had lined up a number of products. Megan asked Lelani's opinion and soon they settled on what Lelani felt were the minimal necessities. "You can always come back for more later," she advised Megan. She briefly considered purchasing the items with her employee discount, but thinking of Mr. Green, she decided not to risk it. She didn't want to lose his trust.

"Are you on your lunch break now, Lelani?" asked Abby, noticing that another customer was waiting.

"Yeah. I'm punched out."

"Why don't I write these up and Megan can get them after your lunch?"

So they all agreed, then Megan suggested they could eat in the Nordstrom café, which was fine with Lelani. She usually liked their soup and sandwich special.

"I picked up paint samples on the way here," Megan told Lelani as they sat down to eat. "Want to see?"

"Absolutely," said Lelani eagerly.

Megan spread the color cards on the table, pointing to a soft sage green. "I'm leaning toward this one for my room."

"That's nice. I wouldn't mind having that color myself. I mean, if it didn't look like I was being a copycat."

"I think having both bedrooms the same color makes sense. And I can get enough paint for both of us if you like."

"Great."

"And I thought maybe this celadon green would be nice in the bathroom. It would lighten it up in there and provide a nice contrast with the darker green tiles, plus it would really make the woodwork pop."

"You already sound like an interior decorator."

Megan laughed, then told her how one of the designers had made it clear, in no uncertain terms, that Megan would "only be an assistant."

"Still, they're lucky to have you," Lelani assured her.

"I'm not so sure that Vera would agree."

"Well, I happen to like your taste in décor, and I'm willing to go with whatever you pick out as far as paint colors go," said Lelani as they were finishing up. "I think both those greens are gorgeous and will be an enormous improvement over that nasty pinkish beige."

"I think they'll make the rooms feel clean and fresh," said Megan as she tucked the samples back into her bag. "And I plan to attack my room this afternoon. I'd like to get it all put together before I start work tomorrow."

"Speaking of work, have you considered your work wardrobe?" asked Lelani. She glanced at her watch to see that she still had more than half an hour left in her lunch break. "I mean beyond today's interview outfit, which is actually quite nice."

"And doesn't totally belong to me," said Megan. "I pretty much don't have any of the right type of working clothes. And, after meeting Vera today, I have a feeling I'm going to need to raise the bar a little higher than jeans and T-shirts."

"I heard there's a good sale in the career department. If we hurry we might have time to pick some things out," said Lelani. "And maybe I could put them on hold and purchase them later with my employee discount." Lelani immediately regretted her offer. Where had that come from?

"That'd be fantastic," said Megan.

"We'll have to move fast since I only have about thirty minutes, but I'm happy to help if you want."

They grabbed their purses and headed to the career section. "I had to do some shopping myself," she admitted as they rode up the escalator. "When I first got here, most of my clothes were either too casual or not warm enough to wear here."

"Hello, Lelani," said Margot as they entered the career wear section. "Are you here to shop?"

"I heard there's a good sale going on."

"We just marked down a lot of DKNY, Calvin Klein, and Jones New York."

"Great," said Lelani. "I need some work clothes, and my friend Megan wants to help me pick some things out." She pointed to Megan's outfit. "As you can see this girl has a real sense of style."

Margot nodded with approval. "Yes. Very nice."

Megan looked slightly uncomfortable but fortunately didn't attempt to explain how her roommates had actually put the outfit together for her. Soon they were perusing the markdown racks and carrying a big pile to the dressing room.

"We don't have much time," said Lelani as she handed Megan a dark brown Jones New York suit. "So I'm going to tell you what Margot told me a few weeks ago. Go for the basics. Start with a suit that fits well, looks good, and is comfortable. Then you mix and match the suit pieces with other items, like the jacket you wore today could go with those brown trousers. Does that make sense?"

"Sort of," said Megan as she slipped into the brown jacket.

"Too big," said Lelani right away. "Let me run back and get the eight. Meanwhile, you try on the Calvin Klein jacket, okay?"

Megan nodded, and Lelani went back and picked up several more items from the rack. She felt slightly guilty, knowing that she would be using her employee discount for a friend, but at the same time, she could actually be purchasing these things as "gifts" for Megan—sort of as an exchange for Megan's help with fixing up the bedroom and buying paint. In fact, that would be a good way to cover her cost for the paint and things. Surely, that made this ethically acceptable.

"I think I've figured out your size," said Lelani as Megan tried on another pair of pants. "You're about the same as me on the bottom half, except that you're shorter. And on your top half, you're about one size smaller."

"That's because you, unlike me, have boobs," Megan pointed out.

"And you, unlike me, have a butt," teased Lelani.

"Ugh, don't remind me." Megan peered at her backside in the mirror.

"Hey, some women would kill for that butt." Lelani looked at her watch. "Oh, I'm going to have to run. But let me gather up some of the things that we know are possibilities. I'll put them on hold for now then come back up here after work to buy them."

"All of them?" asked Megan.

"I'll try to pick out the ones that seem to make the most sense." Lelani was gathering up quite a pile. "But, don't worry, you can try it all on again at home. What you don't want, I'll simply bring back. No problem."

"That's so sweet."

"And I'll see you after work."

"Thanks so much, Lelani."

Then Lelani hurried back to Margot. "Can you hold these for me until after work? Then I can take more time to figure it out. Okay?"

Margot nodded as she hung the items on the "hold" rack. "Your friend really does have good taste, Lelani. This is a very nice selection."

"I'll tell her you said so. She's still in the dressing room." Lelani laughed. "Cleaning up after me."

"Well, I appreciate that."

"See you around five," said Lelani. Then she hurried back to the employees' lounge, shoved her purse back into her locker, and punched back in just in the nick of time. Of course, she felt like she'd been running a marathon instead of having a break. But considering the help that Megan was giving to her, she felt it was worth it. She just hoped it wouldn't get her in trouble.

Oh, she knew that other employees regularly shared their discounts with friends and family. But she also knew it was frowned upon. For some reason, Lelani was one of those people who had been born with a sort of inner moral code. She had a fairly strict sense of ethics and almost always played by the rules. Not that it had always worked for her. But breaking the rules had always gone worse. So now, for the most part, she was committed to doing things the right way. And considering that purchasing work clothes for Megan was a trade off for the home improvements that subsidized her rent made it seem okay.

# Anna

"Felicia sent me down here for the marketing package on Ramsay Rowan." Edmond Dubois stood in front of her desk, jiggling a yellow pencil between his fingers in what was either an impatient gesture or just plain nerves. Edmond, fresh out of college, worked in the marketing department as Felicia Tarquette's "errand boy." Everyone in the editorial department knew of Felicia, head of marketing, as the Queen B (as in B rhymes with witch). Not only did Felicia have zero patience for employees she labeled *incompetent*, which was most of the editorial department, but she also seemed to thrive on torturing the poor souls. Particularly the children's book editor, or so it seemed.

Anna looked up from her computer screen and let out a low groan. "Don't you think I would've sent the package to marketing if I had anything to send?"

"But it's due, Anna."

"I know it's due, Edmond. But have you ever tried to have a conversation with Miss Ramsay Rowan?"

"I heard she's in rehab again."

Anna nodded. "And she's not allowed any outside contact either."

"That's tough."

"And why Mr. Erlinger ever thought that Ramsay Rowan was a good candidate to contract for a children's book has totally escaped me."

"Because she used to be a child?"

Anna sort of laughed. "There are some, including me, who think Ramsay Rowan is still a child."

"Hollywood," said Edmond. "It can ruin the best of them."

Anna sighed. "I used to really like her. I watched all her movies as a kid."

"And you seemed so excited to work with her," Edmond said.

"That's because I assumed we would actually work. So far Miss Rowan hasn't written a single word. Nor has she come up with a book idea of any sort."

"Celebrities seldom do," said Edmond.

"So we're just paying to use their names? We call them authors, but we do all the work?"

"Basically."

"I thought that Ramsay would at least toss me a bone," said Anna sadly. "Just a concept, an idea. Something that has something to do with her life."

"Like a children's twelve-step book?" teased Edmond.

Anna rolled her eyes and groaned again.

"Well, the book is supposed to be fiction, right?'

"Right."

"So, why don't you just make it up then?"

"Maybe I will make it up. And while I'm at it, maybe I'll just make up the marketing information too. Isn't that usually mostly fictional anyway?"

Edmond gave her warning look. "I wouldn't go that far." He leaned his elbows down on her desk now, smiling directly into her eyes. "But if you treat me right, Anna, I might be willing to help you with the marketing package."

Anna studied him. He was actually kind of cute in a nerdish way, with his short, dark, curly hair and horn-rimmed glasses, but his fashion sense was even worse than her own. Like, what had he been thinking when he picked out that lavender-and-yellow striped shirt? "What did you have in mind exactly, Edmond?"

"Dinner?"

She firmly shook her head. "I already told you that I'm not going to date you. I don't believe in dating—"

"And I already told you that I checked on it, and it's okay to date fellow employees as long as you don't work in the same department."

"I still don't think it's a good idea."

"Too bad." He sighed and stood up dramatically. "And I had such a good idea for that marketing package too."

"Is this a bribe?"

"No, of course not. It's just a fellow worker helping another fellow worker."

Anna considered this. She really needed to put together that marketing package on Ramsay Rowan but had absolutely no idea where to start. Ramsay would be in rehab for at least three more weeks. "How about lunch?" she suggested.

He seemed to consider this. "How about a long working lunch?" The way he said this almost seemed to suggest something more than just lunch.

"At a restaurant?"

He laughed. "Yes. Of course. A restaurant of my choice."

"I don't know if I can take a long lunch—"

"I'll check on it for you," he said.

Once again, she rolled her eyes. For an "errand boy" he could be pretty full of himself. Sometimes she wondered how he managed to even hang onto his job. Especially working for Felicia.

"Let me get back to you on this," he said, glancing at his watch.

"Whatever." She turned her attention back to the book she was currently editing. Naturally, it was a project she'd had nothing to do with acquiring—in fact, it was a fairly lame and not very original story about a turtle who wanted to become a sprinter—but she was stuck trying to smooth out the rhyming meter, with lines that ended unfortunately with words like "orange" or "pickles." She would need some luck.

It was getting close to twelve when her phone rang. She had just come up with a new word to rhyme with pickles, but it vanished right out of her head when she answered. It was Edmond, calling to say that their long working lunch was on and that he'd be down to get her in about ten minutes.

"Just great," said Anna as she hung up. Why had she let him talk her into this? Still, if he could help with the marketing package, maybe lunch with him would be worth it. And if he couldn't help, well, she would never agree to something like this again.

"Do you have a car?" he asked when he came down at noon.

"You want me to drive?" she asked.

"If you don't mind. My car's in the shop and I made reservations at Red Lobster."

"Red Lobster?" She frowned. "Couldn't you have picked something closer?"

"I happen to like Red Lobster."

"Well, you're lucky that I did happen to drive to work today." She turned off her computer screen and reached under her desk for her purse.

"I thought you always drove to work."

"I *used* to always drive. That was before I moved."

He held the door open for her. "So you don't live at home anymore?"

She peered curiously at him. Since when did he know that she had lived at home? "You haven't been stalking me, have you?" she asked as they walked to the small parking lot behind the building.

"No, of course not."

"How did you know I lived at home?"

"I asked around."

She started to unlock her car, then stopped. "You're really not a stalker, right?"

"No. I just happen to like you, Anna. It's not like I've kept that a secret." He put his hand on the hood of her car. "By the way, this is a great car. It totally suits you."

She was still replaying the "I just happen to like you" line. And she wasn't sure how to respond. "But this is a working lunch, right?"

"Yes. I told you that." He held up his briefcase as if it were proof. "See, I even brought my laptop to work on."

"Okay." She unlocked the doors now.

"So, you're not dating anyone?" he asked once inside.

"Not that it's any of your business," she said crisply.

"Why don't you just pretend I'm a girlfriend," he suggested. "I mean, don't girls ask each other things like that?"

"Not like *that*. They don't say, 'You're not dating anyone?' like *that*. It's more like, 'Do you have a boyfriend?'"

"So, do you have a boyfriend?"

"Not that it's any of your business," she said again. "But no."

"That's what I thought."

"I think you're spending way too much time thinking about things that have nothing to do with you, Edmond."

"Okay, let's talk about Ramsay then."

"Yes," said Anna eagerly. "Now that would be reassuring."

"For starters, I e-mailed her agent and publicist requesting bio information last week."

"You did?"

He grinned and nodded. "Yeah, I sort of thought you might need some help."

"But why didn't you tell me that this morning?"

"Because that would have ruined everything."

"Did the publicist and agent respond?"

"Yep. I've got a couple of files worth of stuff on Ramsay, starting with how she won a baby beauty contest at the age of seventeen months."

"Really?"

"I'm not making this stuff up."

"Hey, maybe I can pull a book idea from some of that information."

"It might be your best shot at getting anything from her."

"Why?"

"Because her agent just told me that she's doing a sixty-day treatment program this time."

"Not thirty?"

"Nope. And it's in lieu of jail time."

"Oh, great." Anna shook her head as she entered the freeway. "A children's book author who should be doing time right now."

"That's one way to look at it. But you could give it a different spin."

"Like?"

"Like she's a young actress who is learning from her mistakes."

"What makes you think she's learning?"

"I said it was a spin, Anna."

"Oh, yeah."

They bantered like this all the way to Red Lobster, then continued once they were inside. Although Anna had no intention of admitting it, she was actually sort of enjoying Edmond's company. Despite herself, she compared him to Jake and realized that Jake had never been fun and spontaneous like this. Not only that, but Jake had often made her feel uncomfortable—as if the relationship was more up to her than to him. This was different.

By the time they finished eating, Anna was feeling pretty relaxed. And as they started going over the bio stuff and filling in the marketing material together, she was actually starting to get some book ideas, which she jotted down on her napkin. It seemed that Edmond had been right, this really had turned into a working lunch. She just hoped that he'd actually gotten the okay from her supervisor. Still, if a problem arose, she would simply explain that it was Edmond's doing. He could take the heat. And knowing the Queen B, he would get it.

"I think I have an idea that could fly," Anna told him as she drove them back to work.

"What?"

"Well, I kind of got it from your spin about Ramsay learning from her mistakes," she said. "Also from that story in Ramsay's bio about how, as a child, she didn't get a part when her local theater did *Annie.*"

"And now they probably can't afford her."

"Anyway, I'm thinking of a kind of a never-give-up sort of book. Like when you're facing adversity or failure or rejection or ..."

"Or rehab."

Anna laughed. "Or prison."

"Or the bottom of an empty glass."

"Yeah, yeah, but let's hope not. Anyway, the point of the book is that you have to keep believing in yourself. You can't give up when the going gets tough."

"That sounds like a good kids' book to me."

"And it's not too much of a stretch either. I mean think about it, by the time this book comes out, Ramsay may be doing really well."

"Or she may be doing time."

Anna grimaced. "Let's hope she'll have figured things out. Maybe she'll be an example of how you can pick yourself up after falling down."

"And if not, we can simply stop the presses."

"Isn't there a clause in the book contracts about authors who bring shame or embarrassment to the publishing company?"

"I think they exclude it on celebrity deals." He chuckled. "I mean, think about it, sometimes that publicity is actually helpful in selling books."

"Not kids' books."

"No, you're right. It wouldn't help with kids' books. Then again, there was a time when no one would've considered Madonna a likely candidate for kids' books. And she's done several now."

"It's sad when it takes a children's author like Madonna to give me hope." Anna was pulling into the parking lot now.

"Thanks for having lunch with me," said Edmond as they got out of the car.

"Thanks for helping me with the marketing material." Anna looked at her watch and was surprised to see that it was close to three o'clock.

"I'll get it to Felicia right away," said Edmond as he held the door open for her.

"And I'll put together a synopsis for the book this afternoon," she promised. "That should make Felicia happy."

"And hopefully Ramsay Rowan will do her part by getting and staying sober this time," he said as they parted ways at the elevator.

As she walked back to her office, Anna thought maybe she'd been wrong about Edmond after all. Her excuse for not dating him in the past had been based on the fact that he was a fellow employee, but the truth was she had thought he'd be boring and dumb. Now she realized that he was actually pretty smart, as well as a lot of fun. As she sat down at her desk, she wondered if he'd ask her out again—not for a working date this time, but a real one. She hoped she hadn't come on too strong about that stalker thing.

When her phone rang, she found herself hoping that it was him. But it was Mom.

"Anna," she said in a demanding tone. "Why haven't you called me?"

"What for?"

"To let me know that everything is fine."

"Everything is *fine*, Mom."

"Why aren't you answering your cell phone?"

"What do you mean?"

"During your lunch break. I tried and tried to call you, but you wouldn't answer. What am I supposed to think?"

"That my phone was turned off?" Anna shook her head as she turned on her laptop.

"Why is it turned off? Don't you know that worries me?"

"I had a working lunch." Anna opened up the Ramsay Rowan file.

"A working lunch? What is that?"

"It's where you work during lunch." Anna rolled her eyes.

"So now they aren't letting you have a lunch break? That's illegal, Anna, you can't allow them to take away your—"

"It was fine, Mom. In fact, it was fun."

"Oh?"

"Yes. And it was helpful."

"Working during your lunch hour is fun and helpful?"

"I was in the company of a nice young man." There that should make Mom happy. Now maybe Anna could get her off the phone. "And now I have real work to do, so if you—"

"Who is this nice young man, Anna?" Her mom's voice was warmer now.

"His name is Edmond."

"What does Edmond do?"

"He's an assistant."

"An assistant?" Her mom sounded disappointed. "Isn't that like a secretary?"

"Yes."

"Well …"

"Now I really need to get to work, Mom."

"But you must promise to call me."

"I promise to call you, Mom. Just not every day, okay?"

"But I worry, *mi hija.* In the middle of the night I think of my baby girl, living with a bunch of strangers in someone else's house, so close to downtown, and I think of those other girls that are missing and I—"

"I'm perfectly fine, Mom. You just need to let me grow up." She wanted to add, *and get a life,* but thankfully she didn't. That would only prolong this call.

"I know, I know."

"I love you, Mama," said Anna in a gentle voice. "But I really do need to get some work done now. Have a good day. *Adiós!"* Then she hung up. Seriously, the only stalker in Anna's life was probably her own mother!

# Twenty-two

# Megan

"You think that's enough for two bedrooms?" asked Megan as the guy at the hardware store set three gallons of freshly mixed paint on the counter. He was the same man who had helped her and her mom yesterday, and his name tag said Bernard.

"Should do you at least two coats for each room. More'n enough to cover up a beige tone. Now if your base coat was red or even white, you might want a little more. But this is real good paint. It covers just fine."

"And just one gallon for the bathroom?"

"Yep." He set a couple of paint stirring sticks on top of the pails. "You got everything you need then, little lady?"

She looked down at the items in her cart. "Rollers, extension handle, brushes, masking tape, plastic drop cloths, roller trays. Is there anything else you can think of?"

"Looks good to me," said Bernard. "I can ring you up right here if you like."

As she unloaded the painting tools, he asked how the carpet removal had gone yesterday, and she told him the wood floor came out looking beautiful. "But now I wish I'd left the carpeting down while I was painting. It would've made a good drop cloth."

"Maybe. But then you have to be real careful when you take that carpeting out so you don't damage the walls." Then he explained how she could cut the carpet into strips and take it out one small roll at a time. "And that's easier on the back too." He handed her the receipt.

"That makes sense."

"Need help getting that to your car?"

Megan considered this. "Actually I'm walking."

His brow creased. "You're walking? How far?"

"About eight blocks." She frowned at the box of four gallons of paint and the plastic bag full of painting accessories. "Maybe that wasn't such a great idea."

"That paint's pretty heavy."

"I guess I could call a cab."

"We could deliver it for you," he suggested.

"Really?"

"Not until tomorrow. We've already done today's deliveries."

"But I needed to get started painting today." She picked up the box, testing her strength and trying to decide if she could carry it for eight blocks, but already it felt pretty heavy. Plus her boots, while attractive, weren't exactly designed for walking a long way while carrying a heavy load.

"Hey, Frank," Bernard called over to the other cashier. "Mind if I run this young lady a few blocks so she don't break her back carrying this paint home?"

The other cashier glanced around the mostly empty store. "Nah, go ahead."

And within minutes she was back at Bloomberg Place, thanking Bernard and offering him a tip, which he refused. "We're not allowed to accept tips."

"Well, I really appreciate it."

"Have fun painting."

And she did have fun painting. She did all the steps, just like Bernard had told her, masking off the woodwork and piling her furnishings in the center or the room, then covering them and the floor with the plastic drop cloth. Then she used a paintbrush to cut in around the edges along the walls and finally rolled on more paint. And the transformation, even with just one coat on two of the walls, was amazing.

"What's going on in here?" asked a guy's voice.

Megan jumped, then turned to see a stranger standing in the doorway of her bedroom. An extremely good-looking stranger, but a stranger just the same.

"Who are you?" she demanded, holding up the roller like a weapon in front of her. If he was a mugger, perhaps she could paint him to death.

He grinned. "I'm Marcus Barrett."

"But what are you doing in this house?" she asked, still brandishing her roller.

"I came to see Kendall Weis."

"Oh." Megan relaxed a little. "I thought she was home."

"Apparently not. I knocked and no one answered, which isn't that unusual, so I let myself in, which is also not so unusual. But I checked upstairs and Kendall's not here."

"Well, I haven't seen her since this morning," admitted Megan. "She must've stepped out."

He peered curiously at her now. "So are you a painter?"

"I am today."

He seemed to consider this. "You must be one of her new tenants."

Megan nodded and told him her name. "And you must be Kendall's boyfriend."

"I am today."

Megan chuckled. "Meaning you won't be tomorrow?"

"You just never know."

"Well, if you'll excuse me I have a lot of work to do."

"Looks like you're doing a great job of it too."

"Thanks." She dipped her roller into the tray and started on the next wall.

"Mind if I watch?" he asked as she dipped it again. "I've never painted before, but I wouldn't mind seeing how it's done."

She turned and grinned at him. "You could really see how it's done by doing it yourself. Except that you'd probably get paint on your clothes." He had on what looked like casual office wear, neat khakis and a light blue oxford shirt.

"I could run home and change."

Megan laughed with disbelief. "Sure, I'll bet you could."

He glanced at his watch. "I can be back here by four—unless you'll be done by then."

"That's doubtful. Plus there's another bedroom, as well as a bathroom still left to paint."

"Okay then," he said quickly. "See you in about twenty minutes."

"Sure, why not?" she said as she rolled on another full roller of paint. She doubted that he was serious. Still, if he came back, she wouldn't refuse the help. Her arm was starting to get sore.

To her surprise, Marcus got back even faster than promised. And she was more than happy to relinquish the roller to him, standing by and coaching from the sidelines as he applied the second coat of paint.

"This is kind of fun," he said as he swiped on another roller full of paint, dripping some on his old tennis shoes. Before long Marcus finished the room and seemed eager for more, so Megan led him to Lelani's room, where she'd already masked off the windows.

"What about that carpeting?" Marcus asked as she set the paint bucket right on the rug without bothering with a drop cloth.

"We're going to rip it out anyway," she said as she reached for the crowbar.

"What's that for?" He looked slightly alarmed at the sight of the large tool, like he thought she might use it against him. It was quite a bit more threatening than the paint roller.

She explained how they needed to remove the baseboard, then showed him how it worked. "But you have to do it just right so it doesn't crack."

"Pretty slick," he said. "Mind if I give it a shot?"

"Not at all," she said, relinquishing the tool. "Knock yourself out." Now she just sat on the floor and watched with amusement as he slowly worked his way around the room, carefully removing the baseboard. And before long they were both painting again. She cut in around the edges, and Marcus rolled it on.

"Wow, I can't believe how much better this is looking," he said, pausing to admire his work. "I wonder why Kendall didn't do this a long time ago."

Megan almost said it was probably because Kendall was lazy, but stopped herself. After all, Marcus was Kendall's boyfriend. And he was being helpful. No point in alienating the guy. They were just starting the second coat when Megan heard another male voice calling, "Anybody home?"

"How many boyfriends does Kendall have?" she asked Marcus.

He just shrugged and continued to paint.

"We're in here," she called back.

The next thing she knew, Anna's brother Gil was standing in the doorway. "Where's Lelani?" he asked hopefully.

"Probably on her way home from work," said Megan as she dipped her brush again. "But, hey, if you want to help, you came to the right place. This happens to be Lelani's room that we're working on now."

Gil looked around the room and smiled. "This is really Lelani's room?"

Megan laughed, then introduced him to Marcus. "He's Kendall's boyfriend—she owns the house."

"So do you really need help?" asked Gil. "It looks like you've almost got the painting wrapped up."

"Yes. But the carpet still needs to be removed."

"How do you do that?" asked Gil.

So Megan gave him a quick explanation of how it needed to be cut in strips, rolled up, and carefully removed. "You have to watch out for the walls. Unless you want to paint again." She held out the cutting tool. "You want to give it a try?"

He was game. And so she got him started on the side of the room that they had completely painted, coaching him from the sidelines. "You don't want to damage the hardwood floor beneath," she said. "Just make sure the cut goes through the carpet. Take it off first and we can work on the pad later."

"What's going on?" asked Lelani, appearing in the doorway with a pair of large Nordstrom bags hanging on each arm. She started laughing now. "No way," she said happily. "How did you manage to get a work crew together, Megan?"

Megan grinned at her. "It was sort of serendipitous."

"Hey, Lelani," said Gil in a slightly flirtatious tone as he made a long cut through the carpeting—almost like he was showing off. "Remember I promised you I'd come by to help out?"

"And this is Marcus, Kendall's boyfriend," said Megan. "At least for today, that is. Right, Marcus?"

He chuckled. "Yeah, right."

"This looks fantastic," gushed Lelani. "I love the color."

"You mean better than that old grungy brown?" Marcus teased.

"And you're taking out the carpeting, Gil?" She reached down and placed a hand on his shoulder as he carefully peeled a piece of carpet away from the wall. "Thank you so much!"

He smiled up at her. "No problem."

"I'll go change my clothes," she said. "And then I can help." She held up the bags. "I'll put these things in your room, Megan."

"Thanks," said Megan. "And I'll write you a check later."

They kept on working. Lelani and Gil continued to remove the carpeting while Megan, followed by Marcus, moved on to prepare the bathroom for painting. But it was a little too cozy in the bathroom, and after a few minutes, Megan turned and peered curiously at Marcus. "Do you really want to keep painting? Or are you just trying to make brownie points with Kendall?"

He threw back his head and laughed. "Brownie points with Kendall?"

"Yeah." Megan leaned against the vanity and studied him. "I don't know why else you'd be so nice and helpful."

"Maybe I just like painting."

She nodded. "Well, hey, that's cool."

"Or maybe I want to make brownie points with you." He pointed a paintbrush at her and winked.

Now Megan felt her cheeks growing warm, but she was determined not to show her embarrassment. "Well, whatever the case, I'm sure that Kendall will appreciate the home improvements. I know I do. But it's a little tight in here. If you think you can handle this on your own, I'll go start putting my room back together."

"You're not going to help me?" He looked seriously disappointed.

"Hey, if I don't get my room together, I won't have any place to sleep tonight."

He nodded. "Okay. I understand."

Megan wasn't sure what to make of this Marcus character. Was he a cad or simply a hard worker? Was he actually interested in her? And, really, what difference did it make? There was no way she was going to encourage him. Not only because of Kendall, which was reason enough in itself, but also because she was just plain not interested. Marcus had the kind of looks that made Megan nervous. With his perfect-looking highlighted hair, tan face, and straight white teeth, he could pose for the cover of *GQ*. And that, to Megan, suggested a lack of substance. Plus, he was involved with Kendall, which was a huge red flag. Not that Megan wanted to be judgmental, but Kendall had about as much depth as a birdbath.

Megan started removing the drop cloths and peeling the masking tape off her walls and was incredibly pleased to see how great her bedroom now looked with the fresh green against the shining wood floors. Then she began to carefully move her furnishings back into place, and the transformation really seemed nothing short of miraculous. It was perfect.

"Wow," said Anna as she popped her head into Megan's room. "Looking good in here."

"Thanks," said Megan. "Quite a change, isn't it?"

"Yes. Now I'm wishing I'd taken time to do my floors and paint, too."

"It's not too late," said Megan. "Well, I guess it's too late right now. But maybe we can work on your room this weekend, if you want."

"Do I hear my brother next door?" asked Anna suddenly.

"He's helping Lelani take out her carpeting."

Then Megan listened as Anna went next door and started teasing her brother about schmoozing with Lelani. Anna asked him why he wasn't upstairs working on his own sister's room.

"Hey, you're the one who didn't want to do any improvements," he reminded Anna. "You had to have all your furniture in place."

"Well, I expect you to come over this weekend and help me out," she told him.

He just laughed. "We'll see about that, Anna Banana."

"Anna Banana?" echoed Lelani with what sounded like suppressed giggles.

"Oh, brother, *Brother!*" exclaimed Anna. Then she stomped off and continued stomping all the way up the stairs.

Megan continued putting her room back together and, just as she was setting her little alarm clock, realized that it was nearly seven. Perhaps she should offer the workers dinner in appreciation of their help.

"Anyone hungry?" she yelled down the hallway.

"You bet," Marcus called back from the bathroom.

"Count me in," said Gil.

"Me too," said Lelani.

Megan went into Lelani's room now. "So what should I get? Obviously we need something delivered, don't you think?"

"Definitely," said Lelani. "And I get to buy dinner tonight. And not pizza either. I'm starving for something really good."

"Do you like Mexican?" asked Gil suddenly. Both Lelani and Megan eagerly agreed. "Then why don't you let me handle it?" He already had out his cell phone opened up. "Mexican okay with Marcus?"

"Let me check." So Megan went to the bathroom, where Marcus was standing on the toilet and painting a pale green strip next to the ceiling. "Do you like Mexican?"

"You bet!" He smiled down at her. "How's it looking?"

"Like you know what you're doing."

"Even though it's smaller, it's a lot harder than the bedroom." He pointed to the wall behind the mirror and light. "You have a lot more stuff to paint around."

"Well, you're doing great, but you don't have to finish it tonight, you know. We appreciate anything you do."

"I'll work until food arrives," he promised. "We'll see after that."

And so they all worked until the food arrived. And when it did, Gil refused to let Lelani pay. "It's on the house," he told everyone. Then he called up the stairs for Anna to come down and join them.

"What about Kendall?" asked Lelani as Anna trudged down the stairs, still acting as if her nose was slightly out of joint.

"She's not in her room," said Anna.

"I haven't seen her either," said Megan as she set plates on the table.

"She's probably out shopping," said Marcus as they started to sit down.

"This late?" said Anna.

Marcus laughed. "When it comes to shopping, it's never too late, or too early, or too anything. Kendall is a regular little shopaholic."

It turned out that Marcus was right. Kendall had been shopping. She arrived home just as they were finishing up what had turned out to be a delicious meal. Laden with oversized bags, Kendall stopped in the doorway and frowned at the five of them sitting around the table. "You guys having a party without me again?"

"Yeah," said Marcus, holding up a pair of green, paint-speckled hands. "A painting party."

"What?" She stared at him with an incredulous expression. "You're painting?"

"The guys have been helping us out," explained Lelani.

Kendall peered at the takeout boxes of picked over Mexican food. "Anything left for me in there?"

"Not much," admitted Anna. "But you're welcome to it."

"I planned on leftovers," said Gil. "I guess we were hungrier than I thought."

"That's because that was some really great food," said Marcus, leaning back to pat his belly.

"And because we've been working really hard," added Megan.

"So have I," said Kendall defensively, holding up her shopping bags like they were bounty that she'd been out gathering in the wilderness.

Of course, this only made the others laugh. But Kendall scowled and didn't seem to see the humor. And, doing a repeat act of Anna, she stomped up the stairs, slamming the door to her bedroom behind her.

"What a grouch," said Gil, shaking his head.

"Sometimes we wake up grumpy," said Lelani with an odd grin. "And sometimes we just let her sleep."

Everyone burst into laughter again. But, as Megan laughed, she felt a small pang of guilt, as well as a twinge of pity for Kendall. Although she had no idea what she would do, she knew she'd have to think of something to make this up to her landlady.

# Twenty-three

# Kendall

Kendall threw her shopping bags down in her bedroom and dug her cell phone out of her new Hermès purse. It was the latest fall design with real pigskin, and she'd already gotten a number of compliments on it today. She hit the speed dial to Amelia, even though she'd just spent most of the afternoon shopping with her.

"You are not going to believe this, Amelia," she said without even saying hello.

"What?" asked Amelia in a slightly impatient tone. "And make it quick because Arden cooked dinner tonight and it looks fantastic." Then she made what sounded like kissing noises, probably for Arden's benefit. They'd been married almost a year now but still acted like newlyweds. Amelia had gone on and on about Arden today, bragging about his recent promotion and raise and how Amelia would probably never need to go back to work again.

Still, Kendall put that behind her. "It's out of control," she said quickly. "These tenants of mine have gone too far."

"What have they done?" asked Amelia.

"They're taking over and ripping things apart and they've even gotten Marcus involved."

"Marcus? How?"

"He actually helped them."

"Helped them tear things apart?"

"Yes. And then he ate dinner with them."

"They tore your house apart and then cooked dinner?"

"Not exactly."

"Listen, Kendall, you aren't really making sense. What exactly is going on there?"

"It's just totally out of control. These three freaks that I invited to live with me are taking over. They're ripping out carpeting and painting and—"

"That's great," said Amelia. "That place could use a facelift."

"But I didn't even—"

"I really need to go, Kendall. Arden has just taken some gorgeous steaks off the grill." She made a sniffing sound. "Ooh, yummy, honey."

"Some friend," snapped Kendall. "My life is falling apart and you're—"

"Eating dinner." Amelia smacked her lips.

"But what do I—"

"Isn't your brother-in-law an attorney?"

"Yes."

"So, call him for advice."

"Fine," said Kendall, "I will."

"Later."

Now Kendall angrily hit the speed dial for Kate. "I'm having a crisis," she told her sister.

"What's wrong?" asked Kate with only mild interest.

"My tenants," said Kendall. "They are flipping-out crazy."

"What do you mean?"

"I mean they are tearing my house apart."

"Really?" Now Kate sounded interested. "Call the police."

"The police?" Kendall considered this. But what would she tell them?

"Is it a party?" asked Kate.

"Sort of," said Kendall. "I came home and they were just finishing up."

"Finishing up?" Now Kate sounded confused.

"Eating dinner. Without me."

"I thought you said they were tearing up your house?"

"They had been. Then they ate dinner."

"And made a huge mess? Did they break things? What exactly is going on, Kendall?"

"Well, they're tearing up their rooms. And they're kind of taking over. And they didn't even pay me all the rent that I wanted and—"

"What kind of creeps did you rent to?"

"I thought they were okay. But then they sort of ganged up against me."

"Did they hurt you?"

"They hurt my feelings."

"Kendall, this isn't making a whole lot of sense."

"Well, Amelia suggested I talk to Eric. She thinks I need legal advice. Is he home?"

"He's home, but he's in his office studying for an important case tomorrow. He does not want to be disturbed."

"But I need advice."

"Well, run your questions by me. I wasn't a legal aid for all those years for nothing."

"Okay. I want to evict the tenants," said Kendall.

"For starters, did they sign a lease agreement?"

"Well, yes."

"So when did they sign it?"

Kendall considered this. "It was on Sunday."

"So this is Tuesday. That's less than three working days."

"What does that mean?"

"Well, I'm not that familiar with rental laws, but there is a three-day rescission rule in real estate. It might apply to your case."

"Really? I can throw them out?"

"You might be able to cancel their leases."

"How do I do that?"

"Do you still have their checks?"

"Their checks?"

"Yes, didn't they pay you when you signed the leases?"

"Yeah."

"So, it's only Tuesday. Do you still have the checks or did you deposit them?"

"I deposited them."

"Well, that's probably okay. The money's still in your account, right?"

Kendall looked at the bags on the floor and frowned. "Not exactly."

"You mean you spent it already?"

"Well, I had to pay some on my Visa card, and there was this sale and—"

"Kendall, you're hopeless. You probably deserve those horrible renters. It might teach you a lesson."

"I don't want a lesson." Kendall made a sniffing noise, hoping that Kate would think she was crying. "I just need some help, Katie. I need someone like Eric to come and throw these people out of my house."

"Okay, tell me exactly what they have done. Have they actually destroyed property? Are drugs and alcohol involved? Have they broken the law?"

"They tore out the carpets."

Kate laughed.

"And they painted—and they're just making a mess of everything and I want them to leave!"

"Did they get paint on the woodwork?" Kate asked, sounding slightly concerned now. "Because that's original woodwork, Kendall. It's crosscut old fir and in good shape and it should be preserved."

"I know. But they don't even care—"

"And did they remove the carpets properly?"

"Who knows what they're doing," said Kendall. She could still hear them downstairs, laughing and talking and rumbling around her house. "Like I said, it's out of control and I want them to leave. I don't want renters in my house. I can't stand them, Kate. They are making me crazy."

"Maybe you should call the police."

Now Kendall really was crying. "I just want them out, Kate. How can I make them leave?"

Kate let out a big sigh. "Okay, I'm coming over."

"You are?" But even as she said this, she heard the line go dead. She glanced at her watch. At this time of night, and no commuter traffic, it would take Kate about ten minutes to get here. Kendall suddenly wasn't so sure she wanted Kate to come. She hit speed dial again, but this time she got the answering machine. Then she tried Kate's cell phone, but it wasn't on.

Kendall paced in her room. What would Kate do? What would she say? Maybe she would realize, like Kendall had, that these three girls really were taking over. Or maybe she could look over the leases and tell the tenants that they were no good, or come up with something about that three-day rule. Something to end this thing once and for all. Oh, why had she wanted to rent rooms? For the money? Even that was pointless, since Megan had bullied her to lower the rent. She hadn't even told Kate about that yet. Yes, maybe it was time that someone else stepped in and read these young women the riot act. What right did they have to start painting rooms without Kendall's approval? This was her house, wasn't it?

Kendall heard the doorbell and dashed downstairs to answer it. As far as she could tell, her renters had gone back to their rooms to wreak more havoc. Although they had cleaned up their mess in the dining room first.

"Come in," she told her sister, opening the door wide.

"Where are they?" Kate frowned as she looked past the foyer toward the quiet living room and then over to the dining area.

Kendall pointed toward the hallway that led to the downstairs bedrooms. "Back there."

Kate paused to look at the new furnishings in the living room. "Not bad, Kendall. Although the new stuff does tend to make the carpet and walls look pretty dingy."

"I spent a lot of money on this stuff," said Kendall. "Just for my renters. And look how they thank me. I didn't even tell you that they strong-armed me into lowering the rent."

"Strong-armed you?" Kate looked curiously at her.

"Well, not literally. But they ganged up."

"Let's go see what they've done," said Kate, now purposefully heading down the hallway. She stopped and knocked on the first door, the room that Kendall thought Lelani had taken, although she wasn't positive.

"Hang on a minute," called Lelani, "the door is blocked right now."

"See," said Kendall. "She's in there tearing things up right now."

Kate knocked firmly on the next bedroom door, and this one opened.

"Yes?" Megan poked her head out with a puzzled look.

"I'm Kate—Kendall's sister—and I came over to see what's going on here."

Now Megan looked even more puzzled, but at least she opened the door wider. "What do you mean—what's going on?"

Kate peered beyond Megan and into the bedroom, which Kendall was also seeing for the first time, and to her stunned amazement the room looked totally different.

"What have you done in here?" demanded Kendall, pushing past Megan to see the room more fully. Not only was it painted and nicely furnished, but the floor actually looked great.

"Wow," said Kate. "This is beautiful."

Kendall kept staring at the wood floor, trying to take this all in. Then she stared at the freshly painted walls, which actually seemed well painted, and then she looked at Megan, who seemed to be smiling just a little too smugly.

"Thanks," said Megan to Kate. "It was kind of a rush, but I'm starting a new job tomorrow and I wanted to get it wrapped up." She shot a look at Kendall, then held out her hand to shake hands with Kate. "I'm Megan."

Kate walked around admiring everything and nodding. "This looks really professional, Megan. The painting is flawless and the décor is so perfect. Very, very nice."

Kendall felt like gagging on her sister's praise, but instead she just stood there in silence, taking in the room, which didn't seem to belong in this house.

"Thanks," said Megan again. "That's encouraging to hear, since my new job is with an interior-design firm."

"Really?" Kate looked even more interested now. "Which one?"

"Sawyer & Craig."

"No way," said Kate. "Cynthia Sawyer is a friend of mine."

"Really, you know her?"

"Yes. And I think she's one of the best designers around."

"I know." Megan nodded eagerly. "I'm really excited about it. She seems nice."

Kate turned and glared at Kendall now. "Well, I should apologize for my sister. I think she may be losing her mind. She called me up and was all wigged out over the fact that her tenants were tearing things apart."

"Well, we did tear out the carpeting. But we agreed to that in the lease."

"In writing?"

Megan nodded. "Yeah. We agreed to pay less rent in exchange for work. Is there a problem?"

"Not as far as I can see. All you've done is made this place much, much nicer. Kendall should be thanking you."

Kendall folded her arms across her chest now. "You didn't even ask me about the color."

"You never said you needed to approve the color," said Megan. "Is there a problem with it?"

Kate laughed. "Just that it's perfect."

"Lelani's room is the same color."

"Why does she have the door blocked?" demanded Kendall.

"Because they're still working on the floor," said Megan. "I'm sure she doesn't mind showing you."

So Megan led them back to Lelani's room, and after a few seconds and shuffling sounds, Lelani opened the door. She and that really good-looking Hispanic guy did appear to be tearing out some kind of nasty looking pad that must've been underneath the carpet. It was heaped and piled about the room.

"This is Kendall's sister Kate," said Megan. "She wanted to look around."

Lelani pointed to the other side of the room. "We've got the wood floor showing over there. Other than the staples, which I'm pulling out, it's looking really good."

"I can see that," said Kate. "Sorry to disturb your work."

"Do you want to see the bathroom?" offered Megan, like she owned the place. Couldn't Kate see how these girls were taking over?

"Why not?" said Kate, tossing Kendall another withering look. Kendall knew that this was not boding well for sisterly love.

"Marcus did the painting in here," said Megan. She looked directly at Kendall now. "He just left but promised to come back to do the second coat. It turns out your boyfriend is a really good painter."

"Who knew?" Kendall resented Megan even more now. What right did she have to rope Marcus into helping her like this? Who did she think she was anyway?

"Well, this looks great," said Kate. "And again, I compliment you on the choice of color. Not only does it go great with the tile, but it's a nice transition from the bedrooms too. Really well done, Megan. What you've accomplished in just a few days has probably increased the real estate value significantly. Kendall should be paying you."

Kendall wanted to hit something. Or someone.

"Thanks, but if you'll excuse me ..." Megan backed out of the bathroom now, almost like she suspected that Kendall was ready to bring it on. "I'd like to get the rest of my stuff put away."

Kendall wanted to point out that perhaps that wouldn't be necessary, because she was planning to throw her renters, particularly this one, out.

"Sorry we disturbed you, Megan," said Kate. She fished around in her bag for something and finally pulled out a card. "I'm going to give this to you," she told Megan, "because you seem like a responsible young woman. And if my *baby* sister should have any problems, or if you have any concerns about how things are going here, please, feel free to let me know."

Megan seemed slightly surprised but took the card, then thanked her.

As soon as Megan was in her room, Kate actually took Kendall by the arm and literally pulled her back to the living room. "I cannot believe you dragged me out of my home tonight, Kendall," she hissed. "I honestly think that you are seriously deranged, little sister. What on earth could you have been thinking to make accusations like that? All these girls have done is greatly improved your property value. They're hardworking and nice and you—you—" she actually sputtered now.

Naturally, Kendall didn't know what to say. She had no response to Kate's rage, so she simply shrugged. But at least she didn't say, "Whatever."

"Don't you ever pull a stunt like this on me again, Kendall Alexandra Weis. Because, I swear, I will—"

"Oh, lighten up." Kendall rolled her eyes now. Okay, she knew that wasn't such a good idea, but she just couldn't control herself.

"Sometimes I can't believe you're my sister. Or maybe our parents had defective DNA by the time you were born. But you are a real piece of work, little sister." Kate was standing by the front door, and Kendall wasn't sure she'd ever seen Kate this mad.

"You're blowing this way out of proportion," said Kendall in a calm voice.

"Some of us have better things to do than play your seriously disturbed little games, Kendall. Some of us have a life. But you better straighten up, and while you're at it, why don't you grow up too!" Then Kate stormed out of the house, slamming the door so hard that the leaded glass shook.

Okay, Kendall did feel slightly bad for dragging Kate into this mess. But she still wished she could get rid of her tenants.

# Megan

Megan's first two days on the new job went relatively smoothly. But then Vera went out of town, according to Ellen, to work on a five million dollar house on the coast. And Cynthia was tied up with a proposal for a new hotel. Consequently, they left Megan in the hands of the bookkeeper, Judy, and the receptionist, Ellen.

The first task they gave her was to clean out the storage room, which apparently hadn't been cleaned out since the design firm started nearly ten years ago. But, as promised, Megan didn't complain about the hard work, and after two days of sorting, sifting, and tossing, the storage room actually looked pretty good. She was just taking the last load of recycling outside when she heard Ellen calling her name.

"Yes?"

"Vera is on the phone for you," said Ellen. "She said it's an emergency."

"I'll take it in here," said Megan, setting the box of paper down and picking up the phone.

"Hello?"

"Megan," said Vera in a breathless voice. "I need you to find something for me. Can you do that?"

"I think so. What is it you want me to find?"

Vera went into a convoluted explanation about a missing invoice that was probably in her office. And after asking a few questions,

Megan thought she knew where to look.

"Call me back the minute you find it," said Vera before she hung up.

Megan didn't feel comfortable searching through someone else's office, but she figured that was what an assistant was supposed to do. Still, she looked and looked but couldn't find an invoice that fit the description.

"Vera wants you again," called Ellen. "Why don't you take it in her office? Line two."

Megan fumbled a bit, trying to remember how to use the phone, and finally said, "Hello?"

"Don't just say, hello," snapped Vera. "Say, this is Megan—whatever your last name is—and how may I help you?"

"Hello, this is Megan Abernathy," she repeated, "and how may—"

"Not now, stupid! I mean when you answer the phone in general. I *know* who you are."

That wasn't exactly true, since Vera couldn't remember her last name, but Megan didn't say as much.

"Did you find that invoice?"

"I've looked and looked, but I—"

"Did you look where I said to look?"

"Yes, but it's—"

"Did you write down where I said to look?"

"Yes, but—"

"I don't want buts, Megan, I want efficiency."

"I'm looking in all the files and the drawer that you—"

"Don't look in all the files, Megan. Are you a complete idiot? Just look in the Bushnell files and the—"

"Gerbaldi files and the Horchow files and the—"

"Are you being flip with me?"

"No," said Megan in what she hoped was a cheerful tone. "But I did write down what you told me and I have been looking every—"

"Get Ellen on the phone," snapped Vera. "I'm sure she can find the invoice."

"Just a moment," said Megan. Then as she pushed the phone button to buzz Ellen, she noticed that the light on line two had gone off. Had she disconnected Vera?

"Yes?" Ellen said.

"Uh, Vera was on line two for you."

"She's not there now."

"Can you call her?"

"Why?"

"She wants to talk to you."

"Then why did she hang up?"

"I think I may have, uh, disconnected her."

"Oh, dear."

Megan closed the drawers to the files in Vera's office and tiptoed back to the supply room, but she could hear Ellen talking to what she knew must be a very angry Vera. Ellen was trying to smooth things over. "Yes, yes, Vera. I'll go see if I can find it. Yes, I'll call you right back. I'm sorry. Very sorry. Yes, that must be terrible. You just hang in there and we'll see what we can do."

"Oh, dear," Ellen muttered as she hurried to Vera's office.

Megan went to see if she could help. "Vera told me to look in these places," explained Megan, rattling off the names of the files that Vera had specifically mentioned. Meanwhile, Ellen rifled through the papers in one of Vera's baskets.

"Vera doesn't always file things where they go," said Ellen, thumbing through what did look like a stack of invoices. "Then she blames whoever is handy for her own carelessness."

"Oh." Megan just watched, hoping she might learn something.

"It should be a Horchow receipt," said Ellen, "for a very expensive couch and two club chairs that Vera is certain she ordered but have not shown up. The Horchow company insists these items were not ordered. Vera needs the invoice to prove it."

"Oh."

"And the Bushnells, the owners of the coast house, are having a big shindig tomorrow night, and there will be the devil to pay if those pieces don't arrive in time."

"Right."

"But I do not see a Horchow invoice anywhere." She turned to Megan with a desperate expression. "You run and check with Judy on this. It's possible that she's cross-referencing it with their bill." Ellen sighed. "Possible, but not likely, since the pieces haven't been received yet. Oh, dear!"

So Megan went to check with Judy, explaining the dire emergency, and Judy stopped what she was doing and searched, then shook her head. "If I had it, it would be right here." She held up a folder with the name *Bushnell* on it. "They all go right here."

"Thanks." Now Megan ran back to see if Ellen had any success.

"No," Ellen just shook her head. "This is not good."

"What do we do?"

"Call Vera."

"Me?" Megan so did not want to speak to that woman again.

"Yes, you." Ellen nodded firmly. "You're the assistant. I'm only the receptionist."

Then she chuckled as she returned to her desk.

"Hello, this is Megan Abernath—"

"I know who you are! Now tell me you've found that invoice and all will be well."

"No, we haven't been able—"

Now Vera swore profusely, acting as if this unfortunate mishap were totally Megan's fault. It was all Megan could do not to defend herself, although she knew it wouldn't do any good. She also knew that Vera's temper tantrum would do nothing to solve her problem.

"Vera, if I might make a suggestion," began Megan timidly.

"What?"

"Why not just buy a different couch and pair of chairs?"

Vera laughed. In a mean way. "Well, sure, I'll just trot on down to Furniture Warehouse and pick up something. Maybe in a blue velvet or mauve and, while I'm at it, I'll get one of those shiny reproduction paintings to hang over it. Do you know what kind of furniture stores are out here?"

"Well, no, but—"

"There you go with the but again!" she shouted. "Don't give me buts, give me results. I want that invoice!"

"Well, that invoice is not here," said Megan firmly. "Have you considered the possibility that you forgot to order those pieces?"

The line went silent and Megan thought Vera had hung up on her, although the light on line two was still lit.

"Look, Vera," Megan tried. "There are some good furniture stores in Portland. If you told me exactly what you're looking for, I could go and see if there's anything that—"

"You will never find the same pieces," said Vera, slowly, as if addressing a two-year-old. "That is why we order these items directly from the Horchow company. They are specialty items, Megan. They have to be specially made. Do you understand what I am saying to you?"

"I'm not stupid."

"Well, you could've fooled me!"

"So, you don't think it's worth a try?" said Megan. "You'd rather the

Bushnells have their big party with three missing pieces of furniture?"

"No, of course, not. And I'd have Cynthia go look for these pieces if she wasn't tied up right now."

"Would it hurt for me to try?" Megan persisted, actually getting into the spirit of this adventure. "I mean, what if I got lucky?"

"Even if you found something … slightly acceptable, I doubt you could get it delivered in time."

"Let me try?"

"Fine. Go ahead and try."

"You'll have to describe the pieces. Unless you have a photo or something."

"I have the photos with me," said Vera. "I'll fax them to Ellen."

"What about the fabrics?" asked Megan. "Are there—"

"It's not fabric, it's leather."

"Okay, how about the leath—"

"The information is on the fax. You figure it out, Megan!" Then she hung up.

Megan went to the room that held all the furniture catalogs and fabric samples and began to search for Horchow catalogs. By the time she found the large, heavy books, Ellen had received the fax, which was, of course, blurry.

But Megan did her best to decipher the numbers on the fax, matching them to ones in the book, until she felt fairly certain that she knew what kind of leather was involved in the couch and chairs. The couch was a smooth Italian bronze color, and the club chairs were a sandy suede. That didn't sound too difficult. Now she got out the phone book and started to call up the Portland-area furniture stores. First she described what she was looking for, which they all assured her they had or could get—such good salespeople—but when she explained further, saying she needed them to be delivered to the coast by tomorrow, most of the salespeople balked.

Megan felt driven now. Somehow, she had to conquer this dilemma. She would prove to Vera that she wasn't a complete idiot. And so she continued to call, asking questions, describing what she needed. Finally, by mid-afternoon, she had three possibilities. But she had no car. First she called her mom, but got no answer. She considered borrowing Anna's car, but when she called the publishing company she learned that Anna was in an editorial meeting and wouldn't get out until four thirty.

Now, despite the futility of it, Megan thought of Kendall. Although Kendall had pretty much been freezing out all of her renters these past couple of days, Megan knew that the temptation of "shopping" might possibly draw the shopaholic out of her funk. It seemed worth a try. But when she called the house the phone just rang and rang. She was about to hang up when a deep voice said, "Hello?"

"Who *is* this?" she demanded.

"Who is this?" he shot back.

"Marcus?"

"No, it's the painter. Is this Megan?"

"Marcus, that is you, isn't it?"

"Yeah, I had some time off this afternoon and thought I'd finish up the bathroom. I don't like leaving things undone."

"Is Kendall there?"

"I think so, but I haven't actually seen her. I've heard her thumping around upstairs, though."

"So, you just let yourself in again?"

"I'm the painter."

"Right."

"Want me to see if I can stir up Kendall for you?"

"Would you mind?"

"Not if you don't. She's not in a very good mood these days."

"I've noticed."

"I'm on that funky landline with the cord, so I'll have to—"

"Yeah, I know. I can wait." Megan actually prayed as she waited. Maybe some good could come out of this. Maybe she could mend things with Kendall and resolve this thing with Vera simultaneously—like that old saying, she could kill two birds with one stone. Although that killing part didn't sound exactly right.

Megan prepared herself, planning a way to best ask Kendall for help. She would really play up the shopping thing, appealing to Kendall's compulsive need to buy something really big and expensive. It could work. Or not. Megan still couldn't forget Kendall's response to Megan's dinner invitation last night. She'd wanted to take everyone out to celebrate her new job, but Kendall had flatly refused.

As Megan waited on the phone, she thought she heard yelling somewhere on the other end. It didn't sound good.

"She doesn't want to talk to you," said Marcus in an irritated voice.

"Oh."

"Anything I can help you with?"

"I was going to ask her to give me a ride. I need to go look at some furniture, for work. It's kind of an emergency and I thought I could—oh, never mind."

"I can give you a ride."

"Really?"

"Sure. Like I said, I had the afternoon off anyway."

"But you said you were painting."

"I'm almost done."

"And you don't mind? I'll pay for gas."

So it was settled. Marcus was on his way. And as relieved as she was to have a ride, Megan just hoped this wasn't a mistake.

Twenty-five

# Kendall

Kendall was fed up. As if life wasn't bad enough already—what with these renter girls taking over her house and paying less than half of what she'd wanted for their first month's rent, then acting like they owned the place—but besides that, two strange men had delivered furniture this morning. They said they were friends of Lelani, but Kendall had never seen them before. And yet there they were, walking right into her house like no big deal. She had almost called the police on them, but by the time she located her cell phone, they were gone. Kendall suspected that Lelani had given them a key, which was totally unacceptable. Suppose they made a copy? What if they returned in the middle of the night and murdered her in her sleep? Okay, she knew that was overly dramatic, but she'd had it with her renters.

She called a locksmith to see about changing the locks, but when she heard the price, she decided it wasn't worth it. She'd have to think of something else. So far, being cold and silent hadn't done any good. And last night, when she attempted to blast them out with her music, the neighbors had complained, and she was the one who had to speak to the policeman who came out. She tried to blame it on her tenants, but he'd told her that as the owner, she was responsible. Yeah, right!

What she wanted to know was who was responsible for Anna's aggravating habit of singing opera in the shower every morning? That soprano vibrato was driving Kendall crazy. She wondered if she could use an insanity defense if she lost it and reenacted a scene from *Psycho*.

But today was the icing on the cake. There she was, up in her room, minding her own business, when Marcus comes clumping up the stairs, banging on her door, and telling her that Megan wanted to talk to her, that she was on the phone—the landline downstairs. As if Kendall even cared.

"Thanks, but no thanks!" she'd snapped at him.

"Why not?" he demanded. Then she used a bad but accurate word to describe Megan's character, and he'd gotten mad at her. Kendall's own boyfriend got mad at her for saying something about stupid Megan! And to make matters worse, he had the nerve to defend Megan, saying that she was smart and a hard worker and all sorts of ridiculous things. Marcus had never described Kendall like that. Usually he teased her and called her lazy. What was going on with him?

Naturally, Kendall decided to break up with him at that point. She figured that would be one way to make him sorry. She expected him to apologize and to take back what he'd said about stupid Megan. But he just acted like he couldn't care less if she broke up with him. He even told her that he had already broken up with her anyway.

"You did not break up with me!" she shouted as he took off down the steps.

"I did too," he called back. "I just didn't bother to tell you."

"Did not!" she screamed. And then she slammed her door so hard that an old prom photo of her and a cute boyfriend fell off the wall, breaking the glass. And that's when Kendall decided that it was time to take charge. She had to do something to get her life back under control. But what?

She looked at the pile of unpaid bills heaped on her dresser and wanted to throw something. If her stupid renters hadn't changed their freaking leases, she could've made a small dent in that pile. Well, if there hadn't been that big sale at Macy's—who could resist that? But her bills could wait. Right now, she just needed an escape. She felt trapped in this house. Imprisoned by her lousy tenants. But where could she go? Where?

Kate wouldn't let Kendall crash at her house. Kate probably wouldn't even speak to her yet. Kendall had never seen Kate so outraged over nothing. In Kendall's opinion, her sister's act had been a little over the top. And to think their family called Kendall the drama queen.

She considered calling Amelia and begging for a place to stay, but the "newlyweds" had made a commitment to no houseguests for the first year. Where did people come up with this stuff? And Marcus was definitely out. Way out. Kendall wondered how her grandmother would react to an unexpected guest. Her assisted-living apartment had a couch she could crash on, but would her grandmother put up with it?

Kendall wished she had enough credit to go to a really nice hotel, but most of her cards were either maxed out or dangerously close. She went over and looked through her accumulation of mail again. Of course, they were primarily bills, but occasionally one of those envelopes would contain a new credit card—a credit card that could be activated with one little phone call. She picked up envelopes, giving them the tell-tale shake, and finally—bingo! She had a winner.

She ripped open the envelope to an invitation from a credit company that she'd never even heard of before. But at the top of the letter, she saw the words "$5,000 of credit is yours today!" Then, tossing aside the other paperwork, she called the 800 number and, presto, after answering some questions and being recorded, the card was activated.

She ripped open drawers and dumped them out as she searched for just the right items to take with her. Then she tore things out of her closet. She knew she was working against the clock as she packed several bags, making sure to include her latest purchases. Finally, she was done, and she zipped downstairs and hopped in her car and took off. Her plan was to disappear—to totally vanish without a trace. That should make them wonder. Perhaps she could incriminate her renters somehow. Make it appear as if they had done something to her. She wasn't even sure what or how, but she just wanted to freak them out a little. To get even. And, besides that, she wanted to have some fun. It was about time.

She drove into the city, searching for what might be a fun hotel, a place she could hide out, party, and just lay low. She'd keep her car parked, and if she went out and about, she would move incognito. Perhaps she could pass herself off for a celebrity. It wouldn't be the first time she'd be mistaken for somebody famous.

She finally settled on one of the largest boutique hotels right in the heart of the city. She went in and inquired about rooms, and although the rate was a little high, she went ahead and booked it for a whole week. A week should be a good break.

"So you'll be checking out on Wednesday, October the seventh, Miss Weis?"

"Wait," she said as she recognized an important date. "I think I'll stay that night too. I'd like to check out on October eighth."

The clerk nodded. "That's not a problem. A total of seven nights."

"Yes." She smiled brightly. "That's perfect." Then she signed the receipt and arranged for valet parking and, with the help of a young man who had bad skin and an inability to take his eyes off of her chest, she got all her bags into Room 532. Once she tipped the perv and closed the door, she kicked off her heels and did a happy dance, singing "Happy Birthday to Me!" It was a week premature, but that's what this was, she decided— a great big birthday getaway—and she planned to enjoy this one to the max!

She giggled as she carefully unpacked her clothes and shoes. She felt badly for the rush job she'd done packing, but it had been worth it to get away from the house without being seen by anyone coming home from work, which would be happening by now. Of course, Marcus had seen her home a little earlier, but perhaps that would simply add to the mystery. Maybe he would be indicted along with her renters. She could only hope.

Once everything was neatly placed in drawers or hung in the closet—twice the size as the one in her room back at the house—Kendall decided to take a relaxing bubble bath. It was so great to have her own bathroom again. What had made her think she could give up that little privilege? Even though Anna didn't have nearly the amount of beauty products as Kendall, it was inconvenient to share that personal space. Already, Anna had started to complain about Kendall's housekeeping skills, or rather the lack of. Well, that was Anna's opinion. If it bothered Anna that much to see a towel on the floor, why didn't she just pick it up herself? Oh, it would be so great to have a vacation from all those female hormones that were raging through her house.

Yes, thought Kendall, as she sank into the hot foamy water with a glass of merlot that she'd poured from the mini bar. She deserved this little break. And, if she was lucky, it would shake up her roommates ... and possibly entice them to rethink their living arrangements permanently.

# Lelani

"Maybe we should make some kind of roster for fixing dinner," suggested Lelani as she and Anna worked together in the kitchen. Lelani had started dinner, hoping that her new roommates would offer to help. But so far only Anna had shown, and she seemed slightly reluctant.

"Sharing kitchen chores is a good idea," said Anna. "Just as long as you leave me out of it."

Lelani glanced at Anna, unsure as to whether she was serious.

"Just kidding." Anna wrinkled up her nose. "Well, sort of. Just because my family has a restaurant does not mean I'm into cooking."

"Well, maybe we can have a roster for other chores." Lelani filled a pot with water. "Like grocery shopping and cleaning."

"Good luck with Kendall," said Anna. "Not only does she seem allergic to cleaning, but I don't think she knows the way to a grocery store either."

"The food supply in here did seem a little sparse."

"Although she has absolutely no problem with helping herself to whatever she finds in the fridge."

"You've noticed that too?" Lelani was curious as to how much Anna had observed about Kendall.

"Yes." Anna smacked the knife down on the cutting board. "Even after I wrote my name on a box of leftovers, they were gone the next day."

"And my yogurts have disappeared," admitted Lelani. She didn't mention the bananas too. That seemed a little petty, since she'd left them on the countertop like they were up for grabs.

"And my chips and salsa," continued Anna, "the bag was nearly full and should've lasted several days."

"You're sure it's Kendall?"

"The food always goes missing during the day."

"While we're at work," said Lelani as she measured some salt into the water.

"I don't get how Kendall stays so skinny when she eats like a horse. It's just not fair."

Lelani knew how, but she wasn't about to disclose anything. Kendall was obviously bulimic. Maybe not as extremely bulimic as one of Lelani's old college roommates. But she definitely had the bug.

"My bedroom furniture came today," Lelani told Anna, hoping to change the subject. She didn't really like talking about others' personal problems. Not only did it seem rude, but she worried that Kendall might pop in at any moment.

"How's it look?"

"The furniture is actually not that bad. I think the reason Mr. Green called it juvenile had more to do with the bedding."

"He brought bedding too?"

Lelani chuckled. "Apparently. I wasn't here when he delivered it, but it was piled on the bed. Can you believe it? It was Strawberry Shortcake."

"Strawberry Shortcake?" Anna laughed. "Hey, it's probably vintage, maybe even collectable, you might be able to sell it on eBay."

"Maybe so. For sure, I'm not going to use it. Well, maybe just for a night or two until I do some shopping."

"You don't have bedding of your own?"

"No, but I plan to get some."

"Need a ride?" offered Anna.

"Hey, that'd be great," said Lelani. "I'd considered getting some things at Nordstrom, but even with my discount, their stuff is kind of spendy."

"We should go to Bed, Bath & Beyond," said Anna. "I love that place."

"Maybe Megan will want to come too," said Lelani. "She has such good taste. I wouldn't mind getting her input."

"I'm surprised she's not home yet," said Anna. "It's almost six."

"Well, hopefully she likes spaghetti," said Lelani as she stirred the boiling pasta. "It looks like we're making enough to feed a small army, but I suppose it'll make good leftovers."

"And you know what will happen to the leftovers," said Anna.

"Leftovers?" said Megan as she came into the kitchen. "Does that mean I'm late for dinner?"

"It means you're just in time to set the table," said Lelani from where she was washing lettuce in the sink.

"Why are you so late?" asked Anna.

Megan told them about her boss Vera and how she had been searching for leather couches and chairs for the past three hours.

"Any luck finding what you were looking for?" asked Lelani as she sliced a tomato.

"I think so," said Megan happily. "The last store had something that might work and they even agreed to deliver it to the coast. The question now is whether Vera will find it acceptable."

"What if she doesn't?" asked Anna.

"Good question," said Megan. "I plan to fax her photos first. It'll have to be her decision. No way am I going to get stuck with that bill. The three pieces together, plus shipping, cost about seven thousand dollars."

Anna whistled.

"But it's for a five-million-dollar house," explained Megan. "So I suppose that's just a drop in the bucket for people like that."

"Sounds like you're having fun with your job," said Lelani.

"Today actually was kind of fun. Although Vera was incredibly rude. At one point I almost told her off, but fortunately I controlled myself."

"So, how did you get to the stores to shop?" asked Anna as she stirred the spaghetti sauce. "I mean, I did get your message about needing a ride, but it was too late."

"Marcus took me around."

Lelani blinked in surprise. "Seriously?"

"Yeah. And he was very nice about it too."

"Okay," said Anna. "How was it that Marcus played chauffer to you?"

So Megan told them about how she'd been desperate for a ride, how she'd called everyone she could think of. "But I was totally striking out. So finally I decided to ask Kendall. I figured the shopping part might tempt her."

"Yeah," said Lelani, "spending seven thousand dollars would be a real high for her."

"Apparently not," said Megan. "She told Marcus to forget it."

"Marcus was here?" asked Anna.

"Yes. He was here working on the bathroom."

"Oh, yeah, it looked like it was finished," said Lelani. "He's a good painter too."

"So anyway, he felt sorry for me and offered to drive me around."

Lelani peered curiously at Megan now. "And you're not worried about how Kendall is going to react to this?"

"To be honest, I was a little concerned at first, but Marcus assured me they broke up."

"They broke up?" asked Anna. "Are you positive about that?"

Megan set the water glasses by the sink then nodded. "Marcus said it was no big deal and that it was totally mutual. He actually seemed relieved."

"So Kendall's really okay with it?" queried Anna in a skeptical tone.

"According to Marcus, she's fine with it."

"Well, for your sake, I hope that's true." Lelani lowered her voice. "I hate to say it, Megan, but I think Kendall already has an ax to grind with you. And if I were you, I'd go easy with that girl."

"Trust me, I know," said Megan.

"And, if I were you, I'd watch my backside," added Anna.

"Speaking of watching your backside," said Lelani to Anna, "how's that deal with Ramsay Rowan going?" Anna had filled them in on the celebrity book she was working on, and Lelani thought it sounded pretty interesting. In fact, Lelani had decided that both Anna and Megan had jobs that were far more interesting than hers.

"The editorial committee really liked my book idea," said Anna happily. "I think it's a go."

"What about Ramsay?" asked Megan. "Does she like it?"

"We won't know for a while." Anna sampled the spaghetti sauce, then added some salt. "Hey, Lelani and I are going to Bed, Bath & Beyond after dinner," she said. "Want to come along?"

"Or are you all shopped out?" asked Lelani.

"Not at all."

"I need to get some bedding and things," said Lelani. "And I'd like your help—you have such a good eye for color and design."

"I think it sounds like fun," said Megan as she carried water glasses to the table.

"Maybe Kendall will want to come too," said Anna. Lelani and Megan just looked at her. "Well, you never know. I mean it does involve shopping." They all laughed.

"Everything's pretty much ready," Lelani announced as she poured the sauce over the pasta. "Anyone hungry?"

"Looks great," said Megan. "Sorry I wasn't home in time to help more."

"What about Kendall?" asked Lelani.

"I'm not going to get her," said Anna. "The last conversation I had with her, she was all mad at me for singing in the shower. And then I simply mentioned that maybe we should take turns cleaning the upstairs bathroom, and she went totally ballistic on me. Seriously, I was glad she wasn't armed, because she is dangerous."

"Well, I'm not going up there," said Megan. "You already warned me to watch my backside."

"Okay, fine," said Lelani. "You guys go ahead and put the food on the table and I'll go face the lioness myself."

Lelani tried to appear confident, but she was actually bracing herself as she walked up the stairs. Kendall had been anything but congenial these past couple of days. It was clear that she was not the least bit happy with her tenants, and she didn't care who knew it. This made no sense to Lelani. It had been Kendall's choice to rent rooms—and to hold her tenants to a one-year lease. No one had twisted her arm. It seemed a little late, not to mention flaky, to change her mind now.

Lelani took in a quick breath, then tapped lightly on the door. "Kendall?" she called out pleasantly. When no one answered, she knocked a little louder. "We've got dinner downstairs if you want to join us." She knocked again, but it seemed obvious that Kendall was sending them all a very clear message. Or perhaps she'd gone out. Whatever the case, Lelani had no doubt that Kendall wouldn't starve. Not exactly anyway. She would probably help herself to all the leftovers when the rest of them were asleep or at work. And the truth was, Lelani felt relieved that Kendall didn't want to join them.

It seemed Megan and Anna were relieved too. Not having Kendall sulking or tossing mean comments at her renters made for a much more pleasant meal. With just the three of them, the conversation was fairly relaxed and comfortable, although Lelani sensed an underlying uneasiness. She guessed this had to do with Kendall. In some ways, it felt like the three of them were slightly stuck here. But what could they do?

"I'll bet Kendall sneaks down here as soon as we leave," said Anna as they were cleaning up and putting away the leftovers.

"And she'll probably leave her dirty dishes on the counter," added Megan as she put a plate in the dishwasher.

"We really should come up with a cleaning roster," said Lelani again. "Just to make sure things get done and that the work gets shared evenly." And although she felt like she was being pushy and slightly maternal about this, she was determined not to get stuck doing everything. That's how it had been at her aunt's house, and she wasn't about to fall into that trap again.

"You mean sharing the chores evenly among the three of us," said Anna with a slightly bitter tone. "I think we can all be pretty certain that Kendall has no intention of lifting a finger."

"Well, she can't expect us to be her handmaids," said Lelani. Even as she said this, she felt sorry for Anna. She probably would be permanently stuck cleaning up after Kendall in the upstairs bathroom. Either that or she'd have to put up with a filthy bathroom.

"I have an idea," said Megan. "We'll do like you're suggesting, Lelani. We'll make a chore roster with all four of us sharing the housework."

"That will be a waste of time," predicted Anna.

"Wait until you hear the rest," said Megan. "All four of us will be listed,

but if Kendall refuses to do her share, we'll do it for her, and then we'll simply deduct the housecleaning wages from what we pay her for rent."

"That seems fair," said Anna.

"Kendall won't like parting with more rent money," predicted Lelani.

"I'm sure she won't," said Megan. "But she'll have a clean house in
return."

"And if she doesn't want to pay up, she better do her part." Anna
closed the dishwasher firmly, shaking the dishes inside. "You guys ready to
go shopping?"

They had a good time at Bed, Bath & Beyond. And by the time they were
finished pursuing the aisles, Lelani was extremely pleased with her selections. "I am going to sleep like a queen tonight," she told them happily.

"It's about time," said Megan.

Lelani felt a bit concerned about the expense when she unloaded her
cart, watching the items adding up. She'd selected a top-of-the-line mattress
pad, down comforter, and pillows, plus some very high-count percale sheets.
She'd also decided to buy a very cool area rug with a green leafy pattern, a
bedside lamp that looked like it was made of vines, and some cream colored
towels for the bathroom. But she reminded herself that she would've spent
far more for similar items at Nordstrom, even with the employee discount.
And at least she'd made her purchases with cash tonight. She hadn't spent
much more than what she saved by having the reduced rent this month.
Still, she couldn't keep spending at this rate and expect to make it through
a year on salesclerk wages.

Anna and Megan came to see Lelani's bedroom after she put all her
furniture and bedding into place. It felt like a mini open house, and Lelani
was proud of how pretty it looked. Calm, soothing, and slightly elegant.
Quite a change from the horrible mud-colored room from before.

Still, Lelani's unease didn't go away. What if Kendall decided to break the lease with them? What if Lelani was stuck with a nice bed set and no place to put it? Having to move and pay another rental deposit was more than she could handle just now … and she didn't want to be forced to ask her parents for help again. She wanted to show them that she was more mature than they'd given her credit for—she wanted to prove to them, and maybe to herself, that she really was a grown-up.

"Very cool," said Anna as she walked around Lelani's room. "But I'm starting to get seriously jealous of you guys and your chic bedrooms. I feel like I'm stuck with Kendall in the slums upstairs."

"Well, that can change," said Lelani.

"That's right," agreed Megan. "It can all change."

"I just don't see why Kendall isn't a little more appreciative," said Lelani.

"Maybe because Megan has stolen her boyfriend," Anna pointed out.

Megan frowned. "That's not really what happened."

"I know," said Anna quickly. "But that may be how Kendall sees it."

"Kendall definitely has her own unique perspective," said Lelani. Talk about an understatement.

"Well, maybe Kendall will come around when she sees the improvements we'll be making to the rest of the house," said Megan. "I actually roped Marcus into coming over to help this weekend. I thought we could have a big work party and really get this place shaped up. Sort of like those redo shows on the home-improvement channels that my mom likes to watch."

"Like *Trading Spaces*," said Anna eagerly. "I'll trade my room for yours, Megan. Or yours, Lelani."

Lelani laughed. "It's a little late for that, Anna."

"Anyway," Megan continued, "I figured we could start on Anna's room, which should be pretty quick. With all of us working, we should be able to get the living room painted, and maybe even get the carpeting ripped out."

"That would be awesome," said Anna. "That living room carpeting is nasty. I'm willing to do my part. Although I think I'll find some nice heavy rubber gloves." She made a face. "The thought of actually touching that stuff is kind of scary."

"I'm in too," said Lelani.

"And I'll bet Gil would come help some," said Anna. "Especially if he knows that Lelani will be here."

"Sounds like a plan," said Megan. "Now, who wants to tell Kendall?"

No one said a word.

"I'll talk to her," offered Lelani.

"It seems like you have the best relationship with her," said Megan.

"You're lucky you're not sharing a bathroom with her," said Anna.

"Have you seen her at all tonight?" asked Lelani.

"No. And it's been pretty quiet in her room too," said Anna. "No TV or music or anything."

"Maybe she went to bed early."

"Speaking of bed," Lelani stifled a yawn. "I am so sleep-deprived, and that bed looks so inviting …"

"And I'm so outta here," said Megan. "Sweet dreams."

"Let me know how you like those sheets," said Anna. She'd been the one to recommend the high percale count. "I don't know how people can sleep on anything else."

"That's because you're such a princess," Megan teased.

"I think we should all be princesses," Anna shot back at her.

As Lelani went to bed later that night, she thought perhaps she agreed. The bed and bedding felt fabulous, and for the first time since leaving Hawaii, she almost felt at home.

# Twenty-seven

# Megan

"So do you want me to get them or not?" asked Megan. Impatience had crept into her voice, but Vera was being especially stubborn and difficult today.

"Well, that fax you sent me wasn't very helpful," she snipped. "The chairs looked a little doggy to me."

"Doggy?"

"Frumpy."

"They were almost exactly the same as the Horchow chairs that you supposedly ordered, Vera."

"In your opinion perhaps, but you, my dear, haven't been to design school, now have you? You do not have a design degree, do you?"

"Well, no, but—"

"There you go with a *but* again, Megan."

"So, what do you want me to do?"

"Why didn't you take a color photo of the furniture?" asked Vera. Even though they'd already gone through this.

For the second time, Megan had told her that 1) she didn't have a cell phone that took pictures, and 2) she didn't have a digital camera.

"You should have borrowed one."

"Look, I spent a lot of time and energy tracking these pieces down, Vera. It's the best I can do, but if it's not good enough, I'll call the store and cancel the delivery."

"When did you say they'd deliver?"

"The truck is supposed to leave at one."

"Which gets them here when?"

"Around four."

"That's cutting it pretty close, Megan. Are you aware that we're working for some very important clients?"

Megan wanted to ask Vera if *she* was aware, but didn't.

"Fine. Go ahead and have them sent out, but I seriously doubt that I'll use them."

"That's your decision, Vera."

"I can't imagine that the colors will be right."

"The colors were very close to what you ordered."

"Says you."

Megan took in a breath and held it, mentally counting to ten. "So, how do I go about paying for this furniture?" she asked in a perfectly calm voice.

"You should be able to figure that out, Megan."

Megan almost said *but* again, then managed to start the sentence differently. "I've never done this before, Vera. Is there a credit line or—"

"Ask Judy to help you," she snapped.

"Right," she said crisply, eager to end this conversation. "I'll take care of it."

"Just so you know, I am still very disappointed in you, Megan."

"Why?"

"For losing that invoice, of course."

"But I—"

"There you go with another *but!* I simply have no tolerance for such ineptness. Good-bye!"

Megan hung up the phone and suppressed the urge to scream. What was wrong with that woman? If Megan had taken more psychology classes, she might be able to diagnose her better, but for now, Megan would say she was acting like someone with a borderline personality disorder, the kind of person who could appear congenial and well mannered in one situation, then turn into a mean, nasty ogre when things did not go her way. Not quite as far gone as psychotic, but definitely disagreeable. In some ways, Vera was not unlike Kendall, although Megan figured Kendall was simply narcissistic. Kendall really did seem to believe she was superior, that the universe revolved around her, and that all people, including her tenants, had been put on the planet to serve her.

"So what's the plan?" asked Ellen when Megan came out of the little office that they'd given her to use.

"Vera has agreed to have the pieces delivered to the coast," she explained. "Although she's certain they're the wrong color and wrong style and won't work. Also, she's now blaming me for the nonexistent invoice."

Ellen chuckled. "Well, considering you didn't even work here when those pieces were originally ordered, that might be difficult to prove."

"Cynthia won't take Vera's accusation seriously, will she?"

"I hardly think so."

"Anyway, she said to talk to Judy about how to pay for the furniture. This is all new to me."

"Judy does this all the time," Ellen said. "She'll walk you through it."

As it turned out, the process was relatively simple. Judy showed Megan how to fill out a purchase order, then cut her a check. "Now I suppose you need to get this to the furniture store in time for them to deliver."

"I don't have a car," said Megan.

"I'll call a courier," Judy said.

"And I'll call the furniture store and let them know that we're still on."

Soon they had everything all worked out. The salesman at the furniture store assured her that the pieces would be loaded onto the truck and delivered to the correct address by four o'clock. But just to be sure, Megan called back after lunch.

"They are on their way," the woman in the office assured her.

"I just want to make sure the delivery truck gets there on time," said Megan, nervous about the idea of sending thousands of dollars' worth of furnishings to a place she'd never seen. "Is it possible to have someone call here and confirm the delivery?"

"I'll see to it."

"Thank you."

For the rest of the afternoon, Megan kept herself busy straightening up the room that held all the fabric samples and catalogs. It had been quite a mess, but by the time she finished, it looked rather nice. At four fifteen, Ellen told her she had a call on line three. Megan hoped that it was the furniture store confirming the delivery, but to her surprise it was Vera. Megan braced herself for another scathing go-around. Either the furniture had not arrived, or it was there and it was all wrong.

"The couch and chairs are here," Vera said in a flat tone.

"And?"

"And … I suppose they will do."

Megan let out a relieved sigh. "Oh, good."

"Don't let this go to your head, Megan."

"No, of course not."

"Thank you."

"Thank you!" said Megan, even though she had no idea what she was thanking this woman for exactly. "And have a good weekend," she added, for what it was worth.

"Yes. You too."

Megan felt like shouting hallelujah when she hung up, but Ellen was buzzing her to say she had another call on line one. Surely this would be the furniture store, and Megan would thank them profusely for doing what they promised. But it turned out to be Marcus.

"Hey, Megan," he said, "I hope you don't mind me calling you at work."

"No, that's alright," she said happily.

"Did the furniture thing work out okay?"

"Yes! They just arrived and Vera said they were okay."

"Cool. So, now I think you owe me one."

"Owe you what?"

"How about dinner tonight?"

She was about to say no, but then thought, why not? She actually felt like celebrating. "Sure," she said. "That sounds good."

"I'll pick you up at six."

Megan reconsidered. "Uh, wait a minute, what about Kendall? Do you think that's such a great idea?"

"She won't care."

"But I—"

"If it makes you feel better, I won't even come in the house. You just run out to the car, okay?"

"Well, okay." Still, Megan wasn't sure this was so smart.

"All right," said Ellen as she and Judy both poked their heads into Megan's tiny office. "Tell us what Vera said."

"She said it was okay." said Megan with a grin. "Well, those weren't her exact words. I think she said, the furniture 'would do.' And then she told me not to let it go to my head."

They laughed. "That sounds about right," said Ellen.

Then they both gave Megan a high five.

"You survived round one," Judy told her.

"Yes," said Ellen. "You should celebrate."

And so, when she and Marcus went to dinner later that night, Megan did feel like celebrating. Not only had this been a good week and a good day, she had managed to slip out of the house without even seeing, or being seen by, Kendall.

"So have things quieted down at the house?" he asked her after they'd placed their orders.

"Kendall has really been laying low," said Megan. "And I have to admit that it's kind of nice."

"Well, if she had any sense, she'd see that it was very clever to take in three tenants. I mean, not only are you increasing her property value, she gets rent money besides. I guess she's actually a little smarter than I thought."

"Why doesn't she want to get a job?" asked Megan as she buttered a piece of bread.

"You mean besides being lazy?"

"I guess so. I mean if I was her I'd be so bored staying home all day."

"Oh, but she goes shopping too."

"And to yoga," added Megan.

"The bigger question is, how does she afford it?" asked Marcus.

"I've wondered that too. Does she have some kind of trust fund that we don't know about?"

"I don't think she's getting anything from her parents, but maybe her grandmother helps her out more than we know."

"Okay," said Megan. "I really don't want to keep talking about Kendall. Why don't you tell me more about yourself? I know you work in an investment firm. But what else? Tell me about your family and what you like to do in your spare time."

"You mean besides painting?"

She nodded. "Painting is good, mind you. But what other hobbies do you have?"

"I like sports. I used to play tennis a lot. But then I took up golf."

"I was on the tennis team in high school," she admitted.

"We should play sometime."

"Well, I'm probably pretty rusty."

"Me too." Then he went on to tell her about his family. His parents had divorced and both remarried. "So we have this interesting mix of step-parents and stepsiblings and half siblings. It can get confusing. But I have an older brother, a younger half sister and half brother, plus two older stepsisters and a younger stepbrother. Did you get all that down? There might be a test later."

"It must be interesting around the holidays."

He rolled his eyes. "Oh yeah, we're just one big happy family."

Then Megan told him about her family and how her dad recently died. "So, it's really just Mom and me now."

"Pretty easy to keep track of that."

"But a little lonely too. Like our holidays were fairly quiet before with three of us, but now we're down to two. I can't help but envy someone with a big family." She smiled now. "I think that's why I'm kind of enjoying renting a room in Kendall's house. I mean, other than Kendall, it's fun having Anna and Lelani—sort of like sisters."

"Kind of like the show *Friends?*"

"Sort of. Although we don't have an apartment full of guys next door."

"Weren't they all sort of mixing it up after a while?"

Megan nodded. "Fortunately, Kendall didn't want guys living in her house."

Marcus frowned. "Yes, I was informed of that."

"Would you have moved in if Kendall had offered?" Megan considered that she and Marcus were probably worlds apart in their values.

"I might've considered it. Although I had my doubts about Kendall from the start. She really wasn't my type."

"How'd you get together?"

"A mutual friend." He chuckled. "A kleptomaniac, actually."

"Seriously?"

"Yeah. Her name's Shara. If she stops by the house you might want to lock your bedroom."

Megan didn't know whether to believe him. "So if Kendall wasn't your type," she persisted, "why did you keep dating her?"

He shrugged. "I don't know."

"Because she's so pretty?" Megan tried.

"She's okay." Then he smiled at her. "But I like girls who look more like you."

"You mean average?" She almost added, "and pleasantly plump," but stopped herself in time. That was Kendall's opinion, not necessarily Megan's.

He shook his head. "No way. I would not describe you as average. And besides being pretty, you're smart and funny too."

She felt self-conscious now. "Well, thanks."

"And even though I know you're just using me for my painting skills and transportation, I plan to stick around long enough for me to grow on you."

She laughed now. "You're already growing on me, Marcus. But I should warn you about something." She wondered if this was a mistake, but at the same time, she didn't care. Megan wasn't a girl to beat around the bush.

"Warn me?" He got a worried look now. "Oh, no, don't tell me that you're a lesbian or a bi or something."

"No." She made a face. "But I am a Christian."

Now he smiled. "Hey, that's no biggie. I was raised in a Christian home."

"But the divorces?"

He shrugged. "In case you haven't heard, Christians get divorced too."

"Well, I know." She felt her cheeks growing warm. She must sound like the village idiot.

"But to be fair, my dad doesn't go to church anymore. But my mom and my younger half sister still do."

"How about you?"

He shook his head. "Nope. Church doesn't do much for me."

"So, anyway. I just thought you should know."

"Why?"

"Well, I don't know. We're getting to know each other and—"

"Are you one of those girls who doesn't date non-Christians?" His eyes twinkled like he knew something about this.

"I wouldn't say that. Not exactly anyway. Why, have you run up against something like that?"

"Sort of." He chuckled. "And my younger sister made this pact to not date at all. I mean, not until she's ready to get married. And she's only fifteen. I just do not see how that's going to work."

"Maybe it works for her."

"Maybe."

They continued to talk and banter, and Megan was surprised at how comfortable she was starting to feel around this guy. Sure, maybe he wasn't a Christian, but it seemed he was genuinely nice. And at least he knew where she stood. Or sort of. To be fair, Megan wasn't always so sure of where she stood herself. Like when he asked her about dating non-Christians. It wasn't as if she'd ever made a commitment like that. Not formally anyway. And not to God. She knew that her dad's greatest desire for her, well, besides being happy and fulfilled, was that she would marry a Christian man. And that's what she planned to do ... someday.

In the meantime, would it really hurt to look around? Not that she was seriously looking. She wasn't. And not that she planned to get serious about Marcus either. Really, she thought of him more as a friend. And a hard worker, who was handy with a paintbrush. For now that was more than enough.

Besides, she reminded herself as the dessert was served, she still hadn't faced Kendall yet. Despite Marcus's continued reassurance that Kendall didn't give a hill of beans about him anymore, Megan was not totally convinced. For one thing, Kendall had been extremely quiet lately, which might mean she was stewing or brewing or planning some kind of sweet revenge. And, as both Anna and Lelani had pointed out, Kendall had already set her sights on Megan. Who knew what Kendall might do to get even? What if she decided to blame Megan for something again, like the time she'd called her sister claiming that Megan was tearing the house apart? Or what if she created some lame excuse to break the lease agreement and tried to throw Megan out of her house?

Although Megan knew that she could always go home and stay with her mom again, she felt fully invested into 86 Bloomberg Place. She liked the old-fashioned bungalow. She'd gotten used to some of the sounds it made at night. She liked the sunroom and the way her bedroom had turned out. And she was anxious to see the rest of the redecorating completed. Even more than that, she liked Lelani and Anna. She wanted to get to know them better. Despite a rough start, she even liked her new job and being able to walk to work. Megan really wanted this housing arrangement to work out. She just wasn't sure, with Kendall at the helm, that it was possible.

# Anna

"I broke another nail," complained Anna as they were ripping up the carpet in the living room. They'd attacked her room first thing that morning, and she had to admit that it looked really great with a fresh coat of paint and the clean wood floors. But in the mess she'd misplaced her work gloves, and now this hard labor was playing havoc with her manicure. Still, a promise was a promise—and since everyone had jumped in to help with her room, so she knew it was time to reciprocate.

"Hey," she said when she noticed it was getting close to five. "I could go fix everyone something to eat." They'd had pizza delivered for lunch, and Gil had left a bit earlier to work the dinner shift at the restaurant, so she knew he wouldn't be sending out for anything. Besides, escaping to the kitchen sounded a lot better than wrangling with this creepy carpeting. Anna hated to imagine all the microorganisms hidden in it. The smell of that pad alone was making her nauseated.

"Dinner sounds good," said Lelani as she rolled up a piece of carpet. And Megan and Marcus chimed in as well, saying they expected to be ravenous before long.

"I'll have to run to the store," said Anna, thinking that was another good way to use up some time. The others said they planned to slave away until the carpet was completely out, which at the rate Anna was working might take until Christmas.

"Go ahead," said Megan. "But don't think that KP is going to get you out of helping us later."

"Oh, I know," said Anna. But already she was imagining fixing a complicated meal that would require some serious cleanup afterward. She went upstairs to wash up and make a list of ingredients.

As she was getting her purse, she heard her cell phone ringing. She hoped it wasn't her mom. They had already talked today. As usual, Mom was obsessing over the two missing young women, certain that Anna was next on the list. She followed the local news reports religiously, and every time a new suspect or new evidence cropped up, she got all worked up again. Fortunately, Anna saw by her caller ID that it was Edmond.

"Hey, Edmond," she said cheerfully. "What's up?"

"Not much," he told her. "But I was thinking about you and, I know it's last minute, but I wondered if you'd be interested in dinner and movie with me tonight?"

They hadn't actually been on a real date yet. And although Anna was starting to see Edmond in a new light, she wasn't completely sure she wanted to take this encounter to the next level. She didn't know if she was ready to go out with him. Plus she remembered how her mom had reacted when Anna mentioned his job—calling him a secretary, as if that were an unworthy role.

Even so, Anna probably would've gone out with him tonight, just to escape this backbreaking work. Of course, she knew that wasn't an option. But it was tempting. So, thinking it made a fairly good excuse, she explained what they were doing. "So, you see," she said finally, "I really need to stick around until it's done."

"Need any help over there?"

"Are you serious?"

"Sure."

"Well, I doubt we'd turn away any offers of help. But it's hard work, Edmond." She went into some description now, thinking she might turn him off.

"Sounds interesting."

"Interesting?" She sighed.

"Should I come over then?" he asked hopefully.

"Well, do you like to paint?" Anna had decided that she was a pretty lousy painter. Not only was she too short to reach much without a ladder, but her arms got tired more quickly than the others' did.

"I don't know."

"Meaning you don't know how to paint?"

"Yeah, pretty much."

"How about pulling up staples?" she asked eagerly. Her back was still aching from pulling up the ones in her room. There would be millions to pull out in the rest of the house.

"Sure, that sounds like fun."

She controlled herself from laughing. "Great. Come on over."

"I'm there."

"I might be gone when you get here, because I'm heading out to the store to get something for dinner—"

"So does this deal include dinner too?" he asked happily.

"I guess so."

"Cooked by you?"

"Duh."

"Count me in."

So she gave him the address, then informed the others that a new reinforcement was on the way. "His name is Edmond," she said. "And he doesn't know how to paint, but he said he wouldn't mind pulling staples." Naturally, they all erupted into a cheer. It was unanimous. No one liked pulling staples.

Feeling relieved, and hoping that Edmond might replace her as a laborer, Anna happily drove to her mom's favorite grocery store. She took her time to pick out ingredients for tamales and enchiladas and salad, and she even got a brownie mix and a carton of vanilla bean ice cream for dessert. Hopefully she'd make enough tonight to have leftovers for lunch tomorrow. That is, if Kendall didn't attack the leftovers again. Anna hadn't noticed any food missing from yesterday, though.

In fact, Anna hadn't noticed Kendall at all. Still, everyone had been pretty busy. It was possible that Kendall had sneaked past them while they were working away—on Kendall's house. The irony of this had not escaped Anna. The truth was, sneaking out was something that Anna might have done herself if she had thought she could get away with it. She was a hard worker when it came to some things, but she had never enjoyed physical labor.

Even so she was surprised to find that renovating the house was more fun than she'd expected. Not the work itself exactly. But it was interesting watching the transformation in the house. And Megan was really good at selecting paint colors. She'd found a shade of blue, kind of a light periwinkle, that turned out to be awesome in Anna's bedroom. And then she'd brought home a sample of another shade, just a little paler, which actually looked amazing next to the coral-colored tiles in the upstairs bathroom. But they had agreed to wait on that decision. Since Kendall used, and abused, that bathroom too, Megan had suggested they secure Kendall's approval first.

But Kendall had been keeping a low profile. She'd either gone shopping—Anna's guess—or was just laying low. Her absence was probably just as well, since her house looked somewhat chaotic now anyway. No sense in getting Kendall all worked up. Besides, they had enough work to keep them busy without painting the upstairs bathroom as well.

By the time Anna called everyone to dinner, which was close to seven, they had completely removed the carpeting and pad in the living room and hallway, and Megan and Lelani were just starting on the stairs. Meanwhile, Edmond was reported to be a record-making staple puller. And Marcus was painting. Quite a crew.

"This room looks so good," said Lelani as they sat at the dining table. It was the first meal they'd had in here since Marcus had painted it Tuscan Gold.

"And this food looks so good," said Marcus, smacking his lips.

"You cooked all this?" Edmond's eyes grew wide as he stared at Anna with an awed expression.

She grinned and nodded. "Enjoy!"

And it seemed that they did enjoy. And although Anna had never really enjoyed cooking and didn't think of herself as a natural cook— especially compared to her mom and aunt—it was fun to be praised by this crowd.

"Anyone seen Kendall?" asked Megan.

"No," said Lelani. "But I noticed her car's not in the garage."

"Probably shopping," said Marcus with a full mouth.

"I wonder what she'll think when she sees the place," said Lelani.

"She'll probably act like nothing's changed," replied Megan. "So far she seems generally unimpressed."

"She'd be impressed if she could see the increase in her property value," Marcus pointed out.

"What if she decides to sell it?" asked Edmond.

"She can't," said Megan. "At least not for a year."

"She made us all sign a one-year lease," Anna informed him.

"But leases were made to be broken," said Marcus. "And with Kendall, well, you just don't know."

"You don't think she'd do that, do you?" asked Megan with worried eyes.

"She can be a loose cannon sometimes," said Marcus.

"Let's not think about that now," said Lelani.

The others went back at work, and Anna applied herself to thoroughly cleaning the kitchen, taking her time to put things away in places where it seemed they really belonged. She wondered if Marcus could be right. What if Kendall did pull a stunt like deciding to sell her house after it was all fixed up? After all, she was unpredictable. Kendall had made so much noise a few nights ago that the neighbors called the cops. And then Kendall had made it perfectly clear that she wished she hadn't rented out her rooms. What if she did break the lease?

Anna hated the idea of moving back home. It would feel like such a defeat. Of course, her mom would be ecstatic. She'd probably say, "I told you so," and then throw a big party. And after that, she'd probably turn any of Anna's future plans to move out into a major battle. She'd hold this failure over Anna's head for a long time. Somehow, Anna had to get Kendall to see the sense in honoring the lease agreements. Even if she had to clean up after Kendall, even if she had to stop singing opera in the shower, Anna would have to try harder to get along. Too much was at stake now.

It was getting close to nine when Anna finished up in the kitchen, but she was hoping that the workers would be ready to hang up their tool-belts when she tempted them back to the dining room for a late dessert of freshly baked brownies and ice cream. Hopefully the sugar would make them sleepy and everyone could call it a night.

As it turned out, the sweets only fueled their engines. But at least she had more to clean up now. Anything to keep her from breaking another nail.

"Hey, when are you coming out to help pull up staples?" Edmond called from the living room. "I thought we could have a contest."

"In a minute," she said as she carefully rinsed another bowl and placed it in the dishwasher. Finally she could stall no longer, and she was forced back to the trenches of pulling out staples alongside Edmond. She quickly saw it was no contest. He was fast!

"You didn't tell us that Edmond was an Erlinger," said Marcus as he rolled some paint onto a living-room wall. This color was just a couple of shades lighter than the color he'd painted the dining room, and already it looked like a huge improvement over the crusty old beige.

"Yes, he works at Erlinger Books," she clarified. "I already told you that."

"But you didn't say he was part of the family," Marcus said.

Anna stopped from pulling up a staple and peered curiously at Edmond. "That's because he's not. Right?"

He sort of shrugged and focused on a tough staple.

"You're not part of the Erlinger family, are you?"

Now he looked slightly sheepish.

"Your name is Dubois," she reminded him.

Now he chuckled. "Yeah, well, my mom's name—rather her maiden name—was Betsy Erlinger."

"Betsy Erlinger?" This news stunned Anna.

"She's the oldest daughter of Richard E. Erlinger."

Anna cleared her throat. "So, your grandfather was the founder of Erlinger Books?"

He nodded. "Yeah, and your boss ... well, he's my uncle."

She actually smacked her forehead with the palm of her hand now. "That's just great," she said. "Wow, I can't imagine the things I've probably said to you about my boss, or should I say your Uncle Rick? Shall I turn in my resignation now or just wait for the pink slip?"

"It's okay," he said quickly. "Trust me, I totally agree with you about my uncle. He can be pretty uptight."

"And that must be why Felicia can't fire you like she fires everyone else."

He laughed now. "Actually, Felicia is probably afraid I'll try to take her job. My degree is in marketing. Not that I plan to give her the boot."

Anna felt so stupid. Not only had she been snooty to Edmond, thinking that she was his superior, but she'd put down members of his family as well. What an idiot! It's a wonder he even gave her the time of day. And yet here he was pulling out staples. Go figure.

When the clock turned past eleven, Anna was seriously tired. "Okay, you guys, I hate to be a party pooper," she told them. "But I had a long day and a long week and right now, I can hardly see straight."

Fortunately, they all agreed it was getting late.

"We better stop before we make some mistakes," said Megan. "We don't want to give Kendall any ammunition."

"It'll be interesting to see her reaction," said Marcus as he wrapped his paintbrush in plastic.

"I've never met this woman," said Edmond, "but anyone in her right mind would be deliriously happy."

"We're not sure about the state of her mind," Anna quietly told him. The others chuckled.

"Well, I can't speak for the others, but I'm coming back to finish this paint up tomorrow," Marcus promised Megan. "I don't like leaving a job undone."

"It would be nice to get it put back together before the work week starts," said Megan hopefully.

"And before Kendall comes home and throws a fit because all her furniture's out of place," added Anna.

"So you're sure she's not home now?" asked Marcus. "She might've sneaked in the front and gone straight up the stairs while we were having dessert."

"No," said Anna. "I went through the garage to take the garbage out, and her car was still gone."

"She's probably partying," said Marcus. "After all, it's a Saturday. Don't be surprised if you don't see her until Sunday morning. Make that Sunday afternoon."

Even so, as she got ready for bed, Anna felt slightly worried for Kendall. She blamed her concern on her own mother's constant retellings of frightening news reports about young women getting drugged at parties or bars, even raped, robbed, or murdered. Still, Anna felt pretty sure that Kendall could take care of herself. In fact, considering how Kendall had three renters as well as their various friends and relatives all donating their time to renovate her home while she was out partying … well, she just had to wonder who the genius was here.

"Kendall must've partied hardy last night," said Megan Sunday morning as the three of them convened for coffee and a breakfast of muffins and fruit that Anna had picked up at the grocery store during her dinner run. "Her car's still gone."

"Well, if she partied too hardy, you wouldn't expect her to be home this early anyway," said Lelani.

"At least we don't have to worry about waking up Grumpy," said Anna. Then she offered to clean up in the kitchen if they wanted to get to work.

"You're not fooling us with your KP routine," said Megan.

"Can you blame me?" Anna held up her hands to show off how many nails she'd broken. Right now it was five and counting.

"Maybe you should just clip them and join the club," said Lelani as she held up her hands. Then Megan held up hers.

"I know, I know."

"Just think," said Lelani. "We'll be mostly done by the end of the day. Then you can let them grow back."

"Plus you won't be smelling that nasty carpet anymore," promised Megan.

"And everything will look pretty," Lelani added.

"Almost as upscale and luxurious as Kendall's ad promised," said Anna, and they all laughed.

The whole place really turned a corner by midafternoon. With Gil, Marcus, and Edmond still helping, things moved quickly. Soon they put the living room back together and, without pet stains that needed to be disguised, Megan was able to rearrange the furniture, which really opened the place up and made it look nice.

They finished well before five o'clock. Oh, they still had to tackle the kitchen and the upstairs bathroom. But the other living spaces were painted and clean.

"No more nasty carpet," declared Megan after she and Anna rolled up the last strip from the upstairs hallway.

"Except for Kendall's room," Anna pointed out.

"That's her problem," said Megan.

"She hasn't come home, has she?" asked Anna as she put her ear to the door. "I mean, I haven't seen her."

"No one has. And Lelani tried her cell phone a couple of times, but it went straight to voice mail."

Anna knocked on the door now.

"What are you doing?" asked Megan.

"Well, I just got a creepy thought."

"What?" Megan came over and stood by her.

"What if … well, what if something happened to her. What if she's actually in there and, well, she isn't okay?"

Megan got a worried look. "But her car's not here," she pointed out.

Anna nodded. "That's true. But what if someone broke in here and did something, then stole her car?"

Megan actually laughed. "And you're a children's book editor? With your imagination, you should be editing murder mysteries."

Anna made a face. "You haven't met my mother."

"Hey, if it makes you feel better, why not just open the door and look?"

"Oh, I don't know." Anna sighed.

"Come on, Anna. If you really think there could be a rotting body in there, you should take a peek. Just to set your mind at ease."

"Fine," said Anna, knocking loudly on the door this time. "Anyone home?"

"Go ahead."

Slowly, cautiously, bracing herself for something gruesome, Anna opened the door and looked around.

"So?" said Megan.

"No dead bodies," said Anna. "But it is a pigsty in here."

Megan pushed the door open wider. "Wow, it almost does look like a burglar has been here."

"Kendall's not exactly tidy."

"But seriously," said Megan. "Look at those drawers dumped on the floor. And clothes still on hangers by the closet. It almost seems like someone really was in here looking for something, doesn't it?"

"Now who's being paranoid?" Anna teased. Although she had to admit that Megan was right. Something about this scene did look peculiar.

"Or she was just having a hard time finding the right outfit," said Megan.

"That could be," said Anna. "I've had times when I've gone through piles of clothes trying to put something together that looked good. Although I always thought that was just me. I figured someone like

Kendall probably just put on whatever and stepped out looking like, well, like Kendall."

"Yeah." Megan nodded. "I've had that exact same thought."

Later that night, the three girls were all in the living room, enjoying their new digs and a big bowl of popcorn and a chick flick on Lifetime, when a local news blurb mentioned a missing young woman with, "More at eleven."

"You think they're talking about Kendall?" Anna joked, but the question was barely out of her mouth when she actually started to wonder.

"She's still not home?" asked Megan, who had taken an evening nap.

"Her car's not here," said Lelani.

"Her room's still empty. Well, other than the mess."

Then Megan told Lelani about the state of Kendall's room. "It almost looked like someone had broken in to look for something." They discussed the possibilities and started to get somewhat worried.

"How long has it been since anyone has seen her?" asked Anna finally. The movie was back on, but no one seemed that interested.

"It's been days," said Lelani. "Like maybe Wednesday night?"

"Marcus saw her Thursday," said Megan.

"Anyone since then?" asked Anna, feeling like a detective.

Lelani and Megan both shook their heads. And so, despite being tired after a long working weekend, they stayed up to watch the local news.

"It's happened again," said the reporter in a serious tone. "The third young woman in less than a year has just been reported as missing. Portland State senior Tracy Stewart has been missing since Wednesday." Photos of a pretty blonde woman flashed across the screen. "Friends say this is uncharacteristic of this dean's list student. Miss Stewart attended one morning class on Wednesday and has not been seen by classmates or friends since. According to police sources, a suspicious male was seen lurking around the dormitory where Miss Stewart lives. The suspect is described to be a white male, about six feet tall, in his forties, dressed in dark colored sweats, wearing a short stubble beard. No determination has been made to link the disappearance of Miss Stewart to the other missing women, but the FBI is investigating this possibility. Any information on the suspect or the possible whereabouts of Tracy Stewart should be reported to local authorities immediately."

Megan turned the sound down. "Well, it's not Kendall. But it is kind of weird."

Anna nodded, thinking that her mother had probably just watched this same newscast, and Anna could count on hearing from her first thing tomorrow morning. Anna just hoped that Gil hadn't said anything about Kendall not being around. No doubt Anna's mother would go into a serious meltdown over that. Not that Anna didn't feel worried herself. She did. Three college girls missing in this short of a time was frightening.

Megan was holding up a hand and counting on her fingers. "Okay, Friday, Saturday, Sunday. That's three days since any of us has seen Kendall. Right?"

Lelani nodded with a somber expression.

"Should we call someone?" asked Anna in a voice that came out kind of squeaky.

"I don't know," said Megan. "I mean, she could be staying with someone, maybe her friend Amelia."

"Or someone in her family," suggested Anna hopefully.

"And just because a college student is missing," said Lelani, "doesn't mean that anything has happened to Kendall."

"And you've tried calling her?" asked Anna.

"I left a message the second time," said Lelani. "I just wanted to let her know how the redecorating was coming. But she never called back."

"It's pretty late to be calling anyone tonight," said Megan. "I mean like her sister. And I'm not sure how long a person has to be gone before they're considered a missing person."

"Let's just deal with it in the morning," said Lelani.

"Right," agreed Megan.

Anna wasn't so sure. Still, what could they do really?

"And it would be like Kendall to take off like that," Megan pointed out, "just to jerk us around a little."

"Yes," agreed Lelani. "I'll bet you're right."

Still, Anna wasn't so sure when she finally went to bed. And just to be safe, she pushed her TV cabinet in front of the door. Then she hoped there wouldn't be a fire tonight. Fine, maybe her mother was right! Maybe this world wasn't a safe place for vulnerable young women. Oh, why hadn't Anna listened?

# Lelani

"Did you hear the rest of the news about the latest missing girl?" asked Megan as she poured Lelani a cup of coffee Monday morning. "It was on the radio this morning."

"What?" asked Lelani.

"She was a part-time worker at Nordstrom."

"Really?" Lelani tried to remember the girl's face. "I don't think I know her."

"It was probably a different store," said Megan.

"What about Kendall?" asked Lelani. "Do you think she's okay? Do you think we should do something?"

"I don't know. Anna was asking about her this morning too. She just left for work and seemed a little upset by all this."

"It is upsetting. Three girls reported missing, and now Kendall is gone."

"I promised Anna that I'd call Kendall's sister Kate. I just didn't want to call her too early. I mean, I don't want to upset her, especially if it's nothing, which I'm sure it must be."

"Well, it's after eight," said Lelani. "That's not too early, is it?"

Megan already had Kate's business card out, and Lelani stood by and listened as she made the call. Megan handled it in a very matter-of-fact way, and Lelani could tell that she was trying to act as if they weren't too worried.

"I just thought you should know," Megan finally said. "We didn't actually realize she was really gone until yesterday. It's been pretty busy here what with the renovations and all." She paused to listen. "Yes, the work is almost done and it does look nice." She paused again. "Yes, I'll let you know when she comes home. Yes, I'm sure she's just fine. Let me know if you hear from her though. Thanks."

"She hasn't seen her?" Lelani guessed.

"Nope. And she doesn't seem the least bit worried. She said it's not unusual for Kendall to disappear for a day or two."

"Or three or four?"

"Yeah." Megan shrugged. "I don't know."

"Had she heard about the other missing girl?"

"She mentioned it."

"And she didn't think Kendall could be in trouble?"

"She seemed genuinely unconcerned. And she knows Kendall better than we do. She also mentioned that it's unlikely two girls would be abducted on the same weekend."

"I suppose," said Lelani hoping Kate was right. "Unless the abductor was on some kind of spree."

Megan said she'd stay in touch and left for work, and suddenly Lelani felt uncomfortable being alone in the house. She knew it was silly, but all this talk of abducted young women was unsettling.

Lelani decided to head out to work early. She'd get her second cup of coffee in the employees' lounge today. But she carefully checked the locks on the doors before she left. No sense inviting problems.

Naturally, it seemed that everyone in the employees' lounge was talking about this missing girl. The hot topic of the day was Tracy Stewart, the pretty college coed who used to work at Nordstrom. Lelani sat back on one of the couches and listened.

"Did you know her, Geoff?" asked Sara from the children's department. "You worked at the downtown store."

"I remember her," said Geoff. "She worked in the men's department for a while and she seemed really nice—and smart."

"Didn't Mr. Mean work at the downtown store too?" Beth from lingerie asked in a snide tone.

Geoff made a face and looked over his shoulder. "Yes, and if I knew he'd transferred here, I would've tried for a different store."

"Poor you," said Beth mockingly.

"I wonder if he knew the girl," said a guy who worked in shoes.

"Who?" asked Sara.

"Mr. Mean."

Beth got a suspicious look now. "Doesn't Mr. Mean take his days off in the middle of the week?"

"Yeah, right, Beth," said Geoff. "Mr. Mean probably kidnapped Tracy."

"Did you hear the description of the suspect?" asked Sara.

Lelani felt sick to her stomach. She stood and gave the others what she hoped was a sobering look. Then she turned and marched out, punching in early. She didn't care. She couldn't stand to listen to them be so catty and cruel.

Unfortunately, their little morsel of gossip seemed to catch on. Throughout the day, Lelani heard various cruel remarks about how Mr. Green was probably a suspect in the case. Although she tried to act disgusted by these comments, the wildfire spread anyway. She was so relieved when her shift ended.

As she walked home, she wondered about Kendall. Despite her personal feelings toward Kendall, Lelani seriously hoped that she would be home by now. Even if she was in a bad mood, Lelani would be happy to see her.

But by dinnertime, no one had seen or heard a word from Kendall. And now they were all seriously worried.

"Even though Kate didn't seem that concerned, I wonder if we should call the police," said Megan.

"I think we should," declared Anna.

Lelani nodded sadly.

"If nothing else, it might get Kendall's attention if she saw herself on the evening news."

"Alongside that unfortunate college girl," said Anna, shaking her head.

"That girl was all everyone was talking about at work today," Lelani told them.

"Did anyone know her?"

"Yes. A couple of employees had worked with Tracy at the downtown store. To make matters worse, people started insinuating that poor Mr. Green could have something to do with it."

"Your friend?" said Megan indignantly.

"Yes. It's like everyone wants to hate him, to make him into the bad guy. It's so disturbing."

"Wasn't Mr. Green here on Thursday?" asked Megan.

"Well, yes." Lelani nodded slowly. "He and his brother-in-law delivered my furniture."

Megan had a strange look now, not so different from the employees' expressions. "You don't think?"

"No," said Lelani quickly. "Of course not."

"It does seem strangely coincidental," said Anna with suspicion in her dark eyes.

"What are you suggesting?" asked Lelani in a strained voice. She couldn't believe her friends and roommates would suggest such a thing.

"It's just sort of weird," said Megan. "Don't you think?"

"I don't know." Lelani sighed loudly. "Mr. Green is a nice guy."

"What does he look like?" asked Anna suddenly.

"I don't know."

"Come on," urged Anna. "Just tell us and maybe we'll feel better."

"Yes," said Megan. "Like how old is he?"

"Probably in his forties," admitted Lelani. "And he's about six feet tall and, yes, he's a white guy. But there are probably thousands of men who fit that description in the Portland metro area."

Anna looked truly scared now. "And Mr. Green was in this house on Thursday?"

Lelani nodded again. Her throat felt tight and dry. "I loaned him my key."

"Your key?" said Anna with alarm. "So he could've made a copy?"

"But he wouldn't," protested Lelani. "He's a really nice guy. If you knew him, you wouldn't be a bit concerned."

"But you said all your coworkers hate him," Megan pointed out. "That they call him Mr. Mean."

"But he's nice to me."

"I'm calling the police right now," said Anna, standing.

Tears were streaming down Lelani's cheeks. Had she made some huge, horrible mistake? Good grief, Lelani was no fool. She knew that just because a person looked trustworthy didn't make him so. She knew that there were serial killers out there who won their victims over first, guys who came across like a best friend before they brutally raped and murdered a woman. She knew better!

"It's okay," said Megan, placing a hand on Lelani's shoulder. "We'll get the locks changed if we need to."

Now Lelani was sobbing. "I can't believe how stupid I am."

"You're not stupid."

"I am. I am." She buried her face in her hands now. She could hear Anna on the phone, sounding slightly hysterical as she told whoever was on the other end that their roommate had been missing for almost five days. And then she mentioned Mr. Green and how he had known the missing girl Tracy Stewart, and how he had been in their house on the same day that Kendall disappeared.

Lelani felt so sick she thought she was going to throw up. She ran to the bathroom and with shaking knees just stood over the toilet, still crying. Megan's hand was on her back now. "It's okay," she said soothingly. "This isn't your fault."

"It is," sobbed Lelani. "I am so stupid."

Megan continued to talk to her, calming her down until finally Lelani was sitting on the edge of the tub. "It's not the first stupid thing I've done," she admitted. "But it might be the stupidest."

"Everyone makes mistakes," said Megan. "It's going to be okay."

"I just feel so responsible. I never thought that Mr. Green would—"

"The police are here," said Anna. "They just pulled up."

"I better call Kate," said Megan. "You guys go and talk to them. I'll be out in a couple of minutes."

"I'm sorry, Anna," said Lelani as they went to the door. "If I put you in any danger, I am so sorry."

Before long, an officer who introduced himself as Detective Arnold was questioning all three of the girls in the living room. They answered his questions as best they could, but it was a challenge. They really hadn't known Kendall that long. And they really didn't know her friends. But they told him everything they could think of that might be helpful, and Lelani answered all the questions regarding Mr. Green with complete honesty.

"He just honestly seemed like a nice person to me," she admitted. "A lot of the employees don't like him because he's kind of hardnosed about the rules. But that's his job. I always found him to be fair and kind." She started to cry again. "I just can't imagine he would do something—like—like this."

Then Detective Arnold and his partner went up to look around Kendall's room and the rest of the house. They asked the girls a few more questions and when they were satisfied that they'd gathered all the information available, they finally left.

"We'll be speaking to Miss Weis's sister next," the detective said as he gave them each a business card. "If any of you thinks of anything else, please, give me a call."

"And you'll let us know if you hear anything?" asked Megan.

"Yes. And, by the way, I recommend you get those locks changed, or new deadbolts installed."

"Do you think we're safe staying here?" asked Anna.

"Most likely," he told them. "But be careful."

"What about Lelani?" asked Megan. "She works with Mr. Green. Is she safe there?"

"We'll be questioning him soon."

"Will he know that I talked to you?" asked Lelani.

"We'll be discreet." And then they left.

"Maybe we shouldn't stay here tonight," said Anna. "Maybe it's not safe."

"I wish we had a dog," said Megan.

"Or security alarms," said Anna.

"I'm so sorry," said Lelani. "If this is related to Mr. Green … if this is my fault …"

"You can't keep blaming yourself," said Megan.

"That's right," said Anna. "How were you to know that Mr. Green was a—"

"We don't know that he's anything," said Megan. "Remember, innocent until proven guilty. Chances are he is innocent too."

"Maybe." But Anna didn't look convinced. She was pacing and wringing her hands now. "I really don't want to go home," she told them. "Because my mom will have a fit. I'll never be able to live away from home until I get married."

"I'm not going home," declared Megan.

"I'm not going back to my aunt's," said Lelani.

"I know!" Anna held up her phone. "I'll ask Gil to come over. He can sleep on the couch and protect us."

"Protect us?" Megan looked skeptical. "What's Gil going to do to protect us, Anna?"

Anna got a big grin. "Gil is an expert marksman. He has guns."

"Guns?" Lelani felt alarmed now. "Isn't that dangerous?"

"Only if you don't know what you're doing. Gil is well trained and very safe." She was already dialing, and the next thing they knew, she was telling Gil the whole story.

"Really?" she said hopefully. "You don't mind?" She nodded at the other girls. "Thank you! And, oh yeah, don't tell Mom, okay? She's already freaking out over the other missing girl from last week. If she knew Kendall was missing too, she'd probably come over here and drag me home." Then she hung up. "Reinforcements are coming."

"And you'll sleep okay knowing Gil is here?" asked Lelani.

"Oh, yeah." Anna nodded firmly.

Gil arrived at about nine—armed and dangerous. Well, dangerous to any potential intruders.

"You're sure you know how to use that thing safely?" asked Lelani as Gil examined what looked like a very lethal weapon.

"You bet."

"Don't worry," said Anna as she headed for the stairs. "He's won all kinds of awards and things. We're in good hands."

"I'm going to bed too," announced Megan. "I'm not worried."

"It's not that I'm worried," Lelani explained to Gil. "It's more that I feel responsible. Like if I hadn't been so stupid—giving a key to Mr. Green—well, we wouldn't be in such a mess."

"You don't know for sure that you're in a mess, Lelani," Gil said.

"It feels like a mess to me."

"I'm sure it sounds trite, Lelani, but sometimes it really is the darkest before the dawn." Then Gil told her about some of his most frightening moments and some of the problems he had faced, including a time when he was cornered in an alley by several racist guys who hated Mexicans. Somehow—he thought maybe an angel was involved—he managed to get away with only a few bruises. Certainly his challenges were different from hers, but she felt touched that he trusted her enough to be transparent with her.

To her surprise, she started to tell Gil more about herself. She told him about having a child that her parents were raising and why she quit med school.

"Emma's father was a doctor," she admitted. "A married doctor. His name is Ben."

Gil nodded, his eyes filled with concern.

"I didn't know he was married—not that it made it right. But the way he acted, the things he said to me, well, I just never even considered that he had a wife. He didn't wear a ring, and I never saw her. Oh, I knew it was wrong to get involved like that with anyone. But I was kind of swept off my feet.

"Then when I found out he was married, I was crushed. And when he found out I was pregnant, he was furious. He thought I'd done it on purpose. He thought I was going to blackmail him. And then he turned on me."

"That must've been hard."

"It was. He insisted that I get an abortion. But I don't believe in that. And when I refused, he threatened me. I didn't know what to do. He was a powerful person. I was just a med student. A pregnant med student."

"So that's why you took the baby to your parents?"

"I went home to figure things out. And to escape," she continued, glad to let this story out. "I thought my parents would help me. But they were so angry. And they were disappointed, and ashamed. I had been valedictorian of my high school class. I'd had scholarships. Everyone expected great things from me. I let them all down.

"Once my pregnancy started to show, my parents were embarrassed by me. They didn't want me to leave the house. And when I told them I wanted to give the baby up for adoption, my mom threw a fit. And that's when the really horrible fights began."

"She wanted you to keep the baby?"

"Absolutely. And it's not that I don't want children, but I just wasn't ready. Finally my parents gave me an ultimatum. I was to let my mother care for the baby for one year while I came to live here in the mainland, and then we would decide."

Gil frowned. "Wow, that seems a little harsh."

"Do you think so?"

"That's a lot of pressure to put on a person."

She nodded. "But I agreed."

"And how do you feel about it now? Do you miss your baby?"

"I was never really around her," admitted Lelani. "My mom hired a nanny, and as soon as I was well enough to leave, my dad handed me a plane ticket and a check and basically said aloha."

"Doesn't that mean hello?"

"And good-bye."

"Oh."

"I haven't told Anna or Megan these things," she admitted. "I can't believe I told you, Gil. I think this whole thing with Kendall missing … the other woman … and Mr. Green. It's like I just snapped."

Gil reached over and placed his hand on hers. "Well, you're safe to snap with me, Lelani. But you should probably go get some rest now."

She nodded. And she was tired. Seriously tired. She just hoped that her nightmares wouldn't be back tonight. It was reassuring to know that Gil was here. That he was keeping guard for them tonight. Maybe he was younger than she, but he was a good guy, and mature for his age. Any girl would be lucky to get a guy like that.

# Kendall

"My key card isn't working," Kendall informed the desk clerk Tuesday afternoon. She frowned as she set her shopping bags on the floor and waited for an apology. She couldn't believe she'd gone all the way up to her room, lugging these packages, only to discover the stupid key card had malfunctioned. Just for that she should force the desk clerk to carry her bags up for her on the next trip. Then she'd take another nice bubble bath and order room service for dinner. Perhaps after that she'd feel revived enough to go out partying again.

"It seems that we need you to let us run a new credit card for you, Miss Weis." He smiled. "Apparently, the card you gave us is full."

"Full?"

"As in maxed out."

Kendall blinked. Had she really spent $5,000 already? "Are you certain?"

"I can run a printout for you if you like. A list of room charges." He was looking at his computer screen. "It's a rather long list. Have you been entertaining a lot?"

"No," she snapped. "I don't need a printout." She dug through her purse to find her billfold, then pulled out a card that she thought had some room left on it. "Here." She shoved it at him. "This should work."

But it was taking a long time. So she drummed her freshly manicured fingernails on the marble desktop. What was wrong with these people? Hadn't they ever heard of customer service?

"Sorry, Miss Weis. That card was declined as well."

She opened her wallet again. "Try this one." And again it was rejected. After several cards, she was seriously rattled. "What am I supposed to do?" she asked in a low voice, noticing that other people in the lobby seemed to be gathering, standing around not-so-discreetly and observing this little fiasco.

"Martin will escort you to your room," he said. "There you will collect your things and be escorted to your car."

"Oh." She nodded, thinking that wasn't too terrible. Maybe Martin would carry her packages too.

"And our collection services will be in touch with you."

"Right." She nodded, trying to absorb this information as she waited for Martin to join her. Instead of a bellboy, Martin was a rather big guy. He looked more like a security guard, plus he did not offer to carry her packages. And then, when he let her inside her room, he stood over her like a sentry, like he thought she might steal something. Like what? The towels?

Still, she hurried to pack her clothes and shoes, which naturally didn't fit into her original luggage. Eventually, Martin called down for the assistance of a luggage cart, and when it arrived and was finally loaded, he escorted her grimly to the parking lot below the building. It was clear that this ill-mannered man did not approve of guests who stiffed the hotel, and he severely lacked people skills. Perhaps that's why he worked as a security guard. She did not tip him.

Once in her car, Kendall didn't know what to do or where to go. She'd already seen a blurb about herself on the news—reportedly missing and possibly connected to the coinciding disappearance of a college coed. She'd been delighted by the publicity, despite the fact that they'd used some less than flattering photos. Really, she should've left some good ones out on her dresser. Anyway, she just hoped that this little drama would teach those nasty roommates of hers a lesson. Not to mention her sister Kate and the rest of her family—those supposed loved ones who had left her high and dry.

She didn't include her grandmother in this group, though. And she really wouldn't want Nana to be worried. Not that it was likely. Nana, while not completely senile, had long since stopped paying attention to current events and seldom if ever watched the news. Other than *Wheel of Fortune* and *Jeopardy!*, Nana didn't care for TV. She said it made her head hurt.

Suddenly, Kendall knew just where she would go. Just for the night perhaps, or until she figured this thing out a little better.

"What are you doing here?" asked Nana when she opened the door to see Kendall, bags in hand, standing there.

"Slumber party," announced Kendall with a big smile. "You know it's my birthday this week, and I thought it would be fun to spend some time with you."

"With me?" Nana blinked, then looked slightly suspicious.

Now Kendall feigned a hurt expression. "You don't want me here?"

"Where will you sleep?"

Kendall pointed to the rose-colored loveseat tucked between a rocking chair and the small TV. "Right there."

"I don't understand why you want to stay in this little room when you've got my nice big house to go home to, Kendall."

"I thought it would be fun," said Kendall in a hurt voice. "But if you don't want me here, I guess I can just spend my birthday all alone. Mom and Dad left me. Kate is mad at me. And now you don't want me either."

"No, no," said her grandmother, waving her into the small area. "I'm glad to see you. We'll spend your birthday together." She looked up at the clock. "You're just in time for dinner."

So Kendall and Nana went down to the dining hall, which smelled like overcooked cauliflower, and ate a somewhat tasteless dinner with all the other old people. Kendall was the belle of the ball. Everyone wanted to know who she was, and when Nana explained that it was her birthday and that she'd come to celebrate, they made an even bigger fuss over her. In some ways, Kendall thought she could get used to this. The attention anyway. The food pretty much sucked. After that, she and Nana went back to the tiny apartment, where they watched Nana's favorite two game shows. Then Nana announced she was tired and toddled off to bed.

Kendall turned the TV back on only to see that Nana didn't have cable. She got only three channels and not that well. Bummer. Then she snooped around Nana's tiny kitchenette for food, foraging out a box of stale saltine crackers, some instant soup mixes, and a bag of prunes. She passed on the soup but thought the crackers and prunes should do the trick. She hadn't purged in a day or two and was starting to feel slightly bloated.

Unfortunately, that only managed to kill an hour. It was only eight thirty and Kendall was bored, bored, bored. Why had she come here anyway? Oh, yeah, she remembered, she was broke.

Kendall tried to make herself comfortable on the loveseat and, after tossing and turning for about an hour, wondered if playing the missing blonde debutante was worth it. Then she had to ask herself why she was the one hiding out, as if she were some kind of criminal. She had done nothing wrong. It was those losers back at her house who should be suffering.

Still, if her little disappearing act was upsetting them, maybe it would be worth it. Hopefully they'd get so worried or fed up or whatever that they'd all want their leases canceled by the time she went home. And then she could have her house back—all to herself.

Of course, she might need to get a job then. She'd have to figure out some ways to get some money. But if Kendall hated anything worse than being bored, it was work. Work was like boredom times three. Amelia had jokingly suggested that Kendall get herself a sugar daddy. But that was disgusting. There had to be some other way to make ends meet.

She was behind on her bills. Even more so after her little birthday getaway got cut short. Without her parents' help, which they swore they would never give her again, she would never be able to pay off those bills. She wondered how hard it was to file for bankruptcy. But what if they took her house away? Where would she live then? Certainly not here. Sharing this apartment with her grandmother had gotten old fast. Still, she should be able to talk Nana into giving her some money, perhaps for her birthday.

Kendall so wanted a pink lady right now or even a glass of that sleazy minibar wine. But there was no place to get a drink here. And a security guard would probably stop her if she tried to come or go at this time of night. Finally, she opted for her prescription sleeping pills, taking four to be sure that she was fully knocked out. No way did she want to wake up and hear her grandmother snoring tonight. Life was bad enough without having your sleep disturbed. Hopefully she would think of a way out of this in the morning.

❧

"Is she okay?" asked a fuzzy male voice. Then someone grabbed her shoulder and shook her.

"Wake up, Kendall," snapped a woman's voice.

"Should we call for medical assistance? the man asked.

Finally Kendall opened her eyes, blinking in a blurry attempt to see what appeared to be her sister Kate and a uniformed policeman hovering over her.

"She's fine," said Kate in her characteristic grumpy voice. "Physically anyway. There's no telling about the condition of her brain."

"What's going on?" demanded Kendall. She sat up, trying to remember where she was, then realized she was on what appeared to be Nana's rose-colored loveseat. And then she remembered the slumber-party idea. She glanced past her scowling sister to see Nana sitting calmly in the rocking chair, rocking and just glumly shaking her head.

"You turned me in?" Kendall asked her.

"I didn't know you were running from the law, Kendall."

"I'm not running from the law."

"Falsifying a missing person's report is a serious crime," the policeman said.

"I never falsified anything," claimed Kendall. "What are you talking about?"

"So you didn't know that you'd been filed as missing?" said Kate with obvious skepticism.

Kendall blinked as if completely astonished by this. "I'm missing?"

"Where have you been the past week?"

"I took a little birthday vacation," she said innocently.

"And you're not aware that everyone has been looking for you? You didn't know that good people have been extremely worried over your whereabouts, young lady?" the cop persisted.

"No." Kendall slowly shook her head. "I had no idea, Officer. I was just a little stressed out. I just needed a little break. That's all."

"Why are you here with Nana?" asked Kate.

"We were having a slumber party." Kendall frowned at her grandmother.

"Apparently *you* were having quite a slumber party," said Kate. "Nana said you were out cold. She couldn't even wake you for breakfast, and when she went to the dining hall without you, a friend of hers mentioned that he'd seen your picture on the news. You can imagine how that must have frightened her."

"I'm not frightened," snapped her grandmother. "I just want to get to the bottom of this nonsense."

"Well, others were frightened," said Kate. "That other girl who went missing last weekend has been found—rather her body was found."

"And we thought you might be next in line," said the cop.

"Well, I'm obviously not."

"Obviously not." Kate sounded almost disappointed.

"So, what do you want to do with her?" asked the cop.

"Me?" Kate held up her hands like she wanted nothing to do with her.

"She can't stay here," said the cop.

"She's not old enough," said Nana. "Besides, she snores."

"I snore?" Kendall narrowed her eyes. "You should talk."

"I recommend that you take her home with you," the cop told Kate.

"Why?" demanded Kate.

"You're her closest relative, right?"

"Yes, but—"

"I think she needs a psychological evaluation."

"I couldn't agree more," said Kate, "but why is that *my* problem?"

"You're her sister?"

"Unfortunately."

"When we're assured that she is not a danger to herself or anyone else, then she can come and go as she pleases; in the meantime, I want to sign her over to your supervision along with a recommendation that she gets a complete evaluation."

"Can't you just put her in jail?"

He snickered. "Probably teach her a good lesson. But I don't have any legal grounds for it."

"How long will it take to get this evaluation set up?" asked Kate.

"I'll put a call in this morning. Maybe as soon as tomorrow. I'll let you know."

"Okay." Kate pulled Kendall to her feet. "Come on, let's go, little sister."

Before she could protest too much, the cop and Kate had gathered up her things, shoved them into her bags, told Nana good-bye, and were now escorting her out to Kate's Lexus.

"What about my car?" demanded Kendall, pointing over to where it was parked in the visitors' section.

"It'll be fine here," said the cop. "I'll inform the security guard now that it's staying overnight again."

"But what about—"

"Come on, Kendall," said Kate. "You are really trying my patience today."

"Your patience?" Kendall got into the passenger seat and crossed her arms across her front and sulked. "I'm the one who's suffering here."

"Right," said Kate. "It's always about you. Kendall. Kendall. Kendall."

The only thing good about being at Kate's house was that Kendall got an actual bedroom with a full-size bed and a TV with cable. A step up from her grandmother's place. On the other hand, she felt like a prisoner.

And she was bored. But while Kate was on the phone, she did manage to sneak a bottle of wine from the wine cabinet, and that helped to brighten her afternoon and pass the time a little.

As she finished off the pinot noir in front of late-night TV, she wondered if there might be some way to escape. She also wondered what they'd find in her "psychological evaluation" tomorrow. Kate had informed her that she was scheduled. Not that she was worried. She felt certain that she was saner than most people. It was simply that she didn't put up with things. She was not the kind of girl who would roll over and take it. Kendall was a fighter. And a winner. Not unlike Paris or Nicole or Lindsay ... or any of those other beautiful rich girls that the world bowed down to on a regular basis. Kendall *knew* that she was special. She just wished that the people around her would start to get it.

Thirty-one

# Megan

"I thought you'd like to know that Kendall has been found." Kate called Megan on Wednesday just before noon.

"Is she okay?"

"She's perfectly fine physically. Although I can't vouch for her mental state."

"Really?"

"Well, not *really* really. But she is a serious piece of work. And sometimes, like most of the time, it's hard to believe that we're related."

"Where is she?" asked Megan.

"The police asked me to keep her in my custody."

"The police? Is she in some kind of trouble?"

"It depends. But probably not. However, in light of that whole disappearance thing they have suggested a psychological evaluation."

"That should be interesting."

"It's probably not a bad idea and it might give her a reality check. Anyway, I'll keep her here with me until the evaluation tomorrow afternoon. Then, unless someone wants to lock her up, I'll take her back to her house."

"Surely, no one would want to lock her up." Megan thought that seemed a bit harsh.

"You mean besides me?"

Megan didn't know what to say.

"I must sound like a horrid sister."

"Oh, I don't know." The truth was, Megan did know that Kendall was a handful. But she'd been praying for Kendall a lot these past days. Consequently she felt some compassion for her. Funny how that worked.

"Anyway, I'll let you know how her evaluation goes." Kate laughed now. "Ironically, it's her birthday tomorrow."

"Tomorrow is her birthday?"

"Yes. We found her at our grandmother's assisted-living place, saying she wanted to celebrate her birthday with Nana."

Megan thought that sounded pretty weird but didn't say so. Maybe Kendall really did need to get her head examined. "Let me know how it goes tomorrow," she finally said. "And if she's coming home."

Kate sighed. "If she does, I can't help but feel sorry for you girls, having to put up with her."

"Maybe she just needs to be loved," said Megan. Then Kate laughed and Megan wished she hadn't said that.

"Talk to you later."

Megan tried to imagine how it would feel to be in Kendall's shoes. How would it be to have parents who had sold their home and fled to escape you? Or an older sister who thought you were crazy? Certainly, Kendall had brought some of this, maybe even most of it, on herself. But perhaps her collective behavior was just one great big cry for help. Or maybe it was just plain narcissistic selfishness. Whatever it was, Megan was going to keep praying for Kendall. And she was going to hope for the best. In the meantime, she wanted to let Anna and Lelani know that Kendall was safe. She reached Anna at her desk at work, quickly relaying the news.

"I'm so relieved," said Anna. "My mother has been calling my cell phone nonstop since she heard that it was Kendall who was missing."

"And you'll let Gil know too?"

"Yes. But he'll probably be disappointed that he doesn't get to play armed guard tonight. He liked spending time with Lelani."

"Speaking of Lelani, I still need to call her."

"And I have a meeting. You can fill me in on the details over dinner. Tonight will be my treat. I'll have the restaurant drop something by."

"Sounds good." Then Megan called Nordstrom but had to leave a message for Lelani to return her call. "It's somewhat urgent," she told the woman on the phone.

It was only about ten minutes later that Lelani called. "Is it about Kendall?" she asked breathlessly.

"Yes. She's been found!"

"Is she okay?"

"I think so." Then Megan explained about the evaluation.

"Do they really think she's crazy?"

"I guess they're concerned."

"Oh, Mr. Green will be so relieved. It's his day off, but I'll have to call and tell him the good news."

"I figured he would've been off the hook after the police took the murder suspect into custody yesterday."

"You'd think so. But some employees here were ready to convict him."

"Too bad."

"Yes. I'll have to start spreading the word that he had nothing to do with any of it."

"I'm sure you must feel relieved too," said Megan. Lelani had been so torn the past couple of days. On one hand she had remained somewhat loyal to Mr. Green, feeling certain that he couldn't have done something so horrific. But on the other hand, she was nervous, questioning herself and her judgment and feeling that she would be the one to blame if Kendall had been harmed.

"You can't imagine how relieved I am." Lelani let out a big sigh. "I'm happy that Kendall's okay. And happy that this clears Mr. Green. Poor guy."

"They didn't actually lock him up, did they?" asked Megan.

"No, but they questioned him. Fortunately, he had no idea who had given his name to the police and I didn't say a word."

"Yeah ... that would've been awkward."

"Especially after he's been so kind to me."

"Anyway, Anna is bringing home dinner." Megan knew she needed to get back to work. "And I can fill you guys in on anything else then, okay?"

"Sounds great. Thanks for letting me know."

Later, when they sat down to dinner, Megan told Anna and Lelani about her conversation with Kate. "I can understand her frustration," she admitted as she finished up. "But Kendall is her sister. You'd think she might show a little more compassion."

"Did she say where Kendall had been this past week?" asked Anna.

"She was found at her grandmother's assisted-living place."

Lelani looked stunned. "Do you really think Kendall stayed there the whole time?"

"It seems a little weird."

"No wonder they think she's crazy," said Anna.

"Oh, yeah," said Megan. "And tomorrow's her birthday."

"Really?"

"Kate thought it was ironic that Kendall would be getting her head examined on her birthday."

"That's pretty sad," said Lelani.

"Yeah," agreed Anna. "I'm even starting to feel sorry for her."

"What if they declare her insane or incompetent?" asked Lelani. "Do you think we'll be able to stay here?"

"I guess that would be up to the grandmother," said Megan.

"Oh, she's not crazy," said Anna with confidence. "She's just spoiled and shallow and selfish and lazy and eccentric. But not she's not crazy."

"What makes you so sure?"

Anna shrugged. "Just a feeling." Then Anna made a sheepish smile. "I guess I can relate to her—on some levels—because I'm a little spoiled too. And I've been known to have tantrums from time to time. Although I'd like to think I've outgrown them. But I could see that in Kendall. Besides, she's only twenty-two. She's got time to grow up."

"Twenty-three tomorrow," Lelani reminded her.

"Speaking of tomorrow," said Megan suddenly. "What if we put together a little birthday-slash-welcome-home party for her? Would that be weird?"

"No weirder than any of this," said Anna.

"I think it would be nice."

So they set about planning it, calling what few people they knew, including Kendall's friends Amelia and Arden, as well as Marcus and Edmond and Gil. Finally Megan called Kate.

"You're having a party for her?" Kate sounded incredulous.

"It is her birthday," Megan pointed out.

"But she's been such a brat."

"I know." Megan considered quoting the Bible to Kate, the part about loving your enemies or doing good to those who try to do you in, but then decided not to. "I know it probably sounds strange," she admitted. "But we just want to make Kendall feel like part of the family. Maybe it's our way of trying to get this next chapter with her off to a good start."

"You mean if there is a next chapter," Kate said.

"Right. But it is her birthday. No matter what happens tomorrow, it seems like she should be able to celebrate her birthday."

"I guess."

"We thought it would be fun if it could be a surprise," said Megan. "Like maybe you could bring her home at seven and we'll all be here."

"I suppose I could do that."

"And if there's anyone else you know who should come—like your grandmother or husband or whoever ..."

"Okay, Megan. I'll see what I can do. But I have to confess, I'm a little stunned by your willingness to let Kendall get away with this. I mean, you guys were pretty worried and everything, and Kendall could've prevented all that if she'd just called."

"I know. But we want to do this." Megan was thinking about the story of the prodigal son now, how he didn't deserve the welcome-home party that his dad gave him. Maybe this was different, but maybe it would make a difference too.

# Thirty-two

# Kendall

"This has been the worst birthday of my entire life," Kendall told the psychologist as he finished writing something down. He just nodded, peering at her over his glasses and acting like he understood, although she knew he didn't. He couldn't. No one ever seemed to understand her. Sometimes, like today, she didn't even understand herself. Like when he asked certain questions and the answers seemed painfully revealing and fairly embarrassing too. She had tried to be honest.

"So are you writing horrible things about me?" She leaned over his desk now, trying to peek at his notes. "Am I nuts?"

He closed his notebook and smiled at her in a sort of patient, benevolent way. "No, you're not any nuttier than most people."

She frowned. "Really?"

"Did you want to be?"

She shrugged. "I guess not."

"I can see by some of your test results that you're quite intelligent."

"I am?" She sat up straighter and brightened a bit.

"But you're an underachiever."

"Is that a nice word for *lazy?*"

"Perhaps. Or maybe you simply lack confidence or motivation."

"Or maybe I'm just plain lazy."

"I'm sure that's part of it."

She sighed. "Was this evaluation really necessary?"

"Maybe not. But at least they'll have something on record now, in case you decide to do anything that's, well, questionable."

"It's not like I broke the law," she said quickly. "I mean, I was aware that people were looking for me, but that wasn't exactly my fault, was it?"

"Was it?" He peered curiously at her.

She shrugged.

"Well, hopefully you've learned something from all this." He smiled again. It was the sort of smile a person might give a naughty child. "Hopefully, you'll be a bit more responsible if you decide to go AWOL again. Pick up the phone and let people know your whereabouts. It's a pain to worry a loved one. And it's selfish."

"I don't really want to be a pain," she confessed. "I mean, I do like having my own way, but I want people to like me too. I want to be respected."

"It's a two-way street."

"What?"

"Being liked and respected."

"Meaning I need to like and respect people."

He nodded.

"I try to do that," she persisted. "But I guess I want them to like and respect me first. Then I can like and respect them."

He kind of laughed. "That's how a child thinks, Kendall."

"Oh."

"Grown-up thinking, mature thinking, is willing to take the first step."

"Oh."

"I am going to recommend that you see a counselor, Kendall."

"Really?"

He handed her a business card. "Marjorie is an associate of mine. I think she could help you a lot."

"Meaning you think I *need* help?"

"What do you think?"

She shrugged and fiddled with her new Cartier bracelet, an early birthday present to herself.

"You just told me this was the worst birthday of your life, Kendall. So, how would you say that your life is going in general?"

"Not so well."

He smiled a bit bigger this time. "The first step in getting better is admitting there's a problem." He handed her the card. "Happy birthday."

Kate was reading *Newsweek* in the waiting room. She looked up with an expression of mild interest. "The men in the white coats aren't locking you up?"

Kendall rolled her eyes and held up the business card. "No, but I'm supposed to start seeing this shrink now."

Kate looked at the card, then nodded. "Sounds like a good plan to me."

"Can I go get my car now?" asked Kendall. "I'm sure you'll be delighted to get rid of me."

"First you're going to apologize to Nana," Kate said. "And then we'll stay and eat dinner with her so that all of Nana's friends can see that you're alive and well and not locked up in the loony bin."

"Fine," said Kendall. "Whatever. I just hope that no one's broken into my car by now. I have lots of good stuff in there."

"Yes, I'm sure you do." Kate shook her head. "You've probably done some major shopping during your little disappearing act."

Kendall just shrugged. Why did everyone think that they knew everything about her? And why did everyone treat her like a child? Maybe Marjorie the shrink would help her to figure these things out.

Yeah, right.

Neither of them spoke as Kate drove through the heavy commuter traffic. Kendall just gazed out the window and tried not to think about what she would say to her roommates when she finally got home. Kate had already told her that she'd informed them of her whereabouts, and Kendall suspected they would be pretty ticked at her. She hoped to sneak past them, go directly to her room, and then sleep in late tomorrow. Perhaps if she just laid low for a few days, the whole thing would blow over. And, if worse came to worst, she could always apologize. It seemed that Kate was going to ensure that she got some practice with Nana tonight. Not that Kendall wasn't willing to apologize to Nana. She would do that willingly. With everyone else, well, she would have to wait and see.

"What are you doing here?" Nana demanded when she opened the door.

"Hello to you too," said Kendall, pushing the door fully open. Then she hugged Nana as she burst into an apology. "Nana, I am so sorry that I crashed on you like that the other night. And I'm sorry if I upset or embarrassed you in front of your friends here. That was selfish and wrong and I am sorry." Then she let go of Nana and stepped back in time to see Kate blinking in surprise.

"Oh, that's all right," said Nana, grinning now. "You've made me a celebrity in this place. Everyone wanted to hear the story of my missing granddaughter. John Armstrong is just certain that you're a movie star. He swears he saw you on one of those Hollywood TV shows."

Kendall laughed. "Cool. I'd like to meet this John Armstrong."

"We thought we could have dinner with you, Nana," said Kate.

Nana looked shocked now. "Really? Both of you?"

"Is that okay?"

"Oh, I'm sure we can work it out." Nana was reaching for her purse now, linking arms with Kendall. "Well, come on, girls. We need to get going if we want a good table."

Okay, being a "star" in an old-folks' home wasn't the same as walking down the red carpet like Paris Hilton, but it wasn't that bad either. And when John Armstrong, a little bald man with a squeaky walker, asked her to autograph his dinner napkin, she just laughed and did it.

"Nana looks tired," said Kate as Kendall was still chatting with a small group of admirers. "How about if I walk Nana back to her room, okay?"

"Okay," said Kendall. She gave Nana a hug and told her she loved her. Then, deciding to take this apology business one step further, she hugged her older sister too. "I'm sorry for being a pain in the butt to you, Kate."

Kate looked slightly stunned but simply nodded.

"I'll try to do better, okay?"

"Okay."

Kendall stuck around to charm the old folks a bit longer, but the game shows started to come on TV, and she soon lost the attention of her little fan club. Knowing that Nana would be glued to her own TV by now, Kendall decided that it was time to go home and face the music. That is, unless, she could slip past her roommates unnoticed. Perhaps they had gone to bed—although that was wishful thinking. It was just a little past seven.

When she got home, it was obvious that her tenants were not in bed. In fact, the house was lit up and it appeared that, once again, her roommates had invited people over. Well, what was surprising about that? They'd already made themselves completely at home and kicked her out too. Where was she supposed to fit in anymore?

She slipped in from the garage, hoping that she might somehow get up the stairs without being noticed. She could tell by the messy kitchen that they were definitely entertaining tonight. And it was only Thursday.

She emerged from the kitchen, ready to make a dash up the stairs, when she heard everyone yell, "HAPPY BIRTHDAY, KENDALL!" And her three roommates were walking toward her with a big chocolate cake lit up with bright pink candles. And then they were all laughing and joking and greeting her, and Kendall felt pretty sure she was having some weird kind of hallucination or out-of-body experience. Was this for real?

"Welcome home," said Megan as she kissed Kendall on the cheek.

"Aloha!" said Lelani as she slipped an orchid lei around Kendall's neck.

"Happy birthday," said Anna with a big bright smile.

Kendall could not think of a single thing to say. She just stood there staring at the crowd in stunned silence. Several of her friends were there. And even Kate and Eric and Nana were here. How had they done that? And then she noticed her house—or was it her house? In some ways it was just as upside down as everything else. In place of that cruddy beige carpeting was a golden hardwood floor, and that old beige wall paint was now covered in a warm, sunny color that made it look bigger. She just shook her head in amazed wonder.

"I can't believe this," she finally said. "What is going on?"

"We're so glad that you're okay," said Lelani happily.

"We just wanted to welcome you home," added Anna.

Kendall was blinking back tears now. "I don't deserve this."

"Maybe not," said Megan. "But we did it anyway."

"I'm so sorry," said Kendall, wiping the tears that were now streaming down her cheeks. "I'm going to do better."

"And we're going to sing 'Happy Birthday' now," said Megan. "Start us off, Anna."

As the crowd belted out a boisterous version of "Happy Birthday" at the top of their lungs, Kendall thought that this might be her best birthday ever. And, if this was any kind of sign, it might turn out to be a very good year as well. Suddenly, it seemed entirely possible that she had been all wrong about her roommates.

## ... a little more ...

When a delightful concert comes to an end,

the orchestra might offer an encore.

When a fine meal comes to an end,

it's always nice to savor a bit of dessert.

When a great story comes to an end,

we think you may want to linger.

And so, we offer ...

**AfterWords**—just a little something more after you

have finished a David C. Cook novel.

We invite you to stay awhile in the story.

Thanks for reading!


Turn the page for ...


- **Discussion Questions**
- **A Conversation with Melody Carlson**
- **An Excerpt from *let them eat fruitcake***

# Discussion Questions

1. Kendall talks about her parents abandoning her. Do you think that's an accurate statement? Do you think Kendall really believes it's true?

2. Megan decides to confront Kendall because she felt her ad was misleading. Do you think she's being pushy? If you were in Megan's situation would you be able to have this conversation?

3. When Lelani shares her Nordstrom's employee discount with Megan, do you think she's being ethical? Why, or why not?

4. What does Marcus see in Megan that he doesn't see in Kendall?

5. Do you think Kendall is evil or just selfish? Does she have any redeeming qualities? If so, explain.

6. Which of the four girls are you most like? Why?

7. Megan seems interested in Marcus but is hesitant because he isn't a Christian. Have you ever been in this situation? How did you handle it?

8. Kendall comes across as very confident, but she actually has a lot of pain in her life. How does she attempt to deal with her pain?

9. Do you think conflict is always a part of living with other people? How do each of the four girls deal with conflict? How do you?

10. When Kendall's roommates throw her a welcome home party, how does this affect her? Do you think Kendall will change for the better in future books?

# A Conversation with Melody Carlson

**How did you come up with the idea for 86 Bloomberg Place?**

I think relationships between women are fascinating and so I created an ensemble cast of characters and threw them together in a shared house. Naturally, this raises all kinds of "problems," but that's what makes a story interesting. Having four very different young career women with completely different backgrounds all living under one roof is like putting a kettle on the stove and turning up the heat.

**Have you ever lived in a house with roommates? What sort of conflict did you have to deal with?**

I volunteered as a "short-term-assistant" missionary, teaching preschool in a foreign country (Papua New Guinea). During that time, I shared housing with three other single women all from different parts of the world. Let me say that it was very interesting and eye-opening and perhaps the hardest "trial" I faced on the foreign mission field.

**Each of the four girls at Bloomberg Place are dealing with loss on a very deep level. How does their living situation force them to face, rather than escape their problems?**

There's nothing like living in close proximity with others to bring our personal issues to the surface. Whether it's family, friends, or strangers, we tend to "rub against" each other when dwelling under the same roof. And even if it's a little painful, healing often follows. That's my goal with this series. To allow troubles and conflicts to surface, perhaps even get a little "ugly," and then see how the characters work through it.

**What would you say to readers who are dealing with a difficult roommate situation?**

I think most conflicts arise from a lack of understanding. Often we misjudge others and subsequently create "protective" walls that only make our situations worse. But I think empathy is a huge key to connecting with a difficult person. When we learn why people do what they do—whether they're suffering from a broken heart, a dysfunctional family, grief, or something else—we begin to see and interact with them in a whole new way. Sure, that person might not be you new best friend, but perhaps they won't be your worst enemy either.

**Can you tell us a little bit about what happens with the four girls in the next book?**

Well, readers who know me know that I don't outline my books. Like them, I want to be surprised by the story. So all I can say is that these four young women will continue getting acquainted, continue getting into misunderstandings, and hopefully they will get a little bit closer.

# Megan Abernathy

"I am back from the worst Thanksgiving ever!" declared Kendall. She peeled off her coat, discarding it on the sectional next to Megan.

"Too bad," said Megan with a speck of feigned interest. The truth was, she really didn't want to hear about Kendall's day. It wasn't as if Megan's had been particularly good. Before Kendall came in, she'd been absently watching the 49ers annihilate the Seattle Seahawks. The Seahawks were Megan's dad's favorite team, and if he were still alive, they'd be watching the fiasco together, commiserating. Also, this was the first Thanksgiving she'd spent alone—at least until Kendall walked in.

To be fair, it was her choice. Several weeks ago, she'd encouraged her mom to join a friend on a Mexican cruise during Thanksgiving week. And then Megan had declined Marcus's invitation to spend the holiday at the beach with his family. She wasn't ready for that.

"I am utterly exhausted." Kendall flopped down in the club chair, leaned her head back and sighed as if she'd just completed the Portland Marathon.

"And why is that?" asked Megan. She was trying not to be selfish, but it was hard to muster even a twinge of empathy for Kendall right now—perhaps because she'd been having her own little pity party. For a party of one.

"I don't know why I let Amelia talk me into going to their place. It was bad enough that she was cooking dinner, since she barely knows how to make toast, but she didn't bother to warn me that her sister and brother-in-law were bringing both their newborn baby *and* a teething toddler along."

"Did you think her sister would leave her children home?" ventured Megan. She muted the Doritos commercial, although so far the ads had been more entertaining than the actual football game.

"No, of course not. Although she might've considered hiring a babysitter to watch the little monsters in the other room so that the grown-ups could enjoy themselves. Or at least try. Not that we wouldn't have still heard the screaming brats. Who knew two small children could spoil things so badly?"

Megan nodded with sympathy that was about as genuine as Kendall's faux fur coat lying limply next to her like a slain polar bear. "So … it was a bit of a circus then?"

"It was like being held hostage at a screaming, pooping, puking baby fest." Kendall rolled her eyes dramatically. "Note to self: Never have children."

"And never attend holiday dinners where other people's children are present?"

Kendall nodded. "Absolutely."

Megan was about to make some sort of excuse to exit, but she heard the front door open, and then to her relief, Lelani came in.

"Hey, Lelani." Megan hoped she would join them. Kendall could continue to pour out her troubles on Lelani while Megan slipped off to her room.

"Hey, what's up?" Lelani took her time to remove and hang her navy wool coat on the hall tree, carefully unwinding her knitted scarf and hanging it neatly as well.

"Come tell us how your Thanksgiving went," urged Megan. "Poor Kendall's was a disaster."

Lelani sat down next to Megan. "My Thanksgiving was okay," she said without much enthusiasm.

"So everything is smoothed out with your aunt and uncle now?" asked Megan.

"As smoothed out as it can be." Despite her weak smile, Lelani seemed discouraged.

Lelani's aunt had accused her of flirting with her overweight, middle-aged, and balding uncle, which was preposterous, especially since Lelani was a beauty who could catch the eyes of most guys without even trying. Consequently, she had avoided her relatives for more than a month. Finally, the aunt had come forward and apologized to Lelani. Apparently one of her aunt's friends had gently hinted that the problem lay with her husband and not her niece.

"My aunt actually cornered me and begged me to move back in with them." Lelani sounded weary. "She wants me to help with the children in exchange for free rent."

"So you had to spend your day with children too?" asked Kendall with what seemed like sincere compassion. "I am *so* sorry."

"Actually, the children were great."

Kendall blinked. "Really?"

"Yes. It was the adults who drove me nuts. Honestly, I couldn't get away from there fast enough."

"Did you tell your aunt you were tied into a year-long lease?" asked Megan.

"I reminded her of that fact, but she seemed to think it was no big deal."

"No big deal to her," said Kendall with a sly grin. "But I plan to hold you to that lease."

Lelani sort of laughed. "That's sure not how you felt last month."

"Well, things change," said Kendall. "And I'm glad that you're both home. Now if we just had something good to eat." She glanced around. "Where's Anna?"

"Probably still with her family," said Lelani. "Come to think of it, I could probably still show up over there."

"Did Gil invite you?" asked Kendall.

Lelani nodded, then picked at the cuff of her silk blouse. "But I wasn't sure how his parents would react."

"They still don't know that you're dating?" asked Megan.

"We're not really dating," said Lelani quickly.

Kendall laughed. "If you're not dating, what do you call it?"

"Well . . . we can't call it dating," explained Lelani. "Not until I meet his parents."

"You have met his parents," pointed out Megan.

"I've only met them as Anna's friend and roommate," continued Lelani. "Not as their son's girlfriend—not that we're calling me that."

Kendall shook her head. "Me thinks you protest too much."

"Out of respect for Mr. and Mrs. Mendez," said Lelani firmly. "We need to proceed slowly and carefully."

"But I've heard Anna say that her parents treat Gil differently than her. She said that Latinos aren't nearly as protective of sons as they are of daughters."

"Maybe so, but our age difference could be a concern."

Kendall laughed so loudly that she snorted. "You are like, what, a year older than him? That is so ridiculous, Lelani. They need to get over it."

"Maybe."

"What they should be thinking about," said Megan, "is what perfectly gorgeous children you and Gil would have."

Lelani frowned. "That's getting the carriage *way* ahead of the horse."

"Ugh, children!" Kendall groaned then stood. "Please, do not even use that horrid word in my presence today." She headed toward the dining room, then paused. "Hey, is anyone else hungry?"

"Is that a hint or what?" said Megan quietly.

"Duh." Lelani stood now. "She obviously wants us to come fix something."

"And you're going to?"

Lelani shrugged. "I'm actually pretty hungry. My aunt's turkey was a little on the underdone side, and eating pink turkey concerned me."

Megan stood as well. "Come to think of it, I'm kind of hungry too. I had a microwave meal that was a little on the overdone side. Think *wooden* turkey."

Soon the three of them were foraging together in the kitchen. Kendall opened a bottle of red wine and filled three glasses, her contribution to their meal. And Megan managed to put together a fairly decent-looking green salad, topping it with gorgonzola and pine nuts. Lelani fixed a nice plate of crackers and cheese. Still, without a trip to the grocery store, this meal, though pretty skimpy, was probably as good as it was going to get today.

"Hey, everyone," called Anna as she emerged through the garage door carrying two plastic bags as if bearing gifts.

"Is that food?" asked Kendall hopefully.

"Yep. My mom insisted on sending home the leftovers. I didn't think anyone would complain."

"God bless your mom," said Megan eagerly.

They all chattered as they helped Anna to unload the leftovers, heaping sliced turkey and candied yams and even some pumpkin empanadas onto plates and carrying them into the dining room, which Lelani had already set for three.

"We need another place setting," said Megan, quickly running to get it from the kitchen and thinking that this really wasn't half-bad for a Thanksgiving meal. And far better than moping around by herself.

Soon they were all seated around the table—their little makeshift family of four. After Megan said a Thanksgiving prayer, Kendall held up her glass to make a toast. "Here's to holidays without children."

Anna frowned in a confused sort of way, but went along with it just the same.

"Kendall had a bad day with Amelia's sister's kids," explained Megan. Anna nodded. "Oh, right."

"And I want to propose a second toast," said Lelani. "Here's to good friends and happy times throughout the rest of the holiday season."

The response to this toast was much more enthusiastic.

"Speaking of holidays," said Megan, "do you plan to go home to Hawaii to celebrate with your family, Lelani?"

"Yeah," said Kendall eagerly. "Maybe you'd like me to join you?"

"Why just you?" protested Anna. "I'd like to come too."

"Don't leave me out," said Megan quickly. "I'm the one who asked about it in the first place."

"Christmas in Hawaii," said Kendall dreamily. "I'll have to get in to the tanning salon and—"

"Don't book your flight yet," said Lelani calmly. "Unless you're going without me."

"Meaning you're not going home for Christmas?"

Lelani firmly shook her head. "No. I am definitely not. In fact, I'm sure I'll be working right through Christmas Eve and then again on Returns' Day, since half the people at Nordstrom have already begged for time off."

"I would think you could talk Mr. Green into—"

"I already promised him that I'd be around," said Lelani quickly.

Megan suspected that Lelani was still trying to make up for their accusations against Mr. Green when Kendall had gone missing. Accusations that turned out to be way off. Their implicating her supervisor was definitely an event that all four girls wanted to forget.

"Okay, so Hawaiian holidays are out," said Kendall with disappointment. "Anyone else have any exciting idea?"

"You could join me and my family," said Anna in a less than enthusiastic way. "Although, for a change, I would love to do something besides watching nieces and nephews breaking piñatas and fighting over candy."

"Count me out," said Kendall.

"That's right," said Anna. "You've decided you hate kids."

"Hate's a bit strong." Kendall narrowed her eyes. "As the late W. C. Fields used to say, I love children … if they're cooked properly."

"Ugh," said Lelani. "That is disgusting."

"It's a joke," said Kendall.

"Since when did you become an expert on W. C. Fields?" asked Lelani.

"Since I did a paper on him in college."

"A paper on W. C. Fields?" queried Megan with skepticism. "What kind of class was it?"

"Filmography." Kendall grinned. "Here's another W. C. quote: 'I cook with wine. Sometimes I even add it to the food.'"

"He said that?" asked Anna. "My mom has that on her fridge."

"Yep. That was old W. C. Want to know another interesting fact?"

"Sure," said Lelani.

Anna nodded, although she looked slightly suspicious and Megan felt even less sure.

"You're going to like this one, Megan."

"Huh?"

Kendall nodded and continued. "Did you know that W. C. Fields was an agnostic his entire life?"

Megan shrugged. "Why should that surprise anyone?"

"And he was found reading a Bible on his deathbed."

"Seriously?" Megan peered curiously at Kendall now. Was she pulling their legs?

"Yep. He reportedly said that he was looking for a loophole."

Well, they all laughed, but even as Megan laughed, she had to wonder. Maybe Kendall was looking for a loophole too.

"Okay, as interesting as W. C. Fields is," said Lelani, "let's get back to Christmas. I just got a really great idea."

"What's that?" asked Anna.

"Well, since no one seems to have any really firm plans, how about if we have a big Christmas party right here?"

"What kind of Christmas party?" asked Anna.

"An old-fashioned one," said Lelani. "You know, on Christmas Eve."

"This would be a cool house for a party," said Megan. "Craftsman-style homes are great to decorate."

"And even better since you guys fixed it all up," Kendall added.

"And we could get a tree and bake goodies and put up lights and all sorts of fun things," said Lelani eagerly. "I've never had a real mainland Christmas before."

"That's right," said Anna. "That must've been weird celebrating Christmas in eighty-degree weather."

"Oh," sighed Kendall dreamily. "A sunny beach and a cabana boy bringing me a mai tai sounds like a perfectly lovely Christmas to me." She gazed hopefully at Lelani now. "Are you absolutely, positively sure you don't want to rethink going home for the holidays and taking me with you? I could buy your ticket."

"First of all, cabana boys are in Mexico, not Hawaii," said Lelani. "Second of all, no, I am not going home."

"Besides that," said Megan, "you can't afford even one ticket to Hawaii, Kendall. Remember, you're broke."

She made a pouty face. "Thanks for reminding me."

"So, how about it?" persisted Lelani. "Does anyone want to host a Christmas party here?"

Anna and Megan both agreed.

"Fine," said Kendall. "If Hawaii is out, I'll agree to having a Christmas party here. And I might even help decorate, since that sounds sort of fun, but do not expect me to be involved in the baking. As you know I'm fairly hopeless in the kitchen."

"Of course." Anna winked at Lelani and Megan.

"Well, that is, unless you make fruitcake." A sly grin appeared on Kendall's face. "I do know a thing or two about that."

"Meaning?" Megan waited for Kendall's predictable response.

"Meaning you guys make the fruitcake, and I'll add the rum. Or brandy. Or whatever it is they soak that stuff in. Yum!"

"You mean you actually *eat* fruitcake?" Megan gasped.

"Eat it, drink it, sure, whatever," said Kendall with a laugh.

"You must be the only person I know who likes it."

"And you'd actually serve it at our Christmas party?" Lelani looked as if she was rethinking this idea.

"That's right." Kendall's eyes glinted with mischief. "And here's what I have to say to anyone who comes to our party—*Let them eat fruitcake!*"

The other girls chuckled at this, but Megan suddenly got it. Somehow, she knew exactly what sort of party Kendall had in mind. And, although Lelani was probably imagining a sweet, old-fashioned Christmas Eve celebration with good food and gifts and singing, Megan suspected that Kendall was envisioning a rock-out, drink 'til you drop, party-hardy kind of Christmas Eve.

"Does it snow here for Christmas?" asked Lelani with wide eyes.

Kendall laughed. "Don't get your hopes up."

Megan wasn't about to say anything just now, but she knew she wouldn't be getting her hopes up either.

# Other Books by Melody Carlson

*These Boots Weren't Made for Walking*
(WaterBrook)

*On This Day*
(WaterBrook)

*Ready to Wed*
(GuidepostsBooks)

*Finding Alice*
(WaterBrook)

Notes from a Spinning Planet series
(WaterBrook)

The Secret Life of Samantha McGregor series
(Multnomah)

# Don't Miss the Rest of the 86 Bloomberg Place Series

Catch up with Kendall and the gang as their lives take unexpected twists and turns in these great follow-up novels.

### let them eat fruitcake

will be available in September 2008
and spring broke and three weddings and a bar mitzvah
coming in 2009!

*transforming lives together*